Mixed Doubles

'You wanted me from the very first minute you saw me. You enjoy the way I talk to you. It gets you hot. If only you'd admit it to yourself, Natalie.'

He was so powerful. His hand felt so big, wrapped round her neck. She was his prey. She began to relish the sensation of being his; of being small and vulnerable compared to his size, his strength, his mind. For a split second – a horrifying, exhilarating, gut-wrenching, terrifying second – her mind screamed YES.

D1289621

By the same author:

THE SUCCUBUS
THE SEVEN-YEAR LIST
UNDERCOVER SECRETS

Mixed Doubles

ZOE LE VERDIER

BLACK
lace

Black Lace novels are sexual fantasies.
In real life, make sure you practise safe sex.

First published in 1998 by
Black Lace
Thames Wharf Studios,
Rainville Road, London W6 9HT

Copyright © Zoe le Verdier 1998

The right of Zoe le Verdier to be identified as the
Author of this Work has been asserted by her in
accordance with the Copyright, Designs and Patents Act
1988.

Typeset by SetSystems Ltd, Saffron Walden, Essex
Printed and bound by Mackays of Chatham PLC

ISBN 0 352 33312 X

*All characters in this publication are fictitious and any
resemblance to real persons, living or dead, is purely
coincidental.*

This book is sold subject to the condition that it shall
not, by way of trade or otherwise, be lent, resold, hired
out or otherwise circulated without the publisher's
prior written consent in any form of binding or cover
other than that in which it is published and without a
similar condition including this condition being
imposed on the subsequent purchaser.

For Adelle

Chapter One

Natalie Crawford smiled and allowed herself a moment to daydream. One moment – that was all she could spare from her hectic schedule. Every minute of every day had a purpose; every single thing she did was a means to an end.

This tedious job was a means to an end: a way of building contacts, learning the ropes and setting herself up for the future. If she was going to be her own boss by the time she was thirty – in three years, two months and forty-three days – she simply didn't have time to waste on dreams. Even at night, when she was sleeping, her subconscious drifted to work: to sales forecasts, the next presentation, Monday's meeting with the chairman. Her brain never slept. Only after a particularly challenging and rewarding day – one like today – would she treat herself to the luxury of a whole sixty seconds' worth of fantasy. After her six-month trial period, today Natalie had been offered a full contract, and so felt she deserved a little self-indulgence.

She clicked her way out of the company's computer system and sat back in her plush, soft-leather executive chair. At twenty-six, she was young to have one of these chairs. The other managers in the marketing department were all in their early thirties. But she was different from them. They were like puppies, panting frantically in their clumsy dash to be the first to fetch the corporate bone. They would grow up to be the chairman's lapdogs: blindly loyal, hard-working, but brainless. Well, they could stay here all their lives if they wanted, panting and wagging their tails every time the chairman walked by. She had other plans. Company politics and departmental manoeuvrings didn't interest her, and she didn't participate in them unless they could further her own career. She wasn't working here, and working hard, because she had a desire to help Freedom Sportswear make another 2.7 million pounds profit this year. This company was just a stepping stone towards her future. Natalie had it all worked out.

She sank into her dream. Like everything else in Natalie's life, it was precisely controlled – and it had a purpose. Imagining herself with her own business wasn't just enjoyable, it was an exercise in positive thinking. She didn't even need to close her eyes, so strong was the image. She'd conjured it up so many times over the last few years, refining and adjusting it until it was perfect.

There she was, aged thirty, dressed in Donna Karan, sitting in her small but well-designed office in WC1 and fielding calls from blue-chip clients eager to tap into her renowned marketing expertise. Her immaculate male PA (who would have been a model but he had a brain) was making her fresh coffee; just outside her door, her small but loyal staff were working with almost as much energy and zeal as she was. They were in awe of her; she was so good at her job. Unfazed by anything, she was in complete control.

Complete control. No one above her, sanctioning

her decisions, clamping down on her creativity or – worse still – pinching her ideas and claiming the credit. Complete control. The thought gave Natalie a thrill that was almost sexual. The warm glow trickling down the back of her neck had nothing to with the evening sun streaming through the window.

She blinked and was back in the open-plan marketing department, one of ten managers and assistant managers whose 'workspaces' all faced the menacing closed door of the chairman's office. At this time of night on a Friday she was the only one left. Even the chairman had gone home to his wife and his life. But Natalie loved this time of day: she loved the total quiet, and the opportunity to get things tidied up without any interruptions. It felt slightly forbidden too, like going into school during the holidays and sneaking a look inside everyone's desks. And staying late got her noticed: those who put in the longest hours found that there was a quicker way to the top than inching up that proverbial ladder.

Natalie wore a slight, secretive smile as she tidied her desk and stood up. Two more years, two more promotions, and she'd have enough experience and confidence to set up her own consultancy. She already had the name – The Crawford Consultancy. Now all she needed was single-minded determination and patience, and she had plenty of that.

Like a cat waking up, she stretched languidly. Packing her briefcase full of homework, she smiled at the thought of her empty flat, and all those empty hours stretching out in front of her. She'd felt mean, at first, kicking Jason out; but now she was glad. He wasn't right for her: an out-of-work actor who spent all his time sitting around watching cookery programmes, and wanting to 'do stuff' at the weekends, just didn't fit in with the scheme of Natalie's life. She had her own 'stuff' to do at the weekends. Important stuff to keep her one step ahead at work. She'd get herself a decent boyfriend later: one who understood that work came first. She didn't have time for a man right now. Her vibrator kept her happy, and if she needed something more – the feel of real, hard flesh – she knew she could get it. She could get anything she wanted. Right now what she wanted more than anything was an ice-cold beer to celebrate the start of the weekend.

She said goodnight to the security guard as she left the building, and they shared their usual joke about her being the last to leave. 'Don't you have a home to go to?' She faked a sweet laugh, and pushed her way through the revolving doors. Outside, the sunlight hit her face and warmed her skin – what a relief, she hated the false coldness of the air conditioning. She wouldn't have aircon when she had her own company, she'd have windows that opened to let in the summer. She put the roof down on her company-issue convertible, so she could bask in that warmth and feel the wind on her face during the long drive back to London. Checking her reflection in the rear-view mirror, she set off. The traffic wasn't too bad at this time, which was another good reason for staying late at the office. The company had chosen to move its headquarters to suburban Surrey, and the roads were jammed with commuters at rush hour. Or so she'd been told. Natalie had never left the office before eight.

She was cruising down the dual carriageway, enjoying the powerful hum of the sixteen-valve engine, when her mobile rang. 'Yes?' she said, flicking the switch to put the roof back up so that she could hear.

'Natalie? Is that Natalie Crawford?'

'Speaking.' The car roof unfurled soundlessly, enclosing her in near silence again.

'Natalie, this is your uncle, Justin Crawford.'

Natalie laughed to herself. Justin had an endearing habit of introducing himself by his full name – as if

4

she had lots of Uncle Justins. 'My favourite uncle,' she said. 'How are you?'

He came straight to the point, as usual. 'I'm fine, Natalie. Actually, I'm better than fine, I'm ecstatic. Actually . . . I'm gay.'

Natalie glanced at the carphone's mic for confirmation, unsure she'd heard correctly. 'You're . . . gay?'

'Yes. I've come out of the closet. Today – just now. Isn't it wonderful?'

For him, maybe. 'What does Auntie Pat think about this?'

'Don't you worry about Patricia – she's been having an affair with her personal trainer for years.'

'Oh. I see.' Natalie wondered where this was leading. 'Justin, why are you telling me this?'

'Because you've got to help me, sweetheart.'

She wondered how she was going to do that, exactly.

'I'm going to live in Rio. I need someone to take over the club for me. I want you to do it, Natalie. You're the only person I can trust in our awful family. In fact, you're the only person I can trust in the whole wide world – apart from Sinbad, of course.'

She raised an eyebrow and swooped gracefully into the slow lane. This conversation was requiring some concentration; she couldn't cope with overtaking chauvinist lorry drivers at the same time. 'Sinbad?'

'My lover,' Justin said casually. 'Listen, darling, come over now and I'll show you the ropes.'

Natalie shook her head in disbelief. Justin's phone calls were always bizarre, but this one took some beating. 'Justin, I already have a job, which I have just this minute finished. I'm going to go home, have a bath and a beer, and I'll come and see you tomorrow when you've calmed down a bit. All right?'

'No, it's not all right, sweetie. I won't be here tomorrow. I'm leaving on the 2 a.m. flight to Rio de

Janeiro.' He whooped appropriately, as if he was already there, dancing in the Mardi Gras procession wearing nothing but a thong and a smile. 'You have to come over now, my darling. And I've got the bubbly open, so you'd better hurry, or there'll be none left for my favourite niece.'

'Let me get this straight.' Natalie narrowed her eyes and stared into the mic. 'You're leaving Auntie Pat for someone called Sinbad. You're going to live in Brazil. You want me to take over the club, as of now.'

'Spot on. I always said you were a clever girl.'

'Justin . . .' Her mouth gaped as she searched for the words. By now, she shouldn't have been shocked by anything her Uncle said or did. But he'd surpassed himself this time. Knowing him, he would be fully expecting Natalie to drop everything and take over the Crawford Club, and probably had no contingency plan in case she said no – which she'd have to. Natalie would have to find him a temporary manager. Knowing Justin, he'd be back from Brazil in a week, completely heterosexual and wanting his club back. 'I think we'd better talk things through,' Natalie said. 'I'll be there in half an hour.'

'That's wicked, darling. I knew you'd say yes.' He whooped again, and rang off before Natalie could get another word in.

'Wicked?' she repeated to herself, wondering where a fifty-year-old had picked up a word like that; and wondering why she seemed to be the only member of the family who'd ever grown up.

Natalie tried to keep calm as she sat in Justin's office. Someone had to. Both Justin and Sinbad (tall, lithe, androgynous, Brazilian, beautiful – and, at twenty-five years younger than Justin, younger than her, too) were on an unstoppable high. Brains full of champagne bubbles, they were dancing around the office, screaming occasionally the way overexcited queens do. They looked good together. Somehow, Sinbad seemed the perfect match for Natalie's eccentric, dapper uncle. As they kissed and hugged each other Natalie realised that she'd never seen her uncle so happy. Gayness suited him. He'd rarely looked so at ease with Auntie Pat.

Their carefree excitement was infectious, but Natalie fought it. Someone had to take control here; there was a business to run, which Justin seemed completely unconcerned about. Now that Natalie was there, in his office, he seemed to think the problem was solved.

'Justin. Justin.' Natalie raised her voice above the hysteria. '*Justin!* Don't you think we should talk about the club for a minute, before you get completely drunk?'

He giggled and hiccuped, and sat behind his desk in his comically over-sized chair. He motioned Sinbad towards him and, as the dusky-skinned beauty draped his long limbs across Justin's lap, Natalie's uncle feigned an air of seriousness. 'You're right, darling. Let's get down to business.' With a hoot of delight, he popped open another bottle of Moët and took a swig.

Natalie sighed, frustrated at his tipsiness. 'Justin, this is important. We've got to get this situation sorted out. You and Sinbad are buggering off to Rio tomorrow, and you're expecting me to just step in and take over this place. It's not on.' She paused as they sniggered at her use of the word 'buggering'. She huffed and rolled her eyes to the ceiling. 'Can you be serious just for one minute?' she snapped. 'For goodness sake, act your age.' Justin and Sinbad nudged each other like naughty children being told off.

'Right,' Natalie began, glad she'd finally got some quiet. 'I cannot manage the club. I've already got a job. Now, you've no assistant, no deputy – no one else who knows how this place is run. Did you think of a plan just in case I couldn't take over at a moment's notice?'

Justin eased himself out from beneath his lover's spindly body and moved around the wide desk to Natalie's side. Crouching down beside her chair, he took her hand in his. 'Natalie, my darling, you're not going to say no to me, are you? You can't. I'm relying on you. There's no one else who could run this place, no one else I'd trust it with.'

Natalie slowly shook her head. 'But I –'

He put a gentle finger to her lips. 'Hush, now. Listen to what I have to say, please.'

She sighed. It was pointless arguing with Justin. She nodded. 'Go on.'

'You want to run your own business. You've told me so many times you want to be your own boss – well, here's your chance. This is a golden opportunity, Natalie. How many twenty-six-year-olds are handed complete control of a big business like this? There'd be no one telling you what to do – no one to answer to. The decisions would be yours; and failure or success would be your responsibility. Now, you've already told me you hate your job.' He silenced her attempt at interruption with an accusatory finger. 'Yes, I know why you took it – it'll look good on your CV, it'll give you some clout when you set up on your own. And you get to go on "management" training courses.' He curled his mouth around the word 'management' as if it was offensive to him. Natalie's father ran management training courses himself, and there was no love lost between the two brothers: one ex-army, one ex-art school.

Leaning closer to Natalie, Justin tried to infuse her with some of his excitement. 'Instead of running round the woods, building bridges out of pieces of old rope and trying to light fires without matches, why not really learn what's involved in running a business?

8

I promise you, you'll learn more in one day here than you would if you did management courses back to back for the next five years. And, whatever your salary is at the moment, you can double it here. No, treble it.'

She laughed at his eagerness. It was a tempting idea. Taking over the club certainly would give her more experience than she'd ever get in her present job; hands-on experience; just what she needed. But it wasn't quite as simple as that. 'Justin –'

'Unless, of course, you're afraid you won't be up to it.'

Natalie met her uncle's teasing eyes. She knew she was being baited, but still she couldn't help nibbling at the bait. 'Me? Afraid?' She arched a disdainful eyebrow. 'I could run this place standing on my head.'

'I know you could.' Justin's wide mouth spread into a knowing smirk. 'So you'll do it?'

Natalie tutted. 'I can't jack my job in, just like that.' Immediately she'd said it, she realised that, technically, she could. She'd been given her contract today; she was supposed to read it over the weekend and bring it in, signed, on Monday. Only then would she be a fully fledged company member. It wouldn't be awfully fair on her boss, but there would be nothing he could do if she didn't go back to work again.

Justin sensed her faltering. He had a way of doing that; of knowing what she was thinking almost before she'd thought it. 'Go on, Natalie. Go with your instincts. Say yes.'

She wanted to, but she couldn't. Walking out on a good job just wasn't her style. 'It's impossible. Look, I'll help you find another manager, but –'

Justin shook his head and stuck out his bottom lip like a spoilt child. 'I don't want another manager, Natalie. I want you. You're so clever and brilliant, and you're so good at marketing, and this job is all about marketing . . .'

'Flattery will get you nowhere,' she laughed. 'I keep telling you, I already have a job. A bloody good one.'

His expression turned serious. 'Give in your notice.' He held up a hand as she started to protest. 'Natalie, I won't be able to rest unless I know this place is in safe hands. I've worked for years to make this club what it is now. I want to keep it in the family. I want you to run it. I don't want anyone else. You'd be brilliant at it, darling. Just think of it – your own boss, at your age. Wouldn't it be wonderful?'

It would, but Natalie wasn't sure about making such a commitment. Handing in her notice at work, especially when she'd only just established herself, was a big step. And knowing Justin, it would probably be a very silly step to take. 'I know you.' There was suspicion in her voice. 'You'll be back with Auntie Pat in a week. No disrespect to you, Sinbad,' she said, as he collapsed to his knees, whimpered pathetically and clutched possessively on to Justin's sleeve. 'But you do tend to change your mind about things fairly frequently,' she continued, turning her attention back to her uncle. 'When you get fed up of Brazil you'll be back here wanting to run your club again. And then I'll be out of a job.'

Justin shook his head sadly. 'I know I may have been a little . . . inconsistent in the past. But this is it.' He turned to his new lover and gazed into his dark brown eyes. 'I'm in love with Sinbad. This man is my life. There's nothing for me in England any more. I won't be back.'

He sealed his heartfelt words with a kiss on Sinbad's full lips; a kiss so tender, Natalie felt the surge of pure love in the air. She was touched and almost believed that, for once, Justin meant what he said.

Disentangling himself from his lover's long arms,

Justin turned back to Natalie. 'The manager's job is yours, if you want it. Please say you want it. I guarantee that after a week here, you won't ever want to go back to working for someone else. Just imagine it, Natalie . . .' His voice went low and quiet. 'Being the boss . . . being in control . . . Let's face it, you're just one of the "team" in that job, just a little cog in the company wheel.' He grabbed her knees dramatically, making her jump. 'You're not a team player, Natalie. This is your chance to prove to everyone that you've got what it takes to go it alone. Seize it, Natalie. I promise you won't regret it.'

Natalie shut her eyes for a moment. This was all getting too much. Too many thoughts were colliding in her brain. She was thrilled by the thought of being in charge of the club, and already she was imagining herself ensconced in her position of power in Justin's office – her office – overlooking the tennis courts. But Natalie was as sensible as Justin was impulsive; and so there were other, more important thoughts vying for her attention. Justin's reputation as a businessman wasn't good. Within the family, the general consensus was that the Crawford Club was kept afloat more on luck than judgement. Running the club was probably not going to be easy. And Justin's reputation was going to be tarnished beyond repair when the story of his sudden homosexuality came out. How would Natalie explain to her parents that she'd walked away from a brilliant job with good prospects, simply because her wayward Uncle Justin had asked her to? It was insane – and yet, something in her guts was telling her to go for it.

'Have a look around.' Justin stood up. Gently tugging on Natalie's hands, he pulled her to her feet. 'Go on, have a look around the place, have a think about it.' He steered Natalie towards the door. 'Don't rush into the decision. I want you to be sure. No regrets. So take your time. I'll come and get you in fifteen minutes.'

Natalie sat in the Crawford Club's café and tried to put her thoughts in order. Looking around, watching the singles and doubles matches taking place on the courts adjacent to the restaurant, she felt herself wanting this job. It was too perfect to be true, for all the reasons Justin had given her – a short-cut to being her own boss, an overnight promotion to company manager; the thought made her hands shake as she lifted her coffee cup. This was what she had always wanted. And she was sure she could run this place. She'd got her degree; she'd got experience in marketing; she was so good at her job that Freedom Sportswear had head-hunted her from her last company. So although completely confident in her skills, what was stopping her?

She wished she could be more impulsive – more like her uncle. But she couldn't help thinking that there was a downside; and one she didn't want to discover when it was too late. In a few hours her uncle would be thousands of miles away; far too distant to be of any help with the problems he would surely leave her. Should she walk away from her job to run a business she knew nothing about?

Natalie finished her cappuccino and continued her tour of the club. She'd been there a couple of times since Justin had started it from scratch, three years ago, but now she looked at the place in a different light. And the more she looked, the less worried she became. It was becoming increasingly hard to resist the images flooding her mind – the images she'd fantasised about for so long.

She strolled past the tennis courts, stopping to look in each one, and thinking that in a few hours' time, she could be master of all she surveyed. And what she surveyed was fantastic. The Crawford Club was as

12

plush inside as it was outside. Everywhere was immaculate and superbly equipped – a little like the club's members, with their pristine whites and their state-of-the-art racquets. The whole place had an exclusive, secluded air; the air of effortless, unhurried ease which comes with wealth. Here again, the club and its clients were well matched. Both appeared to have plenty of money.

Still, appearances weren't enough to make up her mind. She had to be sure that she was doing the right thing; and something was nagging. Perhaps it was just that the tranquil calmness of the club's atmosphere was such a contrast to her churning mind.

Natalie had been staring into court six for some time before she realised there was no one playing on it any more. A polite cough woke her up. Her eyes unglazed and she turned around. The coach she'd been watching, before she'd drifted off into her thoughts, was now standing beside her.

'Were we that bad?' he asked, smiling.

'Sorry?'

He waved his racquet towards the empty court. 'I suppose it wasn't exactly Borg versus McEnroe, but I didn't realise we were that boring. We finished playing five minutes ago, and you didn't even notice.'

God, he was gorgeous close up – tall; lean; tanned; pale-blue eyes; floppy, sexily messy, dark-blond hair. So gorgeous, it took Natalie a while to answer. 'Oh . . . no, it wasn't . . .' She felt slightly flustered. His eyes were so blue. 'The match was good . . . You're a very good player, I just . . .' She pulled herself together and returned his friendly smile. 'I was miles away. I've got a lot on my mind.'

'Sorry to hear that.' He paused, and Natalie thought she detected a hint of flirtatiousness in his lovely eyes. 'Nothing serious, I hope.'

'Well, it's serious to me,' she said. 'I've been offered

a job here. I'm not sure whether to take it or not. I have –' she checked her watch '– the next five minutes to make up my mind whether to leave the job I've already got.'

She looked up to find him sneaking a furtive glance over her body. His grin widened when he realised he'd been caught. 'I'm Paul,' he said, holding out his hand. 'I'm the head coach here.'

'Natalie,' she replied. 'I'm . . . Justin's niece.'

His thick eyebrows slowly lifted. 'You're *the* Natalie?'

'You seem surprised.'

'I am. You're not quite what I was expecting.'

There it was again; unmistakable this time. He liked her – it was in his eyes and his smile. He was flirting with her. Flattered, Natalie felt a twinge of arousal in her belly.

'And what were you expecting?' she prompted, nerves making her voice sound tighter and higher than usual.

'Well, when Justin described you, he said you were a very clever and dedicated businesswoman.' Paul hesitated, looking deep into Natalie's eyes. 'He forgot to mention how attractive you are.'

She blinked several times, unsure of what to say. This was so different from the politically correct world she'd just come from. At work, any hint of passion was kept cool by the air conditioning and the threat of sexual harassment allegations. No one dared hold eye contact for too long, in case it could be construed as flirting. Now, a man she'd only just met was giving her unmistakable vibes. It felt good.

'And why was my uncle describing me?' she asked.

'I asked him what you were like. He said you were taking over as manager here.'

'Did he now,' Natalie huffed. 'Well I haven't made up my mind, yet. I've already got a good job, you see, and ... Oh, there could be all sorts of problems, knowing my uncle. Besides, I know the sportswear business inside out, but I don't know the first thing about tennis.'

'Neither does your uncle,' Paul said, winking. 'That's my job, to deal with the tennis side of things. Me and Justin work as a team...' His voice trailed off, and Natalie could tell Paul was picturing himself and Natalie working as a team. The idea was rather appealing.

There was a moment's silence. It was probably only a split second, but to Natalie it seemed interminable. Interminable, and delicious. It was like the moment before you first kiss someone new: loaded with anticipation, crackling with tension. Paul and Natalie's thoughts collided. In their minds, the gap between them was gone, their hands were all over each other and their lips were pressed together. Their pupils dilated; their breathing slowed; their pulses raced. Natalie felt the hairs on the back of her neck rising. She felt her bones melting.

'So ...' he said quietly, his soft voice slowly reaching her through the thick silence, 'if you took over from your uncle, you'd be my boss.'

Natalie nodded, strangely aroused by the droplet of sweat trickling down his forehead. 'Would that bother you?' Her voice sounded distant, she was so focused on his eyes and the way they were oozing suggestions.

'Bother me? It wouldn't bother me.' He ran his fingers through his hair, pushing his fringe away from his face. 'It might affect my concentration though, having someone so –'

A voice came over the Tannoy and the moment was broken. 'Paul, telephone call in reception. Paul, telephone call.'

Paul blinked and smiled regretfully. 'Excuse me,' he said sadly, 'I'll have to take that call.' He held out his hand again. His handshake was slow, warm and meaningful. 'It was nice to meet you, Natalie. I hope you decide to take the job. If there's anything I can do to convince you . . .'

You just did, she thought, watching his bum in his tiny white shorts as he walked away.

Trembling slightly, Natalie slipped into the ladies' changing room. It was empty, and she stood in front of one of the many full-length mirrors lining the walls and studied her reflection; studied the image that Paul had just seen.

She was a picture of cool professionalism. Everything about her had been carefully designed to give the right impression: her navy Jigsaw trouser suit; the way her long, dark-brown hair was tied back from her face in a neat pony tail; her understated make-up and simple jewellery. She looked as serious about her work as she was; but, just discernible beneath the cool exterior, was the strong femininity that Paul had admired. There was a good figure hiding in her conservative clothes: a sexy, shapely arse, well-proportioned legs, a slim waist and full breasts. A hint of her cleavage was just visible above the first button of her jacket. And lurking just behind her brown eyes there was something she hadn't noticed in a long time – something wild and different. There was a sense of adventure.

She started to smile at herself as she realised that, against her better judgement, her mind was made up. The idea scared her, without a doubt. She was taking a big risk. But how was she going to be a businesswoman if she was always afraid to take risks? How would she ever be sure she could go it alone – unless she tried it? Of course, she knew that Paul was the deciding factor; but she didn't want to admit that to herself. Work came first, and she was taking this job because of the opportunities, not because of the man.

The man was a perk, and a far more tempting one than the convertible car she'd have to relinquish. Who needed sixteen valves when you could have him – that body, those eyes?

She jumped as the changing-room door swung open. It was Justin, with Sinbad in tow. 'Well?' he said, grinning, already knowing, as he always did, what she was thinking.

'Well.' She smiled back. 'You're looking at the new manager of the Crawford Club.' She sounded nonchalant, but the sweet sharpness of those words on her tongue gave her an undeniable thrill.

In a scene straight out of *La Cage aux Folles*, Sinbad screamed and Justin ran to hug her. 'My darling,' he gushed, holding her tight, 'you won't regret this, I promise you.'

In the darkness, Natalie sneaked a glance across at Paul. Was this real? Could reality be this perfect?

Having signed her contract of employment – which Justin, with uncharacteristic foresight, had had drawn up in readiness by his solicitor – Natalie had kissed her uncle goodbye. She'd sat in his office, which was now her office, and typed her letter of resignation to Freedom Sportswear. Then she'd said goodnight to a different security guard, and headed down to the car park.

Once again, her attempt to get back to her little flat in Battersea had been thwarted. Paul had bumped into her in the car park and, not bothering to disguise his delight that Natalie was now his boss, he'd invited her out for a celebratory dinner. They'd driven in their separate cars into nearby Epsom to eat. Then, high on the unspoken thought that they were going to sleep together later, they'd driven to the headquarters of Freedom Sportswear. Four hours after she'd left work with a year's contract, Natalie was back with a letter of resignation which she left on her boss's desk, along with her company-car keys.

Paul noticed her watching him and took his eyes off the road for a moment. 'What?' he asked, his wide mouth hinting at a smile.

'I was just wondering where the nearest train station is,' she said, her smile hinting at the fact that the last thing she wanted was a train.

'I think you've missed the last train to London,' he said casually.

'Oh.' Natalie bit her lip, to stop herself from saying what she really wanted to say. 'That's a shame,' she said instead. 'I'll have to get a taxi home.'

'Do you have to?'

Paul's attention returned to the road ahead, but Natalie could still see the longing in his eyes. 'Well . . .'

'Because, if you don't have to get back, you could stay the night at my place, and . . .'

There was another interminable, delicious moment of silence as both of them imagined what that 'and' meant. Natalie's pussy clenched and sent a spiral of icy anticipation curling up her spine. She shivered slightly.

'Are you cold?' Paul asked.

'No. I'm absolutely fine.'

'Would you like to stay at my place, then?' (Would you like me to kiss you; to slowly undress you; to gently lick your nipples with my tongue? Would you like me to spread my fingers over your breasts and stroke and squeeze; to press my hard body against your soft body; to ease my way deep inside you? Would you like to spend the night exploring each other; rolling around in my bed; coating our skin with saliva and sweat and the juices of our longing?)

'OK,' she said.

They drove the rest of the way in silence.

* * *

18

Paul's flat was typical of a bachelor: messy, lacking in style, but well stocked with beer and condoms. The beer she noticed when he told her to help herself to a drink; the condoms when she rooted around in his bathroom cabinet. Fridges and bathroom cabinets told a lot about their owners, and Natalie always had to have a look inside them.

His living room told a lot, too. Sipping her beer, she wandered around while Paul went into the bedroom, presumably to tidy up. There weren't many books on the shelves, but there were hundreds of magazines, mainly to do with tennis and coaching. There were trophies from tournaments, and several arty tennis posters. Paul had been a fairly successful doubles player before a knee injury had sent him into coaching; now he was a very successful coach, and obviously proud of his achievements. His coaching certificates had been framed, and pictures of him teaching various celebrities and minor royals dotted the living-room walls. Here was a man whose career meant a lot to him. A man after her own heart.

'Hi.'

Natalie turned and smiled. 'Hi.'

Paul stepped closer. Hesitating, bouncing nervously on his heels, he looked over his shoulder towards the bedroom, then back at Natalie. 'Erm . . .' He gestured vaguely. 'I've . . . er . . . I've changed the sheets. You can have the bed; I'll sleep on the sofa.'

She laughed to herself. Paul's voice had been full of innuendo and confidence ten minutes earlier; now that the delicate moment had arrived, he was suddenly unsure. Had he read the signals right? Did she really want to sleep with him?

'Paul.' Natalie moved closer to him and put her hand on his shoulder. Her heart was pounding fast. 'You don't have to sleep on the sofa. We both knew what you meant when you invited me to stay.'

19

His relief was visible. 'I just didn't want you to think that I'd assumed anything. We've only just met, and . . . I don't usually move this fast.'

'Neither do I.' But Paul was different. The attraction had been immediate, and powerful, and mutual.

'I really like you, Natalie,' he said, inching nearer to her. He ran his palm over the side of her head, stroking her hair, then moved down on to her neck and pulled her still closer to him. His eyes glittered with a sparkling mixture of gratitude, excitement and longing. They gazed into each other, sharing yet another moment loaded with tension – the last moment. In another instant they would know what it felt like to taste each other, to touch each other – to be a part of each other.

'Kiss me,' she said silently, speaking to him with her eyes.

He kissed her, slow and soft at first, his lips nibbling tentatively. Their bodies pressed close together and their heads swayed gently as they mirrored each other in an intimate, lyrical dance. Then, as the first sweet thrill wore off, his kissing became harder; more urgent. He pushed his mouth against hers as if he wanted to use her lungs to breathe. His tongue swirled around hers, tasting her, wanting her.

'Natalie,' he whispered, letting a little desire escape from his lips before they moved down on to her neck. He suckled on her skin, inhaling deeply; inhaling the scent of her body. His hands were everywhere: clasping her face, clutching at her shoulders, slipping down into the small of her back to pull her even nearer. Now, she was so close that their hips were sealed together and she felt the hardness of his cock pressing against her pussy. She felt his pulse echoing in her belly.

Breathing deeply, he tore himself away from the pleasure of her long neck, which was now wet and warm from his lips. His chest rose and fell as if he'd just come off court. He reached behind her head and gently slipped the band out of her hair, easing it free as if it were her inhibitions which were entwined in the long, soft glossiness. Then, watching for Natalie's reaction, he unbuttoned her jacket and pushed it off her shoulders and on to the floor. With fluid fingers, he lightly caressed the heavy swell of one breast through her tight white T-shirt. His eyes were still fixed to hers, but, as she slowly blinked with pleasure, his gaze drifted down over her throat, down her cleavage, and on to his hand. Entranced, he watched his fingers close over her breast and gently squeeze. Electric shocks jerked down Natalie's spine as, encouraged by her sighs, Paul grew bolder. His gentle squeezing became hungrier, harsher, until he pinched her nipple hard.

Natalie gasped, but the shock of the pain quickly dissolved into pleasure and she wanted more of it. Pushing his hand away, she pulled off her T-shirt and threw it down. Reaching behind her, she unhooked her lacy white bra and, as slowly as she could, revealed her pert, full breasts. Heat flickered up from her pussy, up and over her quivering limbs, as Paul feasted his eyes on her. He groaned and lunged for her, enclosing one naked breast in his hand and engulfing the other with his mouth. His tongue circled her wide, aching nipple. His lips sucked hard, pulling on the swollen tip of her breast. His teeth nipped at her tender skin.

Natalie's fingers shook as she ran them through his silky hair. His blondness looked so good against her olive skin, like rivulets of liquid gold. His hair felt so good, too, brushing over her as his head dipped at her breast; a soft contrast to his teeth. She understood why men always want to bite her nipples – they were so wide, so soft and tender, so ripe for a little pain. If she had been a man, she'd have bitten her nipples, hard.

Paul did, and Natalie's body jerked in surprise. He straightened up, grinning. 'Sorry,' he said, obviously not sorry at all. 'I just couldn't resist it. You've got such fantastic tits.'

'You're not so bad yourself,' she said, pulling off his T-shirt. His chest was broad and well developed, kissed by the sun and blessed with just the right amount of hair. Natalie smoothed her fingertips along the wispy path snaking upward from his taut stomach, and spread her fingers across his chest. Copying what he had done, she bowed her head and sucked his soft nipple into stiffness, then nibbled softly, then harder.

He didn't react to her biting as she had done – she wished men's chests were as sensitive as women's; perhaps then they'd spend more time lavishing attention on their lovers' breasts before moving on – and Natalie slowly sank to her knees. Looking up at Paul with a wicked spark in her eyes, she unfastened his jeans and pushed them down around his ankles. His boxer shorts followed his jeans, and then he did react, groaning as Natalie ran her tongue round the swollen end of his prick.

She loved giving head. It was such a position of power, having a man's cock in her mouth – having him at her mercy. She got a physical thrill, a raw ache in her pussy, whenever she felt a man go rigid and helpless; whenever she heard those groans of surrender.

Paul was a loud groaner, and it gratified Natalie to hear his pleasure. She almost moaned aloud herself, his prick was so lovely: long, thick, as tanned as the rest of his body (he must sunbathe naked, she thought. Vain sod, she thought), and as hard as the rest of his muscles. Natalie couldn't fit much of him in her mouth, but what she could fit in tasted fantastic. She rolled her tongue round him, lapping up the unmistakable, musty odour of cock. She sucked him hard, drawing the flavour of sex from his velvet skin. Above her, he sighed and grunted, and his fingers twitched involuntarily in her hair. As she struck up a rhythm – a slow, sensuous rhythm – he joined in, moving his hips ever so slightly backward and forward to meet her mouth. Natalie's lips and tongue worked hard, sucking, flickering, teasing him until she tasted pleasure, hot and sticky in her mouth. He froze, and his fingers gripped her head as Natalie swallowed the sweet, salty juice. Slowly, reluctantly, she slid her lips from his prick and stood up.

His eyes were tightly shut, as if he was embarrassed by his lust. His handsome mouth was fixed in a grimace, and there were droplets of sweat on his forehead and chest. Natalie curled her hand round his neck and kissed him out of his trance. Coming to, he held her round the waist and kissed her back, showing his gratitude. Her tongue poked into his mouth. He flinched – another thing about men that frustrated Natalie. They loved tasting pussy, but why were they so precious about tasting their own come? She grabbed the back of his head and held him in an embrace, forcing him to share the taste of himself.

But he was stronger. He pulled away.

'What's the matter?' Natalie asked.

'Nothing,' he said, smiling. 'It's your turn.'

She couldn't argue with that.

He took her hand and led her into the bedroom. It was dark in there, apart from the candlelight, which lent a romantic glow to a room that would have had no romance with the lights on. As well as hiding the blandness of Paul's bachelor decor, the sweet perfume hid any possible stale-sock smell – the usual aroma in a single man's bedroom. But this room smelt of jasmine, ylang-ylang and patchouli: an intoxicating mixture.

'It smells lovely in here,' she said, looking down as Paul knelt to take off her shoes, her trousers and her skimpy white panties. He peeled her knickers off slowly, delicately, as if he was unveiling a statue to an expectant audience.

'It smells lovely in here,' he mumbled, burying his face in her thick, dark muff.

Natalie squirmed, torn between the thrill of having him there, between her legs, and the nagging worry of what she did smell like.

She didn't know why she should be worried. Every man she'd ever been with had told her that her pussy – all women's pussies – smelt and tasted beautiful. It probably dated back to school days, when the ignorant, prepubescent boys would taunt the girls about fishy smells, and girls who'd never seen a penis except in biology diagrams would retort with jibes about cheesy dicks. There was something in Natalie – in all women, maybe – something infinitesimal but strong, deep inside her, that made her ask every time for confirmation.

'What . . . What do I smell like?' she asked quietly.

Paul looked up, a hazy smile on his face, as if the scent of her had gone straight to his brain. 'You smell like a woman,' he said. 'You smell of sex. It's the most beautiful smell in the whole world.'

And, with that, he pushed at Natalie's hips until her legs gave way and she sat down on the edge of bed, which was just behind her. She lay down as he spread her legs and dipped his mouth to the mouth of her cunt. Supporting her neck with her hands she looked down her body and watched him at work. Within seconds, he was lost in the pleasure of her pussy, licking her like a dog at a spilt ice cream: slurping noisily, sucking greedily, unfurling his tongue deep

24

inside her to catch every drop of her juice. And, within a few minutes, he'd had his fill and was sliding up her body.

Oh, what a typical man, she thought, just couldn't wait to get down to it. For a moment, Natalie was speechless. She put her hand to Paul's shoulder to stop him. 'Is that it?' she gasped.

It was Paul's turn to lose the power of speech. His mouth gaped.

'I made you come,' Natalie said, raising her eyebrows and nodding downward, to make it clear that she expected the same.

'Oh.' Paul's confusion slowly turned into a smile. 'You want me to ... er ...'

'Get back down there,' she laughed, pushing him away.

He looked at her for a moment, surprised and obviously aroused by her confidence. 'You're not shy, are you?'

Natalie shrugged. 'We're both adults. What's the point in being shy about it?'

He returned her wicked gaze, admiration shining in his eyes. 'I love a woman who knows what she wants,' he said. 'It turns me on.'

'Oh, I know what I want,' Natalie purred, 'and what I want right now is for you to get back down there and make me come.' To emphasise her point, Natalie lifted up her legs and wrapped them over Paul's shoulders.

'You're the boss,' he said, bowing his head in willing surrender.

Yes, she thought, I am. The boss of the Crawford Club, and the boss in bed. 'Oh, yes,' she moaned, lifting her hips up further towards him and letting her head fall back on to the bed.

This was more like it. Paul hadn't been lying when he'd said that assertive women turned him on. He attacked his task with gusto now, curling his fingers round her thighs so he could hold her still and stop her writhing. His tongue was as frantic as her sighs, lapping the inner edges of her swollen lips, poking inside her hot pussy, swirling round and round the hard knob of her clitoris. He sucked with his lips too, kissing her, and, as he'd done with her breasts, he lightly nibbled as well, making Natalie gasp and jerk her hips.

Sensing she was close to coming now, Paul grasped tighter round her trembling upper thighs, preventing her from cutting off his air supply – she was squeezing his neck, trying to keep him there for ever. He fastened his pliant lips round her throbbing clit and sucked and flickered and sucked, until sparkles of light flew behind Natalie's eyelids. She let out a long, plaintive moan as her hips began to shake. With a final lap of his tongue over her open sex, Paul prised himself out of her thigh lock.

'Happy now?' he said, easing his way on to the bed beside her.

She couldn't speak. She could barely breathe. Her fingers trembled as she touched his glistening lips.

'Want a taste?' he asked, placing his hands on either side of her shoulders and looming over her.

Unlike him, Natalie didn't hesitate. She liked to taste herself; there was nothing more intimately sexy. Before his mouth reached hers she lifted her hand, grabbed the back of his neck and brought his lips to hers. She slid her tongue on to his, tasting her juices, such a sweet contrast to his.

The taste went to her head. Before her orgasm had even begun to subside, she went in search of another. Rolling over, she pushed Paul on to his back. She straddled him, excitement welling in the pit of her stomach as her oozing pussy poised above his long penis. Grasping him with one hand, she eased herself down on to him.

Oh, Jesus, that feeling ... She hadn't had sex for a month, and her body had almost forgotten how it felt to have thick flesh filling her pussy. Her vibrator was wonderful but it wasn't real – it didn't move inside her unless she made it; it didn't have arms and legs and a beautiful broad chest; it didn't groan with delight as it slid inside her.

She sat still for a moment, just savouring the sensation of being so full. Paul's cock seemed to reach so far inside her that pleasure trickled like oil all over her brain. Involuntarily, she moaned. Paul reached up and cupped her breasts. He was smiling slightly, pride and pleasure mixing in his blue eyes.

'Natalie,' he whispered, his voice faint with awe. 'Oh, God, Natalie.'

She began to slide up and down on his wonderful prick. The friction between the most intimate parts of their bodies was lubricated by the juices overflowing from her pussy, and both of them moaned in unison at the sensation. Effortlessly, she raised and lowered herself, pausing every time he was fully sheathed inside her so she could relish the incomprehensible fullness. Her steady, savour-every-second pace slowly quickened as her lust grew stronger and the sweet shock of having him inside her dulled. Now, she wanted more than just to slide on his thick rod; she wanted to use it, to ram herself on to it, to spear herself with pleasure.

Leaning forward, she planted her hands either side of his head. Behind her, her hips began to pump, banging down hard on his pelvis, drawing them both closer to insane ecstasy. Beneath her, he raised his head to taste her nipples as they dangled tantalisingly towards him. Opening his mouth wide, he sucked on

27

as much of her breast as he could, coating her skin with saliva, lightly grazing her with his teeth.

The sounds of his mounting pleasure echoed against her skin. This was it: they were both about to come. Natalie tilted her hips back so her clit dragged against his prick, and she fucked him frantically, like an animal. Within seconds his head had fallen back on to the pillow and his eyes were tightly shut again. His mouth, contorted into an expression of pain, let out incomprehensible burbling noises. Drawing a few more precious seconds of pleasure from his prick, Natalie sat up and slowly, slowly raised and lowered herself a few more times. Squeezing him tight inside her pussy walls, she milked every last drop of ecstasy from his spent body.

'Oh ... my ... God,' he gasped, as she finally relinquished her hold on his cock and lay down beside him. Opening his eyes, he stared into hers. 'You're amazing,' he whispered.

She shrugged nonchalantly. 'Tell me something I don't know.'

He playfully slapped her thigh. Rolling on to his side, he held her flushed cheek in one of his big hands. 'I mean it, Natalie,' he said, his eyes earnest. 'That was amazing. I haven't had sex that good in years.'

'Neither have I,' she said, although it was a lie – just before she'd kicked Jason out of her flat they'd had one last mad, frenzied session. She'd had four orgasms before she'd stopped counting.

He kissed her: the sort of long, lingering kiss that happens after you've just come together, when you're feeling intimate and satisfied; when you've just slept with someone for the first time, and it was good.

Their lips parted and he stared down at her. 'I've never met anyone like you,' he said. 'I can't quite believe we're going to be working together.'

'You know,' she said, running her fingers through

his hair, 'I make it a rule that I never get involved with anyone I work with.' Her fingers trickled over his sweat-dampened cheek, over his neck, on to his chest. 'It always causes problems at work. It just shouldn't be done, no matter how attracted you are to someone.'

'What are you saying?' he asked, worry tainting the edges of his expression.

'I'm saying . . .' Her fingers carried on downward, reaching for his sticky, semi-turgid prick. 'I'm saying that we shouldn't really see each other again. If I'm going to be your boss, it's probably not a good idea.'

He slumped on to his back and thought for a moment. 'You're right,' he said at last, turning to face her. There was a twinkle in his eyes. 'It'd probably be better if we stopped this now, before it goes any further.' He rolled off the bed, distractedly rumpling his hair. 'I'll sleep on the sofa.'

'Oh, there's no need for that.' She sighed, lightly caressing her breast with one hand and patting the bed with the other. 'I have another rule, you see.'

'Oh yeah?'

'Yeah.' Her fingers moved seductively over her belly and down into her soft, damp hair. 'Don't waste your life playing by the rules.'

Chapter Two

*T*hat weekend – the first weekend Natalie was in charge of the club – began like a dream.

When she was little, Natalie's favourite programme was *Dallas*. At the age of eleven or twelve, she thought that the world she saw on the television screen was perfect, and at night she'd fantasise that she could step through the TV into Sue Ellen's shoes, and into that glossy, money-soaked world. Sue Ellen was her favourite. She wasn't as good-looking as Pammy, and she had the scheming, two-timing JR for a husband rather than the lovely Bobby, favourite of all the girls at school – but she had her own business. She was a strong, feisty woman – or so she seemed to an eleven-year-old.

As Natalie got older, her fantasy became less about being Sue Ellen, and more about being her own boss. Even at the age of sixteen, she longed for the power of being in control of a company, and when her father informed her that 'women aren't logical enough to be in business', she swore she'd make it. At that time, thoughts of her future career were inextricably entwined with her sexual awakening, and her dream of running her own company began to have an erotic twist – although, back then, she didn't realise the significance of the way men were beginning to infiltrate her imagination. At night, lying in bed, she'd imagine herself, power-suited and supremely confident, strutting around her business domain. And she'd imagine that her staff were mostly male, and that they all whispered about her, about how insanely sexy she was, and that there was one man in particular whom she chose to be her lover. And he was tall, blue-eyed and blond, with a body sculpted from perfection. An inexplicable surge of energy would shoot beneath her inquisitive fingertips as she'd reach inside her damp knickers.

Now, she was living that dream. She'd stepped straight into her fantasy, and it couldn't have been better. She had charge of the Crawford Club; she had a staff consisting mainly of men; and she had Paul: tall, blue-eyed, blond, and if his body wasn't perfection she didn't know what was.

She got up from her desk and walked to the window. Her huge office overlooked the show court – the only one with seating, it was used for the club's charity matches and tournaments. She could see the adjacent courts on either side, and, below her office, the corridor which ran the length of the club.

The place was quiet today, but according to Paul that was normal for a Saturday. Standing in the passageway was a middle-aged couple waiting to start their match. On the three courts she could see, slow, sedate coaching sessions were taking place. Directly in front of her, on the show court, Paul was playing a sixty-year-old millionairess. It was tennis, but not as she knew it from watching Wimbledon. There wasn't any aggression here: Paul was placing the ball perfectly, delicately even, so that his client didn't have to run at all. It was gentle and almost hypnotic. Falling into a trance, Natalie watched Paul's thigh muscles flexing and stretching, and she thought of how they'd flexed and stretched last night, and again this morning, and how their bodies had slid together, coated in a film of sweat . . .

'Nat?'

Natalie jumped. It was her secretary, Jenny, a petite, pert redhead she'd only met last night, but who was already treating Natalie like someone she'd known for years. 'Sorry, Jenny, I was miles away,' she laughed softly.

Jenny came in and stood beside her at the window. 'I don't blame you. He's gorgeous, isn't he?'

Out of the corner of her eye, Natalie watched her admiring Paul. She'd only known him a few hours' too, but already she felt a twitch of pride that another woman was lusting after him.

'You're so lucky,' Jenny whispered, almost to herself.

Natalie blinked several times. 'Sorry?'

'You're going out with him, aren't you?'

Natalie's mouth opened but it was a while before anything came out. She stared at Jenny, but Jenny just carried on staring at Paul.

'How . . . How do you know we're "going out"?'

At last, Jenny broke her concentration and glanced at her boss. 'He told me, this morning.' Oblivious to Natalie's shock, she moved over to the desk and began tidying it. 'You're so lucky,' she said, again. 'I've been after him for ages, but he never seems to notice me. Of course, I'm only twenty-one, and he's thirty-two. He probably wants an older woman, well he obviously does. I mean, you're almost twenty-seven, aren't you, and . . .'

Jenny's voice drifted away as Natalie turned her back on her and stared out of the window again. Confused, she looked at Paul, wondering why he'd told Jenny. They'd agreed that morning that their affair – and, by that morning, it was obvious that it was going to be an affair rather than a one-night stand – should be kept a secret. Working relationships were difficult enough without the boss carrying on with one of her staff. It always caused tension, and Natalie didn't want any tension to spoil her relationships with the others on the coaching team.

'He told you?' she muttered, almost to herself.

'Well, actually, he didn't tell me; he was telling the guys, but I just happened to walk into the changing room as they were talking about it; not that I hang around the men's changing rooms but, you know, I have to take the rosters in every morning. Anyway, I was –'

'He was telling the other coaches about me and him?'

Jenny stopped shuffling papers and looked up, finally noticing the annoyance in Natalie's voice. 'Y– yeah.'

Natalie put her hands on her hips. 'And what did he say, exactly?'

Jenny hesitated. Realising she'd said something she shouldn't have, she glanced out of the window, weighing up where her allegiance lay: with her new boss; or with the man she had a crush on.

'Jenny?' Natalie reminded her. 'You're not going to get into trouble you know, I just want to know what Paul said.'

Jenny shrugged slightly, as if she couldn't understand what Natalie was so concerned about. 'He said that, when he met you, it was lust at first sight. Apparently, you two flirted like mad with each other over dinner, and then you went back to his place and did it twice last night and once this morning.'

Natalie's mouth dropped open.

Undaunted, Jenny continued, ticking off the points

on her fingers like a shopping list. 'He said it was the best sex he's ever had, and that you're the most amazing woman he's ever met, and ... Oh yeah, he thinks you're absolutely gorgeous.'

Natalie's anger was immediately, but only slightly, diluted. Paul, like all men, obviously couldn't resist boasting about his conquests; Natalie, like most women, just couldn't resist flattery. Warmth seeped over her skin as she looked down once again at Paul, who had finished his match and was zipping his racquet back into its cover. He glanced up at her at the same time, and their eyes briefly locked. Natalie pointed at him, then beckoned him to come up to her office.

'Anyway, I came to tell you that we've run out of brochures.'

Natalie was confused. 'Brochures?'

'You know,' Jenny explained, 'when someone's thinking of joining the club, we give them a glossy brochure with pictures and bumph all about the club, and a list of events we've got coming up, and –'

'I know what's in the brochures, Jenny,' she huffed, trying not to snap. 'Why are we out of them? Isn't it your job to reorder that sort of thing?'

'Yeah.' Jenny breezed to the door. 'But the printers won't print any more until we pay them.'

Natalie scratched her head. 'They haven't been paid? Well, whose job is that?'

'Paying the bills was Justin's job.' Jenny tutted and pulled a face that told Natalie what she thought of Justin's business skills. 'Still,' she said, handing Natalie the file she'd come in with, 'doesn't look like we're going to need any more brochures, at this rate.'

'What do you mean?' asked Natalie.

'We haven't got anyone interested in joining the club. Our new clients are way down on last year.' She nodded towards the folder in Natalie's hand. 'All the figures you asked for are in there.'

Jenny left her alone. Natalie sighed as she sat down behind her desk, cursing her uncle's name. Unpaid bills were a no-no in any business, but especially in a small town – the club would be getting a bad name for itself. But that wasn't quite as serious as lack of new customers. She opened the file and started poring over the figures Jenny had prepared for her, hoping that the anonymous names and numbers would give her some clues.

'Did you want me?'

She looked up. Paul was standing in the doorway. 'Yes. I've a bone to pick with you.' She stood up as Paul strolled up to the desk, trying to look stern but feeling herself melt, again, at the sight of his long, muscular legs in his shorts. 'According to Jenny, the whole of the coaching team knows about you and me. In some detail.'

'Ah.' He winced. 'Yes, I'm sorry about that. I just . . . I just couldn't . . .'

Natalie folded her arms. 'You couldn't what?'

His shoulders slumped. 'Oh come on, Natalie. You're so gorgeous. I couldn't be expected to keep it to myself that I . . . that we . . .'

Natalie tutted, but she wasn't really angry with him. 'Flattery is not going to help you out of this,' she lied. 'We agreed we were going to keep this – us – a secret.'

'I know. I'm sorry. But I'm a man, and men brag to other men. We can't help ourselves.' He put his racquet down on Natalie's desk and got to his knees. 'We're simple creatures. We make promises we can't keep, but we mean well.' He clasped his hands together. 'Forgive me, please?'

Natalie rolled her eyes. Perhaps it was better that everyone knew from the start. There couldn't be any scandal now.

Taking her silence as a yes, he got to his feet. Natalie watched, trying in vain to keep her eyes steady as he took off his T-shirt and mopped his face with it. Her fingers itched to feel his smooth chest; to feel it crushed against her body again.

Paul was obviously thinking the same thing. Dropping his shirt to the floor, he moved behind her. Stepping up close, he slid his hands around her waist and pressed his lips to her neck.

They stood like that for ever, with his mouth on her neck, his pelvis tight against her arse, his arms holding her firm. Then, one of his hands began to inch its way beneath the waistband of her trousers, searching fingertips squeezing their way over her belly, towards her pussy.

'Don't,' she whispered half-heartedly, grabbing his wrist to stop him. 'Someone'll see us.'

'No one can see up here unless you stand right up to the window,' he said, mumbling into her skin. She eased her grip on his wrist and his fingers continued on, regardless of her muttered protests.

'You've got no knickers on,' he sighed appreciatively. 'You brazen hussy.'

'Yeah, well I never made it home last night, did I?'

'And whose fault was that?' he asked, mocking her. Combing through her fluffy pubic hair, he reached the spot where her juices had already begun to flow again, making her curls damp and her body warm. A fingertip gently nudged its way between her lips. Natalie closed her eyes and held her breath.

Get a grip, she told herself. You've got work to do. Fooling around in the office is not a precedent you want to set.

Reluctantly, she eased his hand out of her trousers. She turned to face him. They stared at each other for a minute, then Paul kissed her lightly on the lips. A light kiss turned into a full one; passion went from lukewarm to simmering; in another minute they'd be peeling each other's clothes off again. Determined not to do this on her first day as manager, in the office, in the middle of the morning, Natalie pushed him away. 'Don't, Paul. Not here. Not now.' She giggled and pushed his hand away as it tentatively reached inside her jacket. 'Behave yourself. I've got work to do, and so have you.'

'What could you possibly have to do that's more important than this?' he asked.

Natalie waved her hand towards the jumbled piles of paperwork on her desk. 'I've got all this mess to sort out; I've got sales figures to look through; there are unpaid bills which need paying. Justin didn't exactly tidy things up for me before he left.'

Paul sighed. He was petulant, like a child whose sister wouldn't play with him because she was busy with her homework. 'It's not fair,' he said, fiddling with himself in an attempt to calm his growing erection.

'Life isn't fair,' she laughed.

'You career women are no fun,' he said, shaking his head sadly.

She raised an eyebrow. 'You didn't say that last night,' she teased, reaching out for the bulge in his shorts. As she squeezed, he froze, and she held him in the palm of her hand again – literally. 'You seemed to be having fun last night.'

'Last night?' His smooth, tanned brow wrinkled as if he was struggling to remember. 'What happened last night, then?'

'You don't remember?'

He shook his head, his blue eyes laughing. 'Something good, was it?'

'I'll show you later,' she promised with a wicked smile, rubbing the heel of her hand over his shorts and up and down along his prick. 'I'll give you an action replay.'

'Promise?'

She nodded. 'But you've got to let me get on with my work now. I'll forgive you for bragging, just this once, but you've got to behave yourself from now on.'

He nodded, his disappointment as she took her hand away mingling with excitement at the thought of that action replay. Picking up his racquet and shirt, he reluctantly went to the door. 'I'll see you later, then.' His voice was soft now, and wistful. He turned in the doorway and blew her a kiss, and as it landed on her it sent tingles jumping over her body.

Natalie sat down behind her desk again and picked up a pen. She tried to compose herself, but, as her phone rang and the person on the other end asked whether he'd reached the new manager, and she told him he had, she couldn't resist a smile. This was just too perfect.

Natalie's hand was shaking as she put down the phone. This dream was rapidly turning sour. It wasn't a nightmare; yet it was one of those troubling, persistent dreams that disturbs your sleep and leaves you feeling slightly uneasy when you wake up. First, there'd been the news that Justin hadn't paid a bill, then the news that new members weren't joining in droves, as her uncle had insisted. Now, this.

Natalie had never been spoken to like that before. Standing unsteadily, she went to the back of her office and opened the sliding doors. Stepping out on to the balcony, she took a deep breath. She looked down at the four outdoor courts and, for the first time, she noticed that they weren't in very good condition. For the first time, she realised that her last job had cocooned her. Nothing she'd had to tackle in the high-flying world of Freedom Sportswear had prepared her for this.

The man on the phone had ranted at her. In a rage, he'd been incomprehensible for a few minutes, until Natalie had begged him to calm down. Then, with sudden, unnerving steadiness, he'd told Natalie that if his bill wasn't paid, today, his business would go under; and if that happened, he'd make sure that everyone in town was aware of the way the Crawford Club treated its suppliers.

The man was right to be furious. He'd fitted the club's air conditioning six months ago, and, despite a thousand reminders, had still not been paid. He was a one-man band; this was a big contract for him. He had to pay his suppliers, who were threatening to take him to court. If he could afford it, he'd said, he would take the club to court. There was no need for that, Natalie had replied, soothing his anger with the promise of a cheque delivered, by hand, within the hour.

Why hadn't Justin paid? He was disorganised, and had no sense of good business practice, but he wasn't heartless. Why hadn't he reacted to this poor man's pleas?

She went back to the desk and rummaged in the drawer, looking for the cheque book. Justin had instructed the bank to accept Natalie's signature, but that instruction wouldn't go through until Monday. He was supposed to have left a couple of signed cheques, but of course he'd forgotten. Natalie got the keys to the safe and opened it, but there was only £50 inside, not even a hundredth of the debt. Trembling slightly, Natalie realised that, if she was to keep her promise, she'd have to write a personal cheque – and practically clear out her bank account. And she had to keep her promise. She wasn't going to run this place like Justin had.

Panicking, she picked up the phone and started to

dial her father's number. He would know what to do. But then, as his warnings echoed inside her head – 'If you've got an ounce of sense in your body, don't touch the club. You've no idea what's involved in running a business. Don't come crying to me if Justin lets you down' – she changed her mind and slowly replaced the receiver. This was her problem; she had to use her own common sense to sort it out. This was what being a manager was all about.

She felt vaguely proud of herself for coming to this conclusion. Getting out her cheque book, she wrote a cheque for £5,750. On the intercom, she asked Jenny to come in to her office, and she dictated a letter of profuse apology to the desperate air-conditioning supplier. By the time she'd sent Jenny off with the letter and the cheque, she felt like she was back in control. She felt good.

There would be problems in this job, and there would be dramas and crises and hassles. But, whatever Justin's legacy threw her way, she would cope. She would have to: she was in charge now.

By Monday lunchtime, the dream was a fully fledged, keep-you-awake-at-night, worry-you-half-to-death, nightmare.

Natalie was writing herself a company cheque, to reimburse herself for the air-conditioning payment, when a letter arrived from the bank. In the embarrassing, terse language that bank managers love to use, Natalie was informed that the Crawford Club's cheques would no longer be honoured. Credit limits had been exceeded and it was time the overdrafts and loans were repaid. Her personal savings had been all but wiped out, spent clearing a company debt. If she hadn't been so annoyed, she'd have seen the irony of the situation. She hated air conditioning.

But using up the savings she'd taken so long to

create was only one of her worries. The lack of new members was a problem, but more serious was the fact that, in the last month, forty members had left. And it seemed that the clients weren't the only ones dissatisfied with the Crawford Club: three coaches had also defected, and another had handed in his resignation to Natalie that morning. He was bored, he said. Not enough customers, no job satisfaction – the club used to buzz with activity, now it felt more like a morgue. Natalie would have asked him to serve his notice but he was right, and she had enough coaches left to cover for him with ease. Suddenly the sedate, almost soporific, atmosphere stopped being relaxing and began to inject panic into Natalie's veins.

All the signs were there. This was a business slowly falling to its knees. Trying desperately to make sense of it all, to find a way of bringing the club back up to its feet, Natalie asked for an emergency meeting with the accountants. She got one, but their message was one of doom, not hope. The club was in debt to the bank, and to a legion of disgruntled suppliers. Last month's outgoings were almost double the takings, and this was becoming the norm. The only way to bring the business back into the black was to attract new clients – a lot of new clients – and fast. 'I'm afraid it'll take something drastic to save the club now,' said a dour, grey-suited Mr Brown of Wiggins, Bennett and Brown, chartered accountants. 'By my reckoning, you have one month before the receivers are called in.' He tutted sadly, wondering aloud why the absent Justin hadn't warned his niece.

'Any suggestions?' Natalie asked, desperation tingeing the edges of her voice.

'Call your suppliers, go and see the bank manager – beg yourself some time. Tell them you're different to Justin. Tell them you've got marketing experience. Tell

41

them you're determined to pay them back as soon as you can. And try to sound sincere.'

She couldn't have sounded more sincere, her voice quavering a little as she worked her way through the list of creditors. It was humiliating work. The bank manager was the worst. He was as embarrassingly terse as his letter had been, making Natalie feel like a naughty child as she pleaded for an audience with him. He asked how old she was; there was a telling silence when she told him. Middle-aged bank managers couldn't understand youth. It wasn't until she gave him a potted résumé, and told him how determined she was to make the club profitable again, that he begrudgingly gave her an appointment. Sighing thankfully, Natalie went to find Paul. She needed a friend.

Paul, as head coach – or director of tennis, to use his official title – had his own office. It was on the ground floor, at the end of the corridor that housed the changing rooms, television room, gym, physio and games room. He was in his office, and he opened the door with a smile when Natalie knocked.

'Well, hello,' he said. 'To what do I owe this honour?' His smile faded as he noticed Natalie's forlorn expression and the tears in her eyes. 'Natalie? What's wrong?'

She blinked back the tears, determined not to cry about this – determined to be an adult even though she felt like a child who'd woken up to find herself in the midst of a very grown-up game. She told Paul what had happened, and that she had a month to save the club – and that she didn't think she was up to the job.

'Of course you are,' he said, steering her down his narrow office to the desk at the end, and easing her into his chair. 'I can't think of anyone better to get this club working again. You'll do it, I know you will.'

42

She looked down at her hands, gripping each other nervously in her lap. 'I don't think I can do it on my own,' she said sadly. 'I thought I was good at marketing – I am good – but this is a whole different ball game.' She didn't even notice the pun. 'I don't know the first thing about tennis. How the hell am I going to attract enough new clients when the staff don't even want to stay here?'

Paul knelt down at her feet and took her hands in his. Prising her locked fingers apart, he gently squeezed her hands. 'We'll get through this together, somehow. You're brilliant at your job, and I know the tennis scene inside out. We'll work something out, I promise.'

Natalie lifted her bowed head and looked into his eyes. She wanted to believe him, but she was a realist, and she wasn't sure she did. 'Paul, do you understand what I've been saying? We have four weeks to turn things around otherwise this place will close down, and we'll all be out of a job.' A shudder ran down Natalie's spine as this thought suddenly hit her in the guts. Out of a job, almost all her savings spent on a company debt, no car – 'What the hell would I do?' she whispered. 'Oh Christ.' Another thought hit her, knocking the breath out of her. 'What *am* I going to do?' she asked Paul. 'The club can't possibly pay me, but I've got rent to pay on my flat in London. I could ask my parents to lend me . . . No, I can't. Shit, what am I going to do?'

'Calm down. There's always a way out,' he soothed her, stroking her hair. 'You can move in with me,' he offered.

'But . . . We hardly know each other.'

Paul shrugged. 'We know that we like each other. What else can you do if you can't afford your rent?'

What else could she do? She didn't really want to move in with Paul this early on in their relationship, but it would solve one of her problems. And they did like each other, a lot. 'You really wouldn't mind?'

'Mind?' His blue eyes shone. 'How could I possibly mind waking up next to you every morning?'

Natalie wasn't sure. She enjoyed being with Paul, but their attraction for each other was propelled by sex. Living together brought other pressures; and there would be enough pressures at work in the weeks to come. But she had no choice. 'Thank you so much,' she said, kissing him on the cheek.

As she pulled away he reached for her, meeting her lips with his. For a moment Natalie forgot her worries as his tender kiss bathed her mind in warmth. Slowly, they nibbled on one another's lips. Natalie's hands slid round his shoulders as he knelt up, and his hands moved round her waist. As their kisses became more passionate, with tongues and teeth and urgency, Paul shuffled closer on his knees. A quiet groan echoed in his throat as he tilted his head to kiss her neck, and Natalie forgot everything and wanted only him, his body. That was all that mattered, for now.

Moving forward on her seat, she sat on the edge and opened her knees so that Paul could close the gap between the two of them. Her short black skirt rode up, exposing a white flash of her panties. His penis, already hard, pressed against her soft, damp sex, pushing against the thin material. Pausing in his kissing, Paul flicked open the buttons of her jacket and, sliding his palms over her skin beneath the material, he eased it off her shoulders. Underneath, she had only a cream camisole and a bra, and Paul sighed to see the soft silk clinging to her breasts. 'You're so gorgeous,' he whispered, cupping his hands to her shape. His fingers moved around behind her, reaching underneath her camisole, searching for the hooks of her bra.

44

'What are you doing?' she asked, glancing nervously towards the door.

'I want to take your bra off,' he said. 'I want to feel your tits.'

'What if someone comes in?'

'No one'll come in. They know not to, when the door's shut.'

Natalie wasn't convinced. But she was convinced that she wanted to feel his hands on her breasts, and to feel her breasts naked beneath the silk of her camisole. Deftly, as only a woman can, she flicked her bra open, slid the straps from her arms and pulled it out from under her top.

'Oh,' he gasped, his eyes drinking her in. She dropped her head to see what he saw, and it was lovely. The sight made her pussy ache. The sensual shape of her breasts, pert and full, was obvious now beneath the thin, clinging material. Her nipples were dark discs through the satin, wide and soft, and every detail of her was outlined in the flimsy fabric. Biting her bottom lip, she watched as Paul's fingers gently teased one nipple into stiffness, rubbing his fingertip round and round the tender circle of flesh until it poked brazenly forward, its hardness a sharp contrast to the soft silk. Sighing deeply, Paul bent his neck and teased the other tip with his mouth, suckling on it through the material. When he pulled away there was a dark patch where his saliva had wet her camisole, and her nipple was even more prominent – shocking even, a small but potent sign of her arousal.

A bigger sign was twitching between her open legs. Paul's prick was at its full hardness now, and it was pulsing; yearning for entry into her succulent flesh. For a second Paul hesitated, tearing his eyes away from Natalie's swollen breasts and erect nipples, and gazing deep into her eyes. Shall we do it? he was asking, unsure whether the 'no sex at work' rule still applied. Shall we make love here, in my office, where there's the slight chance that someone will walk in on us?

Lifting her hips from the seat, Natalie tugged at her skimpy panties. She wriggled them over her hips, over the sheer black of her hold-up stockings, and threw them to the floor. Now when she opened her legs her pussy was open too, waiting for Paul to fill her. With a pounding heart, she endured the long, slow moment while he stared greedily at her triangle of dark hair; the angry, pink nub of her clit; her juicy, swollen lips – and the dark gap between that led to infinite pleasure.

'You're fantastic,' he whispered, pulling down his tracksuit pants and the shorts beneath.

'You're pretty hot yourself,' she said, stroking his long, slightly curved erection with the palm of her hand.

Holding on to her hips, Paul edged forward on his knees. Natalie edged forwards to meet him, until only a slither of her arse was still perched on the chair. Planting her feet as far apart as they would go, she held her lips apart with one hand and reached for him with the other. Guiding him towards her pussy, she held her breath as he got ever nearer. In a second their bodies would be joined; in a second pleasure would flood her senses; in a second . . .

'Ooohhh,' she groaned, relief and ecstasy mingling in the back of her throat as he filled the aching chasm inside her. He began to slide, rocking his hips backward and forward, holding her still in her seat. The pleasure was soft and slow, filtering through to her brain like the gradual kick of warm brandy. The friction between their bodies was eased by the juices flowing in her pussy. His movements were fluid and measured as his gaze drifted over her: her face, her breasts, the place where their bodies met. Her attention drifted too, moving through a dream, unable to focus on anything. His blue eyes, concentrating on her; his gentle grip on her hips; her legs spread wide for him; his long penis sliding into her – it was all part of the intoxication of two bodies becoming one.

Reaching down, her fingers moving slowly so as not to wake herself from the reverie, she reached for her clitoris. The tiny knob of hard flesh reacted to the lightest touch, sending shivers of bliss careering down her trembling legs and up her arching spine. Dropping her head forward, she watched as her fingers teased, just above his lunging penis. Just as he thrust again, she rubbed the infinitesimal, imperceptible point, the core of her pleasure, and impossible thrills swirled through her lungs and came out as a short, sharp, loud gasp. Suddenly, as if it was a signal, both Paul and Natalie came to from their dream and found their focus. Concentrating all their attentions on Natalie's cunt, they went for it, like sprinters finding a last burst for the line.

Paul held on tight and began to thrust harder, faster. Natalie, wanting her pussy more open, more vulnerable to his plunging, opened her legs still further, until she felt her inner thighs stretching painfully. Her fingers became frantic, twitching uncontrollably over her clit, sending involuntary spasms into her thighs. With her other hand she gripped Paul's shoulder, urging him further, urging him to keep going, urging him to push so hard that her troubles were crushed by the pleasure. Her breasts bounced as he complied with her silent plea and pumped into her until they both came in quick succession. Groaning, they collapsed into each other's arms.

'Oh God,' she gasped, glancing quickly at the closed door again, just to make sure it was still closed and hadn't magically opened to allow the other coaches a free show. 'Oh God, I needed that.'

'Always pleased to help a woman in need,' Paul said.

'You're such a gentleman.' She smiled back at him.

He gently stroked her hot cheek with the back of his hand. 'So, do I take it that sex at work is no longer out of bounds?'

'Well, I still don't think it's a good idea.'

He looked sad, like a puppy that had just been told off for getting overexcited.

'Look, Paul, I'd love to spend all day making love with you. But there's a reason why relationships are discouraged in the workplace. It alienates the other staff if they think people are carrying on while they're working. It creates a bad atmosphere. I still think we should confine our relationship to after working hours.' She shivered as she felt the aftershock of her climax. 'But, thanks. I really needed this. I needed you.' She kissed him gratefully. 'Everything's going so badly.'

'We'll work it out,' Paul promised. 'I've got an idea.'

'You have?'

He nodded. Slowly withdrawing from the tender clutches of Natalie's pussy, he stood up. Grabbing the nearest thing – which happened to be Natalie's bra – he used it to soak up the come dribbling from his prick. She snatched it from him, startled by his cheek. He continued: 'All the coaches who've left recently have defected to another club. The Shilton. Heard of it?'

Natalie nodded. The Shilton Club was in nearby Esher. She used to pass it on the way to work every morning. It didn't look very impressive.

'I've kept in touch with a couple of the guys who left to go there. According to them, the place is doing really well. Only started a year ago, and it's had to close down its membership books already. They must be doing something right.'

Natalie retrieved her panties and readjusted her clothing, making herself look respectable again. 'So, maybe you should go, take a look at what they're doing. Do a little spying?' Yes, that was a good idea. 'There's no time to waste. Go as soon as possible. How about this afternoon?'

Paul shook his head. 'I'm booked this afternoon – a rich widow we can't afford to piss off. Besides, they wouldn't welcome me if I turned up at the Shilton. Everyone there would know I was director of tennis here, and they wouldn't tell me a thing. You should go. No one will know you.'

An even better idea. She gave him a full-on kiss to tell him so. 'I'll go this afternoon,' she said, 'before I tackle the bank manager.'

The Shilton Racquet Club had only one thing in common with the Crawford – tennis was played there. The rival club looked like a poor relation that had fallen on hard times. Situated in what looked like an aircraft hangar – whereas Justin's premises were purpose built – it was a mess of peeling paint, drab colours and worn carpets. It had no outdoor courts, and the indoor ones were in need of tidying up, with their sagging nets, cracks in the glass doors where balls had been smashed against them, and broken racquets discarded in the corners. Unlike the Crawford's plush, exclusive air, this place was tatty and worn. The atmosphere couldn't have been much more laid back.

And yet, the place was full. The quiet calmness Natalie had found so soothing – and then so worrying – at the Crawford, was a stark contrast to the lively buzz of this place. It was packed out. The café, the courts, the corridors – everywhere she was shown on her guided tour there were people laughing, talking, having a good time. The coach who'd left this morning had been right: the Crawford was like a morgue compared to this place.

But what was their secret? As a friendly male coach (a little too friendly, she thought, resting his hand just a little too low on her waist, showed her around, he gave no clues. He pointed out the amenities, which were far inferior to her club's, and he made no attempt to sell the place on its facilities. Rather, he emphasised the Shilton's unique atmosphere, and the fact that coaches liked to give individual attention to their clients, and the fact that this was a place for relaxation as well as sport. 'A place to forget all your troubles, forget who you are for a while . . . and let us pamper you.' He winked, touching her arm.

He was too tactile. He was annoying her. 'Can I wander around on my own for a while?' she asked. 'I'd like to watch some matches.'

'Sure.' He smiled. 'Ask for me at reception if you need me . . . for anything.'

She pulled a face behind his back as he turned and sauntered away. His tone of voice was unmistakably suggestive. He was flirting, fairly openly. How unprofessional, she thought. What sort of impression did that give to potential members?

The right impression, obviously. As Natalie strolled down the passageway, looking into the courts, she noticed that the majority of people there were women. And the majority of the women were middle aged and veneered with wealth: tanned, gold, bottled blondes. Perhaps her guide's attitude worked with them; made them feel attractive and wanted and sexy. This was a very wealthy area of Surrey, and, judging by appearances, these were some of the richest women in the area. And rich women had time on their hands – time to flirt with handsome young tennis coaches.

All the coaches were handsome. And, as she looked in on the matches taking place, Natalie noticed that all of them were as tactile as her guide had been. They seemed to take every opportunity to touch their pupils, standing behind them, pressing up close to them, wrapping their arms round them to demonstrate the nuance of a perfect backhand stroke, or a fluent forehand, or a devastating lob. The women were plainly lapping it up, and Natalie couldn't blame them. But she was a little disturbed by the sight, nonetheless. Was this what she needed to do to lure customers back to her club – encourage her coaches to flirt with their clients?

'Never,' she muttered angrily to herself, stopping at the last court. This was a show court, like the one at the Crawford but not as impressive. The coach playing on it was very impressive though, and as she watched him she felt a frisson of pure, animal attraction in her cunt. Squeezing her inner thighs together, trying to keep her lust under control, she stared.

He was fascinating. His body was beautiful, every movement as strong and fluent as a big cat's. He wasn't as classically gorgeous as Paul; but he had a raw, gut-wrenching attraction that gripped her. He had big hands, thick forearms – God, those forearms, so masculine – heavy, muscular thighs and broad shoulders. He was about six inches taller than her, with a smooth, shiny bald head; smooth, shiny black skin; a wicked smile; and dark-brown eyes that, as he felt her watching and glanced over to where she was standing, pierced her.

A tiny, faint 'oh' jumped from her open lips as he caught her admiring him, and she immediately looked away, guiltily. But out of the corner of her eye she could see him staring at her, or rather she could feel him, feel the heat of his dark eyes singeing her and making her blush.

The match began again and Natalie waited for a long time, until she was sure she'd given it a safe interval, before glancing at him again. Immediately he met her gaze, again, as if he'd been expecting her attention. Then, smiling lazily, he gave a correction to the tall, attractive woman who was his doubles partner. Standing close behind her, he held on to her wrists and went through the motion of a serve with her. Shuffling nearer, he pressed himself right up against the lucky woman, and rested his chin on her shoulder. Slipping his fingers up along her arms, over her shoulders and then down, he squeezed her round the waist. Pulling her body still further into his, he gently thrust his pelvis into his pupil's arse. The woman smiled, showing how much she was enjoying the contact; he smiled too, looking up at Natalie at the same time – showing how much he was enjoying his job.

Natalie gasped. What a show-off. What inappropriate behaviour. What a stunningly, arrogantly sexy man.

What would it feel like to have him inside her?

Chris wanted her the minute he saw her. But then, he wanted every woman who ever gave him a second glance. And those who didn't give him a second glance he wanted even more. It was an ego thing, and he knew it. He wasn't ashamed of the size of his ego. What was so wrong in acknowledging how attractive he was to the opposite sex; in using his looks to get what – and who – he wanted, whenever he wanted it; in flaunting his libido like he flaunted his muscular body? He was only doing what women had done since the beginning of time. Women were the experts in using their looks to get what they wanted.

He wouldn't mind betting his unashamedly phallic-shaped car that *she* used her looks. And what looks they were. As their eyes met and, embarrassed, she glanced away, he gave her a lingering once-over.

Wow. She was fucking horny.

She wasn't beautiful. She wasn't what he'd call pretty. She was deeply, strikingly attractive, and he wanted to fuck her. He wanted to mess up her slicked-back, glossy dark hair; to pull it out of her neat, no-nonsense pony tail and feel it brush over his chest as he pushed her face down towards his cock. He longed to run his tongue over her delicious olive skin. He ached, desperately, to push up her immaculate black skirt, to crease it up round her hips; to rip off her jacket; to tear the flimsy cream silk of the camisole which he could just see peeping over her jacket's top button. He wanted to see her dark eyes cloud with dirty pleasure, her pure cheeks stain with the pink of arousal. God, he wanted to fuck her.

And he would do. Maybe not today, but he'd have her. He always got what he wanted in the end. Women just couldn't resist him. It wasn't just his hard, perfectly toned body that got to them; his wicked arrogance turned them on, too. It was funny, but, in this age of political correctness, Chris had really come into his own where women were concerned – especially with career women. They were so clever, so self-assured, so bloody untouchable. They thought they had it all worked out; they were in complete control, and God help the man who stepped over their carefully drawn line. But Chris knew what they really wanted – what was lurking just beneath their smart, designer-suited, feminist exteriors. What women craved, deep down, was for a man to take control in bed. They were dying to throw the political correctness out of the window and get down to some good, old-fashioned sex: the man on top, physically and psychologically, making the decisions and setting the pace. Chris knew this, and not just because it was written all over their faces. He knew this from experience.

He knew it from the way Mrs Antonia Spencer froze for a second when he wrapped his taut body around hers to demonstrate where she was going wrong with her serve. When he gave his corrections, speaking into the back of her elegant, long, pale neck, he felt her shudder when his deep voice caressed her skin. He ran his hands firmly down her arms and a giggle twisted and stuck in her throat. Then, for his *pièce de résistance*, he gripped her slender wrists tightly in his thick fingers and slowly, evilly, suggestively, he thrust his groin into Antonia's freshly liposuctioned arse.

Mrs Spencer didn't say a word. She never did. She wouldn't say a word, later, when Chris walked into the ladies' changing room and caught her semi-naked. She wouldn't make a sound when he pushed her gently but firmly to her knees; and then, she wouldn't be able to say anything, even if she wanted to. Her pretty, perfectly lipsticked mouth would be full with him, giving him pleasure, and her mind would be overflowing with the intensely wicked thrill of submitting to Chris's powerful needs, before showering and changing and reapplying her lipstick – and going home to her husband.

Of course, Chris didn't really need Mrs Spencer. But she had to feel that he did. That was what she paid her extortionate membership fees for – not for the use of the courts, or the expert tuition, or the club's barely adequate facilities – but for the personal attention she got from her coach. That was what brought in all the Shilton Club's clients. And giving his personal attention was what kept Chris in the mind-numbingly boring job. That, and the obscene hourly rate he was charging.

Chris loosened his grip on Antonia's middle-aged but well-maintained body, and flicked a glance back at the window to see what effect he was having on the woman watching. He was having an effect, all right, but not the one he wanted. She had turned away, and was striding off down the corridor.

He couldn't let her get away – not without getting her phone number first. He had never let anything he desired just walk out of his life. Once he'd met a woman's eyes, and that instant of pure, primitive attraction – that thought, 'I wonder what it would be like to fuck you' – had twisted its way into his guts, then he just had to talk to her. He had to get close enough to really look into her eyes; to smell her perfume; to feel her presence. Promising his three pupils he'd be back in a minute, he ran in long, purposeful strides to the door. 'Hey!' he said, his low, smooth-edged voice echoing in the empty passageway. 'Wait a minute.'

She stopped, turned and waited. He sloped towards her, smiling to himself as he saw her blink several times. She was clearly embarrassed by what she'd just seen, on court. She was obviously attracted to him. Well, why wouldn't she be? He was fit. All the women told him that – as if he didn't already know.

'Hi,' he said, coming up to her. 'I . . . er . . .' Oh Jesus, her eyes were fantastic: the colour of melted milk chocolate; wide, innocent and clever at the same time; and fringed with incredibly long, sexy lashes. 'I'm Chris,' he said. 'I'm the head coach here.'

She hesitated for a moment. 'Oh. Right. Nice to meet you, Chris.'

She held out her hand. Chris clutched it, holding on far too firmly, keeping her in his grasp for far too long. She looked down.

'What's your name, then?' he prompted.

'Natalie,' she said quietly. She blinked again, lifting her head as Chris finally let her fingers slip out of his.

'That's a lovely name,' he said smoothly. That's a lovely body you have underneath those conservative clothes, he added silently, letting his eyes drift downward.

'Thank you,' she said, laughing nervously and putting her hand in her jacket pocket, out of his reach. Then there was a long silence. Chris let it develop, enjoying her growing discomfort. 'Erm ... did you want something?' she asked, when the silence became embarrassing and she couldn't bear it any longer.

Oh yes, he thought. I want to fuck you.

'I haven't seen you here before,' he said. 'I was just wondering whether you'd like me to give you a guided tour of the club?'

'I've already been shown around, thank you.'

'Shame,' he said, thinking how he'd like to give her a tour around his body. 'Can I show you the café, then? Can I buy you a drink?'

Confused, she glanced back towards the doorway he'd just come out of. 'But you're in the middle of a match.'

He shrugged. 'So?'

'So, it's not very professional, is it, leaving your pupils in the middle of a lesson?'

Chris waved his hand dismissively towards Mrs Spencer and her cronies. 'Oh, they won't mind.'

'They won't?' She raised an eyebrow in disbelief. 'If I was paying the membership fees here, I'm afraid I would mind if my coach walked out mid-lesson.'

'I'll make it up to them later.' He grinned. 'I'll give them each some ... private tuition.'

There was another strained silence while she seemed to be pondering the suggestive tone in his voice. Chris used her moment of uncertainty – what did he mean by 'private tuition'? Did that smirk on his face mean what she thought it did? – to move in. Very slowly, as if he was approaching a wild cat, he inched closer to her. Uncomfortable with his nearness, Natalie took a step backward. But she found her back up against the wall and, as Chris moved nearer still, she had nowhere to go. Like a trapped animal, she looked up into his eyes, wondering what her fate was.

A surge of power shot through Chris's body as he placed a heavy hand on the wall by her head. He was quite a bit taller than her, and he loved the feeling of a woman looking up to him. That was how it should be – the man above her, in control. He relished the thought that, if he put his other hand on the wall and pressed his body into hers, she'd have no way of escaping. She'd be pinned beneath his strength, help-less. But most of all, he savoured the fact that, right now, there was room enough between them for her to walk away, and she didn't. 'I could give you some private tuition, if you like. Call it a free introduction to the club.'

She swallowed, averting her eyes from his. 'No, thank you,' she said unsteadily.

'Oh go on.' He smiled. 'Let yourself go, for once. You know you want to.' Gently, he placed a finger under her chin and raised her eyeline back up to his. 'I know you want to,' he said softly.

That was it; he'd crossed the line. She stepped away from him and told him, by folding her arms tightly across her chest, that she was not playing this game. 'What the hell . . . What sort of coach are you?' she gasped.

'A very good one.' He winked. 'The best, according to my lovely ladies.'

'Oh really?'

'Yes, really.'

She shook her head slightly. 'I find that hard to believe. You walk out on your clients, who are paying you good money to teach them, so you can . . . come on to me?' Her eyes were wide; the fluid pools of chocolate had hardened. She was flustered, fidgeting, shifting her weight uneasily from foot to foot.

'You're a very attractive woman, and you know it,' he said slowly, tilting his head and flickering his eyebrows laddishly. 'You can't possibly blame me for coming on to you. I'd have to be mad not to.'

She met his eyes for a split second. Flattery had found a chink in her armour. Chris smiled to himself; a chink was all he needed. She was as good as his. 'What's your phone number?' he asked.

Her dramatically shaped eyebrows slowly dipped. Her small, sensual mouth opened slightly. She said nothing; instead, she huffed indignantly.

'What's the matter? You're acting like you've never been chatted up before.'

She huffed again. 'You're incredible.'

'Thanks.' As if to show her that he was, he lifted his tennis shirt with one hand and used it to wipe the sweat dripping from his face. He did it slowly, allowing her a good look at the smooth, dark tautness of his stomach. Women always went weak at the sight of his stomach.

But when he dropped his shirt and looked at her again, her jaw was set hard with determination. 'Well, it was nice to meet you, Chris, but, if you'll excuse me, I have another appointment.' She turned and walked away.

Chris wasn't put off that easily. He took a skip to catch up to her. 'Are you going to join the club, then? I'd like to see you again.'

She stopped in her tracks and swivelled to face him. 'I don't think that's very likely.'

'What? You joining the club, or me seeing you again?'

'Either.' She gave him a small, insincere smile. 'I already have a boyfriend.' Her eyes were different now; she was sure of herself, back in control. 'And I already have my own tennis club.'

She flounced away. Undeterred, and intrigued,

Chris caught her arm and stopped her. 'What do you mean, you've got your own club?' (The boyfriend bit didn't bother him – boyfriends and husbands had never got in his way before.)

'I'm the new manager of the Crawford Club,' she announced proudly. Then, looking down disparagingly at his hand on her wrist, 'So, if you'll let go of me, I've got work to do.'

But he didn't let go. '*You're* Natalie Crawford?'

She nodded.

He shook his head. 'Bloody hell,' he whispered. 'You seem very young to be running a business like that. I hope you know what you've let yourself in for.'

She bristled, snatching her wrist out of his fingers. 'Yes, I do, thank you.'

He turned down the corners of his mouth. 'Good luck to you,' he said, stroking his chin and not bothering to disguise the doubt in his voice. 'You'll need it.'

Anger began to colour her cheeks. It was very sexy. 'And what do you mean by that?'

He shrugged. 'So many of your members have left and joined here, I'm surprised you've got enough still with you to keep the club going. And four of your staff have defected here in the last month. One came here looking for a job this morning. We heard the Crawford was dead.'

'Well, you heard wrong.'

'Well, I'm glad to hear it.' He smiled, teasing her. 'So, how many members do you have? We've had to shut our books here, we're at our limit – two hundred.'

She balked visibly. 'W – we don't have quite that many. We don't have enough at the moment. But we'll get them back, believe me.'

A lock of her silky hair had come free from her pony tail and framed one side of her face. She fiddled with it, twisting it round her finger before tucking it determinedly behind her ear. Chris's fingers twitched. He longed to grab her neck, to kiss her hard, to run his fingers through her hair and mess it all up. Turned on by her prickly defensiveness and her sweet indignation, he was tempted to try it. What would she do? What would she do if he backed her up against the wall – if he kissed her, hard? Would she let him slip his tongue on to hers? Would she let him slide his heavy hand beneath her jacket, over the silk of her camisole, on to her soft breast?

He daren't try; not yet. Natalie was not one of his bored, rich clients with 'I'm gagging for it' written indelibly across their faces. Natalie was going to be a challenge.

'And how do you intend to get the members back?' he asked. 'What's your ingenious plan?'

'I'm going to ... My head coach and I are going to ... Well, we –'

'You haven't got a clue, have you?' he said, as his own devious plan was beginning to form in his mind. 'What experience have you got, exactly, of running tennis clubs?'

'I have plenty of experience,' she snapped. 'I've a degree in business and marketing and I've just come from a job as a marketing manager at Freedom Sportswear.' Her voice was tight. 'Before that, I worked as a brand manager at ... Oh, this is ridiculous!' She flung up her hands, exasperated, looking away from him. 'Why am I trying to prove myself to some pushy bastard I've only just met?'

She set off down the corridor, again. Chris strode alongside her. 'I heard the Crawford was in dire financial straits. I heard you're a month away from calling in the receivers.'

Again, she stuttered to a standstill. There was shock and distrust in her eyes. 'Where did you hear that from?'

'From your accountant. He's a member here. I teach him.'

Astonished, she put her hands on her hips. 'And he discusses my business with you?'

Chris nodded. 'A tennis coach is like a therapist. I have to listen to it all on court – business problems, inattentive husbands, who's sleeping with who.'

'Great.' She sighed heavily. 'So everyone knows the club's on its knees.'

'Not everyone. Just me. I don't talk about what I hear on court – although there have been rumours flying around that the Crawford's closing. Justin wasn't exactly a good ... Oh ... are you related?'

'He's my uncle. But it's all right, you can insult him all you want. Believe me, I've called him every name under the sun in the last couple of days.' She sighed again. For a moment, her disappointment won over her other emotions; her jagged, broken glass-topped defences came down, and the truth came out. 'I just can't understand it. The Crawford's so much nicer than this dump.' She looked around, shaking her head slightly at the worn, stained carpet and the chipped paintwork in the passageway. 'Why on earth should our club be failing, when this shit-hole's thriving?'

She looked up at him and, for a split second, she was his. Her eyes were wide with worry and expectation. Vulnerable, childlike, she was waiting and hoping for a response from him. An insider's tip. A helping hand.

He gave her one. 'It's simple,' he said. 'The Shilton Club has me; the Crawford doesn't.'

She blinked, and her expression instantly hardened. 'You?' she sneered.

'Yeah.' He winked. 'I'm the secret of this place's success. Our clients don't come here for the decor or the state-of-the-art facilities. They come for me.'

'*You?*' she repeated.

'Believe me, before I took over as head coach here, this place was on its knees too.' He gave her a slow nod. 'It's true. Ask anyone here.'

Her eyes narrowed.

'I could do the same for you, if you wanted.'

Unsure of what he was offering, she glanced from one eye to the other, left to right, left to right. 'What do you mean?'

'I could turn your club around in a month. That's all it took me, here. This place had forty members when I arrived – within four weeks we had one hundred and forty.'

Involuntarily, her sexy mouth opened. Chris could see the numbers computing in her mind. A hundred and forty members, a hundred and forty membership fees ... Her eyes cleared. She was interested. 'And how did you pull that off?' she asked.

'Simple.' He grinned, remembering just how he'd arrived back from the States and swept into the Shilton with his very individual teaching methods. 'Give me a job, and I'll show you.'

'I can't afford to take on any more staff.'

'I'll work for you for nothing, for a month. If I haven't made your club a success by then, you can kick me out.'

She laughed. 'Are you serious?'

'Try me.'

Her smile faded and her brow creased. 'You'd leave this place and work for me, for nothing?'

'For one month.'

'Why?'

'Why not? I'm self-employed. I've plenty of money in the bank. They need me here – it'll do them good to realise how much they need me. It'll do me good to have a break from this place. I love a challenge. And besides ...' He paused, looking far into her eyes. 'It'll give us a chance to get to know each other better.'

She hesitated. She was faltering, confused by his offer and the sexual overtones quite obvious in his voice. 'I told you,' she said, quietly but firmly, 'I already have a boyfriend.'

He ignored that. 'So what do you say?'

Nervous, her fingers twitched to her stray lock of hair again, which was refusing to stay neatly behind her ear. 'I don't know.' She looked away, as if the answer was written on the wall. 'I don't know. I've got to do something, but –'

'You've got no choice but to say yes. This is the best offer you're going to get, Natalie. I'll work for nothing, and I'll bring you a hundred new members. At least. Come on,' he urged. 'You know it makes sense. What option do you have?'

'But why should I believe you? I don't know anything about you. You say you're the answer to my prayers, but –'

He grabbed her hand and marched her back down the corridor. 'Ladies,' he boomed into the court he'd abandoned. 'If I decided to move to another club, would you come with me?'

Mrs Spencer and her two identical blonde, gold-decorated friends confirmed what Chris already knew. 'We'd follow you anywhere, darling,' Antonia simpered.

Triumphant, Chris turned back to Natalie. 'What more do you need to know about me? I have fifty pupils. Fifty pupils who would come with me if I moved to your club.'

She studied his expression. He studied hers. Chris could tell that the promise of fifty new members was tempting her. 'Well,' she admitted at last, 'I've got to try something.'

'Is that a yes?'

Her nod was almost imperceptible. 'But there are

conditions. We already have a good head coach –
you'd have to work underneath him –'

'You've got to be joking,' he laughed. 'I'm offering
to help you – for nothing – and you want conditions?
Uh-uh. You let me do things my way, or there's no
deal. I take over as head coach; you run the marketing
side of things exactly as I tell you to; and I promise
you you'll have a profitable club in one month, max. I
am the answer to your prayers – as you put it.'

'And what do you get out of it?'

'We'll discuss that when the month's up.'

She lowered her gaze. She was trapped, and she
knew it. The power Chris felt was sexual; but he felt
sorry for her, too. It wasn't nice to be press-ganged. It
wasn't nice to be left in charge of a failing business.
He softened his voice and touched her hand. 'We'll
turn the club around, together. We'll make it as busy
as this place. I promise.'

When she eventually looked up, there was surrender in her lovely face. 'When can you start?'

'I'll be round first thing in the morning,' he promised, 'with a list of all the members I'll be bringing
with me. Deal?' He offered her his hand.

'Deal.'

Chris looked down at her small, slender fingers
enveloped in his thick, strong hand. It took all his
strength to stop himself from pulling her into him,
holding her close and keeping her there until his prick
grew hard. It wouldn't have taken long. This was a
woman who could give him a hard-on with her eyes.

She slipped her hand away before he could do
anything. 'Thanks,' she said. 'I still don't understand
why you'd want to do this, though.'

You will, he thought. He gave her a careless shrug,
as if it was nothing. 'Whenever I see a woman in need,
I just have to help.'

'What a gentleman.' Sarcasm tainted her soft voice,

and her eyes twinkled with amusement. Despite herself, was she beginning to like him?

He paused, deliberately letting tension fill the air. There was an infinitesimal moment of recognition between them; a spark so quick it was invisible to the naked eye; the same spark he'd felt the first time their eyes had met, when he'd been on court and she'd been watching. It was undeniable. There was a faint glimmer in her mink brown eyes, and the slightest hint of a smile on her lips. It was a sign. That smile, even though it was a tentative one, told him what his whole body was yearning to hear: she wanted him.

'I'm no gentleman,' he said. Moving through delicious, syrupy slow motion, he dipped his wide mouth to her lips. In a second, half a second . . .

'And I'm no pushover.' Her small and surprisingly strong hand pushed his chest; pushed him away. She jerked her head towards the court. 'Shouldn't you get back to work now?'

His stomach lurched. That anger; that fire. It was so fucking sexy. 'I'd rather work on you,' he leered.

Her fury burnt his skin. 'Look,' she hissed, drawing herself up to her full height – still six inches below him, 'I'm very grateful that you're going to help the club. But I am not a part of this deal. I want you to be clear about that before you start working for me.'

'With you.'

'Huh?'

'With you. I'll be working *with* you, not for you.'

'Whatever.'

Her mouth was mean. He wanted to bite her lips. 'Look, Natalie, we'll be working closely together. We've got to get on with each other.'

'We'll get on, as long as you keep your hands to yourself.'

He held up his arms in surrender. 'Relax,' he laughed. 'Christ, you're so uptight. Hasn't anyone ever flirted with you before? I was only going to kiss you on the cheek. Seal the deal, as it were.' Before she could protest any more, he did it, brushing his lips against her flushed cheekbone.

Her skin was so soft. Her perfume, faint and purple-smelling, seeped inside his mind. The momentary closeness of their bodies made his bones ache.

They parted. She glared up at him. 'Yes, well, I'd rather you didn't flirt with me from now on, OK?'

He saluted her, mocking her. 'Yes, boss.'

She sighed. 'I hope I won't live to regret this,' she said, almost to herself. 'I'll see you tomorrow then, Chris.'

The sound of his name on her lips echoed in the pit of his stomach. 'First thing,' he promised. 'And you won't regret it. This'll be the best decision you've ever made.'

She rolled her eyes. 'I'm only agreeing to this because I've no choice.'

He watched her walk away, whistling soundlessly. He watched her calves, taut in her high heels; her shapely legs; her lovely arse. He watched the back of her sexy neck. 'Turn around,' he whispered, remembering a Clint Eastwood film he'd watched on video the week before. 'If she turns around, she wants me. Come on, come on. Turn around.'

Just before she reached the end of the corridor, she quickly glanced over her shoulder. She smiled uncertainly.

'Yes,' he breathed, his smile wide and sure. 'She wants me.'

Most women wanted him. So why did this feel like the sweetest victory?

Out of the door, Natalie almost ran to the car park. In the safety of Paul's car, and the welcome dimness of the car park, she sat and tried to catch her breath. It

66

was as if she'd been holding it in the whole time she'd been talking to Chris. She was hot, too. There was a thin film of sweat on her throat, which had turned cold as she'd hit the air outside. And she was trembling.

'Pull yourself together,' she muttered angrily. Taking off her jacket, she laid it on the seat beside her. She flipped the sun visor down and looked at herself in the tiny mirror.

She looked flushed and flustered. Her cheeks were pink; her hair was a mess; and there was something in her eyes she'd never seen before.

What had she done? Why had she let that arrogant, cocky sod talk her into this? Why, when she'd looked into his eyes, had he made her feel like a child playing at being a businesswoman?

'Pull yourself together,' she said again, smoothing down her jacket. Her hands were shaking.

She sat back and tried to make sense of what had just happened. She was furious with herself. She'd looked stupid in there, and desperate, and naïve. She was a manager now, for God's sake. She was a grown-up, with responsibilities. His laughing eyes had made her feel like a kid again. In fact, she realised with a shock, he'd treated her just like her father always did – patronising her, mocking her, manipulating her thoughts. Making her feel inadequate and vulnerable.

It was a greater shock to admit to herself that she'd enjoyed it. But as her breathing slowed, she couldn't deny that just those few, super-charged minutes with Chris had left her deeply aroused. He may not have been as typically gorgeous as Paul, but there was something about him that had made her feel desperately horny. Was it his voice? His eyes? His wicked laugh? The way he looked at her, lust spilling from his smile?

'Oh God,' she whimpered, wondering what she'd

let herself in for. She was supposed to be the one in charge here: in charge of the club, her life and her future. But in the last two days she'd given up a good job, a flat and a car, moved in with a man she'd only just met, and now – fuck knows how she was going to break this to Paul – she'd been persuaded, in the space of five minutes, to replace her new boyfriend as head coach with a man she knew even less than Paul. Why, all of a sudden, when she'd always prided herself on being independent and self-sufficient, had she put herself in this position – completely reliant on two men she barely knew? Her future, and the future of the club, was in their hands. This wasn't how she'd imagined it; being her own boss.

But no one could blame her, she thought, comforting herself. Excusing herself. Just as she had to move in with Paul, for now, so she had to take a chance on Chris. If he was right about bringing fifty new members with him, those extra fees would certainly buy her some breathing space. And it would give her something positive to tell the bank manager this afternoon.

Chris. As she thought of him again, her pussy clenched, sending a shudder spiralling upward through her damp body. She didn't know what it was about him, but something had reduced her to a sweating, blushing, wreck. She felt like a thirteen-year-old who'd just met the pop star she had a crush on.

She checked her watch. Plenty of time before her meeting at the bank. Slumping back in her seat, she closed her eyes and tried to calm herself. But, instead of nothing, she saw him behind her eyelids. Like a film playing in her head, her encounter with Chris reran itself inside the darkness of her mind.

The moment they'd made eye contact, and she'd had to look away. The way he'd held that woman, his pupil, so close she must have felt his penis pressing into her flesh. His calling out to her, running lazily down the passage after her, asking for her phone number. His frighteningly masculine body looming over hers, making her feel small. *The way she'd longed to let him kiss her.*

Chris had that skill, she thought, that look that makes you feel vulnerable in his presence. Without her bra on underneath her camisole, she'd felt intensely naked when he'd been near her, as if the shape of her breasts was obvious and he could see that her nipples were stiffening, and stiffening because of his raw sexuality. She'd become very aware of the dampness in her knickers, and a strange, subversive thought had flashed almost subliminally across her brain. She'd longed for him to put his hand up her skirt, to feel the wetness between her legs, and for him to know that the wetness wasn't just because her boyfriend had fucked her less than an hour earlier.

Reaching down, she trickled her fingertips over her stocking top and under her skirt. Ruffling up the soft material, she felt what he would have felt, and tried to imagine what he would have said and how he would have looked. 'You're wet,' he would have whispered, and she whispered it to herself. His eyes would have drifted downward; his fingers would have reached inside her jacket; he would have cupped her breast, rubbed her nipple through the silk –

'Sorry to interrupt.'

In the time it took for her eyes to jerk open, a violent colour had flared all over her face and down her throat. She hadn't heard his footsteps as he'd approached the car. Oh God. Oh God.

'You forgot this.' He grinned, holding up her briefcase.

Oh God. Oh God. What could she say? What on earth would explain why he'd caught her with one hand up her skirt and the other on her breast?

She didn't say anything. Once again, he was in control of the situation. He opened the car door, handed Natalie her briefcase and said, with a lopsided, laddish smirk, 'I'll leave you to it, then.'

As she watched him walk away, with long, loping, confident strides, her heart pounded in her ears. 'Oh *God*,' she sighed, as her head fell forward into her hands.

By the time Natalie had finished with the bank manager, she was firmly back in the hot seat. Shaken up by her experience with Chris, and mortified that he'd caught her touching herself, she'd gone into the bank feeling uncharacteristically nervous. But then she'd met the manager – a typical boring, middle-aged, middle-class nobody – and she'd quickly reasserted her sense of control. Her meeting was a master-class of fine acting, and couldn't have gone better if she'd spent hours planning it. Mr Feeney – who, as she now knew, was a pupil of Chris's at the Shilton – was very impressed that she'd managed to poach Chris and, with him, fifty new clients. (Of course, in her version, it was Natalie who'd struck this deal with ruthless business sense, rather than having it thrust upon her by Chris.) Feeney had quite obviously found Natalie attractive, which helped matters too. A subtle look here, a flash of her camisole there, a glimpse of her stockings when she crossed her legs and her skirt rode up – it all helped. Within five minutes he was putty in her hands, a slave to this charming, vivacious, ambitious young lady who 'quite obviously had what it took to run a business'.

'Thank you,' she'd said, smiling. 'So I can have the extra overdraft facility I need, just until I get the cash flow flowing again?'

'Of course.' Mr Feeney's handshake was wet and

slimy. 'And, if you need anything else, please don't hesitate.'

He would look forward to seeing her at the Crawford Club, he'd said. He'd be joining, now that Chris was moving there.

The sun was shining on her when she stepped out of the bank.

Chapter Three

*I*t was a dull morning, the next day, when Chris swept in on a cool breeze and started rearranging things. There was obvious tension as Paul showed his successor around the club; tension which Chris did nothing to ease. Natalie followed them, watching Chris's swagger, listening as his confidence boomed out and muffled the sound of Paul's charming, soft voice. It hadn't been easy, explaining to Paul that he'd been usurped, and he wasn't coping very well. Chris was everything Paul was not: loud, brash, macho, arrogant – and the resentment was obvious. To make matters worse, Paul had known Chris, years ago, when they'd both been young professionals on the tennis circuit. Paul had found Chris in bed with his girlfriend, and he'd never forgiven him.

'The guy's an arsehole,' Paul muttered, when Chris called a halt to his guided tour to take a call on his mobile phone. 'Do we really need him?'

'We need the fifty members he's bringing with him,' Natalie whispered. 'I know this must be hard for you, but I'm in trouble here. I need all the help I can get.'

Paul's jaw gripped as he ground his teeth. 'He was

72

the bane of my life when we played the circuit. I thought I'd finally got away from him when I took up coaching.' He flashed Chris a withering look. 'Seems he's determined to follow me wherever I go, and ruin my life.'

'Oh come on,' she soothed, sliding her hand up his long arm and gently squeezing his tense shoulder muscles. 'He might be an arsehole, but he's done wonders for the Shilton Club. It's a miracle that place is so packed – it's a dump. We need a miracle too.'

'We could have sorted this place out, without his help,' he hissed.

Natalie shrugged, wincing as Chris laughed loudly down the phone. That laugh – it was so wicked, so dirty. 'Neither of us could have conjured up so many new members within twenty-four hours.'

'What worries me is his motivation,' Paul continued, ignoring Natalie and burning holes in Chris's broad back. 'That shit never does anything unless it benefits him.' Paul's blue eyes narrowed. 'Why's he doing this? What's his ulterior motive?'

Natalie shrugged again. Chris turned round and their eyes met. He was still smiling and chuckling from his phone call, and she felt herself wishing she knew him well enough to make him laugh like that. Her mouth faltered into a smile as he rejoined her and Paul.

'Right,' he said, resting one heavy arm on her shoulder, and one on Paul's. 'Natalie, the first of your new members will be here in ten minutes. The Right Honourable John Webster and his charming wife, Eleanor. You'd better be ready to greet them – they'll expect the full red-carpet treatment.'

'What are you going to do?' she asked, a little miffed at being given her instructions.

'I am going to brief the coaching team,' he said, turning to Paul. 'So, if you'll get the boys together for

73

me . . .' He looked at his watch, squeezing his arm around Paul's neck so he could see it. 'Yes, I've just got time before my first lesson. If you'll check the lads are all here, I'll see them in the staff room. I'd like to give them a few pointers. There are going to have to be some changes round here.'

Paul looked at Natalie. She nodded. With undisguised annoyance, Paul disentangled himself from beneath Chris's arm and sloped off towards the coaches' changing room.

'What sort of changes do you have in mind?' she asked.

Chris tapped the side of his long nose. 'Don't you worry your pretty head about it. You concentrate on your thing, and let me get on with my job. I know what I'm doing.'

'I'm sure you do.' It was the fact that *she* didn't know what he was doing that worried her. 'But I am still the manager here, Chris. I'd like to be kept informed of what's going on. If you've got changes in mind, I think we should discuss them, before –'

He stopped her, silencing her with a finger on her lips. Natalie flinched.

'Sh-sh-sh.'

God, he was so patronising.

'I thought we agreed that we'd do things my way. Now, run along, good girl. See to the Websters. Leave the rest to me.'

Seething, Natalie pushed his hand away. 'Don't touch me again. And don't *ever* call me a "good girl".'

'Why not?' His black eyebrows jumped salaciously. He took a step closer to her, and leant down until his mouth was beside her ear. 'Would you rather be a bad girl?'

I don't know what I want to be, she thought, frozen to the spot. There she was again, confused and

74

aroused, annoyed at him and annoyed at herself for hating him and yet enjoying being so close to him.

'Chris?'

She jumped at the sound of Paul's voice, and looked over Chris's shoulder at him. Chris didn't turn round. Slowly straightening up, he just stared at Natalie, half a smile on his mouth. 'Yes, Paul?' he said.

'We're ready for your meeting.' Paul's voice was hard.

'I'm coming,' Chris replied, without bothering to look at him. 'Go on now,' he whispered to Natalie, nodding towards the club's entrance behind her. 'The Websters'll be here any minute. Go and welcome them, like I asked you to. We can't stand around here talking all day.'

She spun on her heels and stormed off.

'Good girl,' he said.

She bit her lip and didn't look back.

By the end of that day, Natalie had a smile firmly fixed on her face. She'd spent nine solid hours welcoming new customers, showing them around, introducing them to the staff and completing their membership forms for them. She'd had no lunch; she'd barely had time for a drink. But she didn't care. The club's membership had swelled to almost double what it had been when she'd taken over, three days ago. She could see light at the end of the tunnel. All of a sudden, the task of saving the club didn't seem such an insurmountable one.

She didn't know what Chris's secret was, but he was obviously a fantastic coach. The people who turned up to take a look around were devoted to him. So many of the women said to Natalie – often quietly, so that their husbands didn't hear – that they'd follow him to whichever club he went to, that she began to thank her lucky stars he'd offered to come to the

Crawford. These women, and some of the men too, said that he was the best teacher they'd ever had: he had 'a golden touch'; he gave them 'personal attention'; and, according to one immaculate, beautifully dressed heiress, he'd 'changed my life'. That seemed a little dramatic, but then Natalie had seen Chris in action, and she could understand why these women, dripping with jewels, reeking of money – and bored senseless – would enjoy the type of attention Chris lavished on his clients.

Without exception, as well as being disciples to Chris's 'wonderful method of teaching', they were all wealthy. Not one questioned the membership fees, which Chris had doubled from the normal rate in preparation for the influx of new clients. The Crawford was now far more expensive than the Shilton Club, and probably more expensive than most London clubs. 'There's more money in Surrey than you'd imagine,' Chris had insisted. He was right. And, now, a little bit of it was in the top drawer of Natalie's desk, ready to be paid into the bank tomorrow.

It was seven o'clock now, and the club was reassuringly busy. Not buzzing, like the Shilton had been yesterday, but a gentle hum, which was a great improvement on the silence of the day before. Beaming, Natalie looked out of her office window at the activity below. Beneath her, striding along the corridor, was Chris. He was on his way to the most secluded court, number ten, which for some reason he'd claimed as his own. It wasn't the best court in the club: it was cut off from the others, and a little darker than the rest, since it didn't have a wall of windows. But Chris had insisted.

He looked up at Natalie and waved, winking as he nodded towards the husband and wife walking in front of him. Natalie had shown them around the club earlier – they were a funny pair, quiet and shy, and

76

yet, according to Chris, the man was a businessman who'd earned a billion from ruthless insider dealing. Natalie didn't care how he'd earned it, but the fact that he'd decided to put a little into the club gave her a warm feeling all over. Chris read her thoughts, rubbing his fingers together behind their backs to show her that these two were loaded.

'Thank you,' she mouthed to Chris.

He wondered whether she would thank him if she knew why his clients were so loyal. He doubted it. Natalie was good at her job; she was clever, and witty, and brilliant at dealing with the clients. But she was a little uptight. A little naïve. Just a little anally retentive.

He shuddered at the thought of taking Natalie up her heavenly arse, but immediately banished the image from his head. He could relish that fantasy later, when he was lying in the bath and stroking his thick cock into an erection. Now, he had to concentrate on the job in hand: the Forsythes.

It took a lot of concentration. Bella Forsythe was as hopeless at tennis as she was gorgeous: tall, blonde, with impossibly long legs, a ridiculously short tennis skirt and a deep tan cultivated during summers in Nice and winters in Aspen. The Forsythes were rarely in the country, but when they were they spent their time playing tennis. It was surprising they weren't better at it.

Bryan was just as bad as his wife, whom he didn't match at all. She was a trophy wife, like a perfect diamond bought to detract from a bent, knobbly, wrinkled finger. Bryan was twenty years older than Bella, at least, and was as short, fat and saggy as she was slim and pert.

And yet they were happy together. They never said much, to each other or to Chris, while they were playing. But it was obvious there was a strong rapport between them. They understood each other well. And Chris understood exactly what they wanted.

It was always the same routine. The long, protracted build-up while the Forsythes played their poor excuse for a tennis match. Chris would intervene occasionally, giving one or the other a correction, and demonstrating what he meant. When he corrected Bella, he would do what he did to all the women, standing too close, holding her a little too long, letting her feel the presence of his heavy body behind hers. Bryan would watch silently, the only sign that he was aware of what was going on being his slight shuffle from foot to foot. Then, when the match had finally sputtered to an end, Bryan would give the signal. He would pick up his towel and zip away his racquet, and, with emotionless eyes and a low voice, would say, 'Well played, darling. Shall we adjourn to the café for a cool drink?'

As usual, Bella smiled lovingly at her husband. 'You go, sweetie. I'll be there in a tick. I just want to ask Chris about my backhand.' She turned to Chris. Her green eyes were wide with fake innocence. 'Would you mind showing me again where I'm going wrong? I just can't seem to get the hang of it.'

Chris smiled at her, his cock already thickening at the thought of what was coming next. Then he turned to her husband, gave him a wave goodbye and said, 'We'll catch up with you, Bryan.'

'All right.' Bryan's voice was steady. The only hint of his mounting excitement was an almost unnoticeable twitch at the corner of his mouth. 'I'll leave my wife in your capable hands, then.' With that, he hung his towel round his neck, picked up his tennis bag and walked towards the door.

'So, Bella. We're all alone. What would you like to do?'

She fluttered her long eyelashes shyly. 'Could you . . . Would you . . . help me with my backhand?'

'Sure.' Putting his racquet down, Chris walked over to her. She took up her usual stance, as if she was waiting to receive a shot: legs slightly apart, knees slightly bent, both hands on her racquet in front of her. Chris took up his usual stance. He was so close his legs moulded into hers. His arms reached round her and held on to her racquet, clasping over her fingers. 'Now step across,' he said quietly, speaking into the back of her neck. They moved as one, as Bella took a step to take an imaginary shot. Conducting her movements, Chris pushed the racquet forward, turning her shoulders and making her sweep at the invisible ball. 'Perfect,' he breathed, as she moved back to her original position before trying again. 'Perfect.'

Bella tried it again and again and, as their bodies moved together, heat began to flare up between them. It was as if the friction of their clothes had started a gentle fire. It had also made Chris's prick quite hard.

'Bella,' he said quietly, pulling away from her. 'You've got the hang of it now. Try on your own.'

She spun round. 'Not yet. It feels so much easier when you do it with me. Do it a couple more times.'

He shook his head. 'I can't.'

Bella's eyes were shining. 'Why not, Chris?'

He swallowed hard. Sometimes this was so difficult. She was so pretty, so perfectly coiffed and manicured and softly spoken and – even after a match – so *clean*, he just longed to put his hand up her skirt and get on with it. But he couldn't. This was the way the Forsythes wanted it.

'I don't want to have to stand so close to you,' he mumbled.

'Why ever not?'

He hung his head, as if he was ashamed. 'It gets me horny, being so near to you.'

79

'Have you got a hard-on?' she asked.

Chris looked up. Her head was tilted coyly. He nodded.

'So?' She smiled. 'Come here. Let me feel it.'

Chris hesitated.

Suddenly, Bella's smooth voice grew sharp. 'Come here, Chris. Now. I'm paying you for this lesson. You do what I say or I'll tell my husband you touched me up and he'll get you fired.'

'Yes, Bella,' he muttered. She turned round again, and he sidled up close to her. Wrapping his arms over hers, he pulled himself into her until she could feel his prick nestling in the crack of her arse.

'Oh, I can feel it,' she whispered. 'You are very hard, aren't you?'

'Well, you're very attractive. You wear such short skirts. It's difficult for me to teach you. I can't stop looking at you.'

'Do you want me, Chris?'

'Mmmm,' he groaned, as she arched her lower back and rubbed herself on him. 'You know I do,' he said.

'Then, take me.'

Chris closed his eyes as the words shivered down his spine, through his stomach and into his cock, which twitched in response. 'I can't,' he sighed. 'Your husband could walk in at any minute. He'd kill me.'

'Bryan's gone,' Bella said. 'He's gone for a shower. He always takes ages.' She pulled her hands out from underneath Chris's and threw her tennis racquet to the floor. 'I don't care whether he finds out, anyway. I'm desperate for your cock,' she gasped, pushing Chris's hands down on to her skirt. 'Touch me, Chris. I'm so horny I could die. I need you.'

Her voice ended in a strangulated tangle of pleasure as Chris did what he was told. Rumpling up her short tennis skirt, he rubbed his hands over her knickers. He wrapped one arm round her tiny waist to hold her

80

steady as he delved inside her wet panties. She bucked slightly as, without hesitation, he slid a finger deep inside her tight cunt. He gripped with his forearm, making her gasp for air at the pressure on her stomach, and the pressure on her senses. He fingered her hard, rubbing the heel of his hand over her clit; he couldn't see but he could feel, by the way her body suddenly went loose, that he'd found the right spot. Jesus, it felt good to have her in his arms, to know that she needed this, that Bryan needed this – and to see, out of the corner of his eye, that Bryan stood at the door, watching.

Bella cried out as Chris took his fingers away. She was soaking wet; she was ready. He pushed her over to the centre of the court, where she did what she always did. She clung on to the net while Chris lifted up her tiny skirt and tore down her tiny panties. 'Take me,' she whispered. 'Take me, now.'

He took her. He flung down his shorts and his prick unfurled angrily, the head darkly purple with pent-up fury. His penis looked so threatening, so black and fierce compared to the pert white purity of her buttocks. With one hand, Chris pushed at her back until she was bent forward, and with the other he grabbed his prick and guided it towards her pussy. He could see her lips, swollen and pink and framed with angelic blonde curls; and he could see the small dark hole between, welcoming him, beckoning him inside.

Then he could see nothing. His eyes closed tightly as his thick rod was sheathed inside the tight warmth of her pussy. Holding on to her hips, he rocked in and out of her, his groans mingling with hers. Immediately, he wanted to come, as he always did with Bella. It was too much, knowing this was going to happen – it was hard for him to hold back. He tried, concentrating on replaying last year's Wimbledon final in his head. He was concentrating so hard he almost forgot his dialogue.

A faint, embarrassed cough from the far corner of the court reminded him. 'Oh,' Chris sighed. 'You slut. You filthy, horny slut. What would your husband say if he could see you, bending over like this? He thinks I'm coaching you. You slut, Bella. What would Bryan say?'

'I'd say my wife was a dirty bitch.'

Chris and Bella stopped their groaning and rocking and looked up. Bryan was at the door, as expected. He stomped across the room and stood in front of them. Ignoring his wife, bent over and clinging for her life on to the sagging net, Bryan addressed himself over her head to Chris.

'My wife's a slut, Chris. She can't keep her hands off men. I'm always walking in and finding her. If it's not the gardener, it's her personal trainer. Or the butler. Or the chauffeur. Now you.'

'Bryan, I'm sorry. She asked me to –'

Bryan held up his hand. His other hand was busy at his crotch, unfastening his shorts and prising out his cock. 'No need to apologise, Chris. She's the one to blame.' At last, he looked at his wife. Bowing his head, he took a step towards her. 'You naughty, naughty girl. You've embarrassed me in front of Chris. You'll have to be punished.'

She whimpered. A moment later her whimpering was silenced by Bryan's thick cock sliding into her mouth.

Slowly, Chris slid his penis out of her pussy. Her muscles clutched at him as he retreated, but it was no use. This was it; his role was over. Putting his still hard, still throbbing prick away, he grabbed his stuff and went to the door. Even before he got there, he could hear the sound of Bryan coming into his wife's mouth. In another minute, there'd be the sound of spanking, of Bryan's flat hand against his wife's pink bottom. Chris often stood at the door himself, to watch that bit. But not today. Today he needed to masturbate, to get rid of the excitement weighing heavy in his balls.

And he knew just what, and who, he was going to think about while he did it. He waved at Natalie as he passed her office, on his way to the shower.

Chapter Four

Chris paced the office like a panther, waiting for her reaction with evil in his dark eyes and masculine aggression in every movement. Natalie watched him, thinking over what he'd said and trying not to want him. But it was difficult. He was as beautiful as a big cat. And, she thought, probably as dangerous.

'No. It's not a good idea,' she said at last.

He stopped his pacing and slowly turned his face towards her. The disdain in his expression would have made most women give in; but Natalie, as another strong woman once said, was not for turning.

'It's not the image I want for the club,' she explained firmly.

Chris sneered. Slumping with careless, tooth-achingly sexy ease into the chair opposite her desk, he raised one eyebrow. 'OK then, Miss Marketing Expert. What's your suggestion?'

Trying to look as casual as he did, Natalie sat back in her chair and crossed her legs. The trouble was, she didn't have a suggestion – only a vague idea. She hadn't expected to be launching an advertising campaign for the club only a week after taking over.

Bogged down with the more pressing problem of keeping the place open, this was not something she'd given a great deal of thought to yet. 'I'm not sure,' she admitted. 'But I'd rather go for something understated, and classy. Something exclusive-looking. The poster campaign should show that this is a very expensive, very upmarket place. I want the Crawford's image to be traditional. Perhaps we should redesign our logo, use the same colours as Wimbledon. I know some good designers, they could –'

'That's absolute crap. Forget it.'

Annoyed, she pursed her lips. 'I beg your pardon?'

'I said, that's crap. Traditional, understated, classy . . .' He dismissed them with a shake of his head and a flick of his big hand. 'No one's interested in all that shit. Sex is what sells. Sex will sell this place.'

'I said no. It isn't right. This is a tennis club, not a strip joint.'

He rolled his eyes. 'For Christ's sake, lighten up a bit, will you? I'm talking about doing the photo shoot with our shirts off. We're not going to get our cocks out.'

'You won't be getting anything out – or off. This campaign is going to be classy, Chris.'

Exasperated, he ran his fingers over his smooth head. 'You have no idea, have you? Think you know about marketing? You know fuck all,' he muttered, half under his breath.

That was it. Natalie had had enough of this. Gripping the edge of her desk, she eased herself up from her seat. 'I know a damn sight more than you,' she hissed. 'Show me a little respect. I've worked in marketing, remember? You're only a tennis coach. I've listened to your ideas, and I don't agree with them. I don't intend to fight with you about it.'

'Oh go on,' he smirked, standing up too and leaning

over his side of the desk towards her. 'Let's fight. You look so sexy when you're angry.'

He was so patronising. Fury made her breathing shallow and quick. 'You're impossible,' she said.

'You're wrong,' he said. 'We ran a campaign like this when I joined the Shilton Club. I may only be a tennis coach, but it was my idea. The day the posters went up, we had over a hundred phone calls.'

Natalie was silent. A hundred phone calls. Would a classy, understated advertising campaign bring in a hundred phone calls in one day? Probably not. He was probably right. But she couldn't bear to admit it.

'I haven't much in the budget,' she said. 'What if you're wrong? I'll have wasted money I haven't got.'

'OK. If I'm wrong, I'll pay for the posters and leaflets myself,' he said. 'But I'm not wrong. Sex sells. Why do you think all my clients followed me here at a day's notice? Because I'm fucking sexy.'

'Is that so? I thought it was because you were a brilliant coach.'

Slowly, teasing her with his laughing eyes, he shook his head. Leaning further over the desk, he brought his face within a few inches of hers. It took all Natalie's determination to keep still. He was too near. It was an invasion of her space. But she wasn't going to let him know how uncomfortable he made her feel. She wasn't going to lose this particular battle.

'I am a brilliant coach,' he whispered. 'But I'm also fucking sexy.' Closer still, and his mouth was only a breath away. 'The women like me. I get them wet.'

'Really?' She looked into his eyes. She wanted to scream. 'I can't think why. You don't get me wet,' she said.

He stared at her, trying to make her flinch with the intensity of his gaze. Ever so slowly, a smile broke out across his face. 'Liar,' he breathed.

He was right. As they stood there, an instant away

from each other, Natalie felt every cell in her body screaming, 'Kiss him! Kiss him!' God, she wanted to. She wanted him to feel what he did to her; how fast he made her heart beat; how wet her knickers were.

But she wouldn't ever let him know. Men like Chris were nothing more than egos, only interested in adding another notch to their bedposts. Admit you fancied them and you were lost. Stretching the elastic strands of tension holding them together, Natalie straightened up. 'When can your friend take the photographs?' she asked, pretending nothing had happened.

'This afternoon,' Chris replied. 'It's all arranged. So you've given in? You'll do it my way? You admit I'm right?'

'I'll admit you're right when we get the hundred phone calls.'

She sat down. Wrenching her gaze away from Chris, she stared down into her notebook and began flicking through the pages, telling him she'd finished with him; trying to impress upon him that, despite the fact that she'd lost this argument, she was still the boss here.

But Chris didn't go. 'And when will you admit you want me?' he asked, a smile in his voice.

Natalie didn't raise her eyes. 'Never.'

'That's all right.' He turned and went to the door. 'I can wait.'

'You'll be waiting a very long time,' she said, without looking up.

'We'll see.' He paused in the doorway. Natalie could see his dark frame out of the corner of her eye. 'I reckon you can keep this up for a week, max.'

She glanced at him. 'Keep what up, exactly?'

'This pretence that you don't fancy me.' He winked. 'You'll have to admit it, sooner or later. It'll drive you insane.'

She tried her best to copy the disdainful expression

he'd shown her, before. 'But I don't fancy you, Chris. I already have a boyfriend who's far better-looking than you are. And less of a big-head.'

He shrugged. 'Paul's boring. All he ever talks about is tennis.'

'Whereas you only ever talk about yourself.'

'I'm an interesting subject,' he smirked.

'Believe me,' she urged, 'Paul's far more interesting than you'll ever be. And he's kind, and considerate, and . . .' She wanted to say something to shock Chris; to shut him up. 'Paul's a wonderful lover.'

Chris nodded, turning down the corners of his mouth and raising his eyebrows at the same time, to show that he didn't believe it. 'If he's so good, why do you close your eyes when he's fucking you and pretend it's me?'

The air was knocked out of her. 'Get out,' she managed. But her voice was soft and pathetic compared to the sound of his laughter as he walked away.

Natalie stood in the shadows at the back of the studio. Her jaw was aching, and all of a sudden she realised she'd been grinding her teeth. Watching Chris directing the other coaches was making her temper simmer violently. This was *not* how she wanted it. But there was nothing she could do – Chris was in control.

It annoyed her that she'd given him his way over this. And yet, watching the guys posing for the photographer, she could see he had a point. Sex sells, he'd said. And if this advert didn't sell the club, nothing would.

Her staff looked great. Chris was brilliant at organising them, and, together with the photographer, they'd worked out some good poses. The coaches he'd chosen to go to the photo shoot – Paul, Robert, Mark and himself – were the best-looking blokes in the club, and these shots were bound to 'give all those loaded, horny housewives frothy knickers', as Chris put it.

But she couldn't help thinking that a poster – featuring four men with bare, baby-oiled chests, water dripping from their hair and filthy thoughts quite obvious in their faces – was a step downmarket for the club. She'd sparked up her argument again when they'd arrived at the studio and she'd seen exactly what Chris had in mind, but he'd shouted her down. 'Stop your whingeing, woman! How can the club be going downmarket?' He'd shouted across the room, while the others had looked embarrassed. 'We've just doubled the joining fees. It costs a fortune to be a member at the Crawford, now.' He'd tutted and sighed, looking at the others and rolling his eyes; making her look like an idiot. 'I told you this morning,' he said, speaking very slowly so this silly, stupid woman might have a chance of understanding, 'there are hundreds of bored, horny, filthy-rich women out there with husbands who are too busy or too dull to look after them. We're selling them a fantasy. We're selling them sex. That's what they want. They're not interested in the number of courts we've got, or the fact that we've got an in-house physiotherapist – they're interested in us.'

'But you look like strippers!' she'd said, her voice taut with frustration.

'Yes? And?'

He'd got his way. And the guys had enjoyed posing; they seemed to lap up Chris's laddish banter, as he told them all the girls in Surrey would be after them when they saw these posters. Even Paul temporarily relaxed his hatred of Chris, and sniggered along with his dirty jokes. It was strange to see them laughing together. Even stranger for Natalie when she noticed that, despite the fact that Paul looked like a model compared to Chris, it was Chris's body her eyes kept drifting towards. There was something mesmerising about his heavy muscles, his smooth skin, the tufts of dark hair on his chest and the way he swaggered and posed. Luckily, the studio lights were bright in his face: he wouldn't be able to see which one of them she was looking at as she lurked in the background.

'Right.' Chris clapped his hands as Hanif, the photographer, stopped to readjust one of the studio lights. 'That'll do it, guys. See you back at work.'

Paul, Robert and Mark trooped out. Natalie edged closer to thank Hanif and to ask when the contact sheets would be ready.

'You and me now, Nat.'

She looked over at Chris. 'What?'

'You and me.' He jerked his head and held out his hand, inviting her to join him. 'Let's do a few together.'

'You've got to be kidding,' she said.

He huffed impatiently, lunged for her and grabbed her arm. 'Come on, don't be shy. We'll try a few, just you and me.'

'Don't be silly,' she laughed, turning to the photographer for help. 'Tell him, please. I'm not photogenic.'

Hanif bent down to look through the viewfinder. 'The camera loves you.' He smiled, straightening up again.

'See?' Chris said, pulling her in front of him.

'We should have a shot of you, for the leaflet,' Hanif said. 'The pictures of the blokes will attract all the women, but there's nothing like a pretty girl to pull in a few male members.' His eyes flickered to Chris's as they shared the innuendo. But, unlike Chris, Hanif didn't snort dirtily. 'There's no harm in trying a few, anyway. I've half a roll of film left. You're paying for it – you might as well use it up.'

'I'd rather not.'

'Relax.' Chris put his hands on her waist and positioned her where he wanted her. 'You're so fucking uptight, Natalie. If I didn't know better, I'd think you were frigid.'

She swallowed hard. She'd show him. 'OK. Tell me where you want me.'

He turned to his friend. His eyebrows flickered lasciviously. 'Now there's an offer, Hanif. Told you she had the hots for me.'

Natalie sighed. 'Just get on with it, Chris.'

'OK.' He eased her body round so she was diagonally on to the camera. Standing by her side, he told her to put her hand on his shoulder. His hands were in front of him, casually holding his racquet. 'Look directly at the camera,' he said. She did, while he looked down at her. She could feel the warmth of his eyes. 'Take it,' he said to Hanif.

The camera clicked and whirred. Chris moved her around, making tiny adjustments to their poses between each shot. For once, he shut up, and after a few shots, with murmured encouragement from Hanif, Natalie began to almost enjoy herself. She couldn't deny it was arousing, being so close to his body. He smelt so good, of baby oil and aftershave. It felt so good, having his gaze on her. Feeling his power. She understood why the women wanted to be coached by him. His presence was startlingly sexual.

'This is great,' Hanif said from behind the camera. 'Try looking at each other, this time. Give it some sexual tension.'

Natalie looked up at Chris. Hanif clicked the shutter. Chris smiled: a wide, lazy, confident smile. 'I saw you looking at me before.'

'When?' she asked.

'Before,' he insisted. 'When the others were here. You weren't looking at Paul then, were you? I saw you, leering. You couldn't keep your eyes off me.'

Furious, Natalie felt herself blushing. 'You can't

possibly ... What makes you think I was looking at you?' She narrowed her eyes. 'Christ, you must have a high opinion of yourself.'

His lascivious tongue, so pink against his dark skin, swept slowly across his top lip. 'It's all right to admit it, you know. It's not a weakness on your part. All the women look at me.' He leant closer; too close. 'All the women want me,' he whispered against her neck.

Natalie flinched at the warmth of his breath on her skin. 'I can't think why,' she lied, trying to keep cool. A fire was raging inside her.

'You're blushing,' he sneered.

'It's hot under these lights,' she snapped, looking away from him, back to the camera.

Chris continued, relentlessly. 'You were looking at me, weren't you? You were dying to run your fingers all over my body. You should have said. I'd have let you rub the baby oil into me, if you'd asked nicely.'

Natalie's lips parted, but she didn't say a word. She was mortified; Chris was speaking so calmly, so clearly, that Hanif could hear every word. Behind his camera, he seemed oblivious, which made it even worse. She wanted to run, to escape to the car, where she could crumple up and cry. But she wasn't going to let him win again. Besides, she didn't have a car of her own any more, and she needed a lift back to the club.

Chris slid one arm round her waist, pulling her nearer to him. Testosterone seeped from his every pore, making her feel light-headed. Keeping her eyes firmly fixed on the camera, she tried to ignore the fierce, impossible attraction that was overwhelming her. You hate him, she told herself. Don't let him get to you. Don't let him see that he's having an affect on you. Think of Paul. Think of Paul. Gorgeous, blond, kind, caring Paul.

'I know what you were thinking,' he said.

'When?' she asked, glaring at him.

'When you were watching me before. The same thing you were thinking the day we met, and I caught you in the car park, with your hand up your skirt.'

Her cheeks burnt. His voice was like a flame licking her skin.

'I know exactly what you were thinking.' With his hand in the small of her back, he pulled her so close to him that she could feel the bulge in his shorts, pressing against her. 'You were wondering what it would feel like to have my cock inside you.'

That did it. Spitting anger, she wrenched his hand away and glared up at him. 'You disgust me.' He reached out for her. She blocked his hand with her forearm. 'Don't touch me, you pig. Don't ever touch me again.'

Chris glanced at Hanif. 'Oh dear. Seems I've hit a nerve.' His attention returned to Natalie. His dark eyes were laughing. 'What's the matter? You're very moody today. You premenstrual or something?'

Everything went into slow motion. She saw Hanif straighten up. She saw the expression in Chris's eyes change as she drew back her right hand. Harnessing all her fury, all her hidden sexual energy, she channelled it into her arm. She slapped his face as hard as she could, surprising herself with the force. Chris's head was flung to one side.

In that instant, every pore in her body was zinging with pure, uncut arousal. Every hair was erect. Her nipples were stiff. A million nerve endings in her clitoris pounded in time with her pulse. Her pussy walls wept with juice. In that instant, she wanted him so badly it was more than a craving; it was life or death; it was the line between existence or infinite nothingness. If he'd pushed her to the floor, and rumpled up her skirt, and plunged his salty cock into her, she would have come immediately, intensely, insanely. She would have let him have her.

'Wow,' he said, as he slowly turned back to face her again. For a long moment, he stared into her eyes. There was admiration in his face, and excitement, and lust. But not contrition. 'You are so fucking sexy when you're angry.' He laughed incredulously, holding up his hand as if he was waiting for something. 'I think I'm getting a hard-on.'

Everything changed. She hated him with a passion that made her guts hurt. She wanted to hit him, to slap and punch and bite him until he gave in. She was about to storm out when she realised that that would give him the upper hand, yet again. No, he should be the one to leave. 'Get out,' she spat.

He didn't move.

'Get OUT! NOW!' She gripped his oily shoulders and turned him round towards the door. She gave him a push. 'Go on. Go!'

'You don't mean that.'

'Get out,' she said, through gritted teeth.

He looked over his shoulder. He was about to argue, but Natalie propelled him away from her with the hatred in her eyes. Shrugging and smiling to himself, he picked up his gear and strode slowly towards the door. 'We'd finished anyway. Catch you later, Hanif,' he said, as if nothing had happened.

Natalie turned to Hanif, just as he took a photo. 'What are you doing?' she asked, amazed that he was still working.

'Sorry.' Unlike Chris, he looked genuinely apologetic as he emerged from behind his camera. 'I couldn't resist it. You ... er ... You do look very beautiful when you're angry. Photographer's instinct – I just had to take it. I take portraits, you see. That's what I do, when I'm not doing this corporate shi– stuff.'

She glared at him for a moment. He grinned sheepishly back at her, and her expression slowly softened. She held her cheeks in her sweaty palms. 'Jesus, you must think I'm mad,' she said. 'I'm sorry about all that, but he . . .' She shook her head, looking towards the door Chris had swung through. 'He drives me up the wall. He's such a . . . Is he a good friend of yours?'

''Fraid so. I've known Chris for years, ever since he moved back to England. He's a good laugh to be with, unless you're a woman. I can't say I agree with the way he treats the birds – er, ladies. Ladies,' he repeated, as if to be sure of not offending her.

'He's a sexist pig,' she said. 'I've never met anyone so full of himself.'

Hanif nodded, smiling. 'Yeah, he's an arrogant son of a – but he seems to get all the girls. I don't understand it, but they all go for this bad-boy stuff. We can go to a nightclub in town together, and I'll sit and chat to a woman all night, be really interested in what she has to say, be charming and sensitive – then Chris'll come up to her and tell her he . . . Well, tell her he wants to . . . you know. I can't say it, but you can imagine. And she'll go home with him, instead of me. It just isn't fair. The bad guy always gets the girl.'

'Not always,' she promised. She slid her hands round the back of her neck. Her muscles were gripped with tension. 'Ohhhh, *God*,' she sighed, talking to herself. 'What the hell was I thinking when I said he could work at the club? I've enough problems without him.'

'He might be a pain in the arse, but he knows what he's doing where tennis is concerned.' He nodded encouragingly in reply to Natalie's look of doubt. 'The Shilton was about to close before he arrived. It's none of my business, but, if you take my advice, you'll stick with him. He's good at his job.' Hanif stepped into the light. Moving behind her, he gently eased her hands away and pressed his fingers to her shoulders. 'Here. Let me do that.'

'Mmmm.' His fingers were cool and soft, and so pliable she felt the stress flowing from her muscles almost instantly. 'You're good at that,' she sighed, rolling her neck. 'Do you give all your clients massages?'

Behind her, his laugh was quiet and gentle. 'No. But then, not all my clients have fights in the middle of their photo sessions.'

'I'm sorry,' she said again.

'You don't have to apologise to me.' He stopped his massaging and moved around to her side. 'I can imagine what it's like working with Chris. He . . .' Hanif's brown eyes fluttered nervously. What a welcome change from Chris's arrogance. 'It always makes him ten times worse when the woman he fancies doesn't fancy him,' he said. 'You do know that he fancies you like mad, don't you?'

Despite her still-simmering anger, Natalie's pussy clenched at the thought of it.

'I mean, he wouldn't act like that, unless he was really keen on you. It's a compliment in a way.'

'I've had nicer compliments.'

'You don't like him at all?'

'I've already got a boyfriend,' she said. 'Paul – the tall, blond one who was here before.'

Hanif nodded. 'He's very good-looking.' He walked back to his camera. 'So you don't fancy Chris?' he asked again, as if he couldn't quite believe it.

Natalie didn't think she should be discussing this with one of Chris's friends. But being with Hanif was so soothing compared to being with Chris. Everything about him was soft and comforting: his voice, the colour of his skin, his shoulder-length, wavy black hair and his limpid eyes. 'Chris is attractive,' she admitted. 'But he isn't my type. He's too . . .'

'Sexist? Macho? Chauvinist? Foul-mouthed?' Hanif grinned as he reeled off the options. 'Aggressive? Domineering? Selfish? Pig-headed? Boorish?'

'All of the above,' she laughed. 'You do know him well.'

There was silence for a moment while Hanif fiddled around with his camera. Natalie watched him, wondering how such a softly spoken, sensitive guy came to be friends with such a pig.

'He does have a heart, underneath all that posturing,' Hanif insisted, reading her thoughts. 'Would you mind if I used that photo?'

'Which photo?'

'The one I took of you, just now.' He came forward again, handing her a portfolio. 'I think it'll be a fantastic shot. It's not often I get the chance to capture genuine rage on film. I've got an exhibition of portraits coming up next month at the art gallery – you know, the one in town. I'd like to include a photo of you, if that's all right.'

Natalie took the book from him. Opening it up, she was stunned by one of the most erotic images she'd ever seen. It was a portrait of a woman lying on a bed, her red hair fanned out across the white pillow. The fingers of one hand were twisting in her hair. Her shoulders were bare and Natalie assumed, partly because of her bare shoulders, partly because of the look on the woman's face, that she was naked. She wasn't beautiful, and yet she looked gorgeous, and sensual, and exotic. Her green eyes were dripping with longing. Her eyelids were drooping heavily. She looked like she'd just come. It was an intimate photograph; so intimate that Natalie felt like she'd walked into the woman's bedroom by mistake.

'She's amazing,' Natalie said, looking up. It was slightly embarrassing being confronted with a picture that seemed so private.

'She was my girlfriend,' Hanif said. 'We'd just made love when I took that.'

'Oh.' Avoiding his open, honest gaze, Natalie looked down again. She quickly turned the page. Taking refuge from her embarrassment at such a blatantly sexual image, she pored over the other photos.

They were all amazing, and strikingly intimate. They were all of women, of every variety: young, old, voluptuous, lean, innocent, knowing. Each one was looking into the camera with an expression so intense that Natalie felt like she was eavesdropping into private conversations between these women and Hanif. Some were wistful; some were bored, or sad; many were flirting with the camera. All of them were communicating so strongly with Hanif that for Natalie to look at the pictures made her feel uncomfortable, as if she was a voyeur. And although all the shots were only close-ups or head and shoulders, Natalie could tell by the looks on their faces that every woman was naked. Thinking of all those women, baring their flesh and their souls for the camera – for Hanif – made her feel strangely aroused. Involuntarily, her eyebrows pushed upward and her cheeks began to colour again.

'Were these all your girlfriends?'

He looked down at the book. 'No. A couple were. Some were models. Some are friends. Some were just women who came into the studio for something else – like you. I'm fascinated by women, especially by the way they act with their clothes off. They act very differently, you know. That's why, when I take a portrait, I always take nudes. Some of these girls were incredibly shy when they came into the studio, but somehow, when they were naked, they came out of themselves completely.'

Natalie could understand that. Hanif had the sort of

voice and eyes that could make a woman want to show him her inner self.

'All these shots are for my exhibition. It's going to be a celebration of women. I love women,' Hanif said quietly. 'I'd love to put you in the exhibition.'

Quickly, she glanced up at him. 'Me?'

He nodded. 'Can I? Can I use that shot?'

She was flattered. 'Well, if you think it's good enough.'

'Can I take some more pictures of you?'

'Well, I ... I couldn't, I mean, I couldn't possibly pose without my clothes on.'

'Why not?' He took the book from her. Closing it, he bent down slowly to put it on the floor. Moving tentatively, as if he might scare her off, he stepped a little closer to her. 'The camera wouldn't see your body – only your face. You've got a lovely face. And you're a natural in front of the camera.' He lifted his hand. Lightly, he brushed his fingertips over Natalie's cheek. She flinched.

'Oh, I'm sorry,' he said, stepping away, breaking the spell. 'I'm being a bit forward, aren't I? It's just that ... Well, from a photographer's point of view, you're ...' He gaze switched from one eye to the other. He seemed slightly nervous. 'You're very attractive.'

'From a photographer's point of view?'

He looked down at his feet with a shy smile. 'OK. From my point of view. But, I want you to understand, I'm not making a pass at you.' He met her eyes again. His expression was sincere. 'I'm not like Chris. I know you've got a boyfriend. I just want to take a photo of you.' He saw her hesitancy. 'Look, you don't have to take your clothes off. It's not compulsory.'

They looked at each other for a moment. Natalie couldn't believe this. There was sexual tension flowing in the air again. But this time it was sweet and cool, and gentle as the softest summer breeze. The hairs stood up on the back of her neck.

Chris made her feel nervous, and panicky, and vulnerable; Hanif made her feel beautiful. 'OK,' she said, feeling excitement bubble up in her stomach as the words left her mouth. 'I'll do it.'

Hanif's elegant mouth broke out into an unexpected smile. 'Really?' he said. 'You'll pose for me?'

She nodded. 'Sure. It'll be fun.'

Looking back on it later, Natalie would realise why she'd done it. It was Chris's fault: he'd made her feel angry and vulnerable, and when she felt angry and vulnerable she always had to do something wild and assertive, to prove to herself that she was the one in charge. It had been the same with her father, when she was younger. Every time he'd patronised her and treated her like a child, she'd gone out and done something to prove to him how grown up she was; something to really piss him off.

Now it was Chris she wanted to get back at. Perhaps there were better ways than taking her clothes off for a man she'd only just met, but at that moment – her brain addled with rage – she couldn't think of any. This seemed wild, and assertive, and empowering. And besides, Hanif had the sort of eyes that made her feel like her clothes were already dripping off her. He had the sort of smile that made her want to show him her body.

And so, as she sat on a faded red velvet chaise longue, straight on to the camera, with her knees clasped together and her hands on her knees, and Hanif suggested she unbutton her blouse, she barely hesitated. 'Just the top two buttons,' he said. 'You look a bit too businesslike.'

She did as he asked, quite willingly. His shoulders dipped again as he looked through the viewfinder, but he straightened up with a thoughtful look on his face. 'Could you . . .' He stepped around from behind his tripod and approached Natalie. 'May I?'

'Go ahead.' She watched him as he bent over and tentatively adjusted her shirt. His touch was so light on her throat as he pulled at the collar that she found herself wishing she could feel his fingertips all over her body. Down her throat, over the sides of her breasts, all over her back, down . . .

'Hmmm.'

'What? Something the matter?' she asked.

'Well, I don't want to push you to do anything you don't want to, but it would be nice if we could . . . See a little more . . . That's a lovely shirt, but it's fairly conservative, and I suspect you're not all that conservative, deep down.' His dark eyebrows twitched slightly. He smiled. 'I like to get to the core of my subjects, see the real them. Like I said, that's why I take portraits of women with no clothes on. There's nothing to hide behind if you're naked. You have to be yourself.' He held up his hand. 'I'm not suggesting anything drastic, but it would be nice if you looked less like a manager and more . . . Well, more like yourself.'

Natalie's pussy clenched as excitement began to swell inside her. 'I could . . .' She hesitated, gulping the words back down, but they came straight back up again. 'Maybe it would be fun to . . . Maybe I wouldn't mind posing naked for you.'

He was clearly taken aback. 'You sure?'

She nodded, nervous but exhilarated. 'I feel comfortable with you.'

He studied her for a moment, as if he was weighing up whether she had what it took. 'You really want to do this?'

'Sure. All the other women have done it. It's no big deal, is it?' She was trying to convince herself. 'Anyway, I was thinking, a photo of me might be a nice present to give to my boyfriend.'

He let out a soft laugh. 'You don't have to justify your decision to me, Natalie. My subjects all have their own reasons for wanting to be naked in front of the camera. I don't want to know what your reasons are. I'm just flattered you trust me enough to let me do it.'

She shrugged, pretending it was nothing, while her heart was racing out of control.

Hanif went back to the camera. 'You know, doing what I do, I like to think I'm a good judge of women. But I guess I'm not, really.' He took his camera off the tripod and turned back to Natalie. 'When you came in here today, I thought, now there's a woman who'd never pose for me in a million years. She'd never let me in. You looked so businesslike, so straight-laced. I hope that doesn't offend you.'

'Not at all,' she said. But if she hadn't already made up her mind, those words would have got her clothes off, for sure. 'It just goes to show, you can't judge a book by its cover. Just because I wear conservative clothes for work, that doesn't mean I'm –'

'Do you mind if I take some while you're getting undressed?'

'No, I suppose not.'

Now that she'd offered, he seemed keen to get on. She was, too: if she thought about it for too long, she'd change her mind. Before she could, she looked up into the lens and unbuttoned her shirt. She dropped it to the floor, then stood up and slipped off her skirt and heels. While Hanif moved closer, and the camera shutter clicked and the motor whirred, she reached behind her back and unhooked her bra. There was silence as Hanif paused, lowering the camera from his face for a moment. High on his attention, Natalie didn't pause as she rolled down her tights and, with a

102

lurch of anticipation in her throat, eased down her knickers.

'Is there something wrong?' she asked, when the silence went on for a little too long. His gaze was running all over her body, sliding over her skin like warm oil. 'Hanif?'

'Sorry.' He blinked several times, as if he'd just realised what he'd been doing. 'Nothing wrong.' He met her eyes again. 'You've got a great body. I was just thinking ... God, Chris'd be green with envy. He'd kill me if he could see you.'

That thought made her smile, too. 'Well? Where d'you want me?'

'On the chaise longue. Just sit however you feel comfortable, and we'll take it from there.'

She felt very comfortable, wrapped in the heat of his longing. He was professional, and emotionless, and cool. But he wanted her; it was obvious in the quiet restraint of his low voice, and in the way he paused frequently to suggest a different pose for her. Every time she moved he touched her, resting his hand on her shoulder, easing her arm into the position he wanted it in with just his fingertips. There wasn't any conversation between them; not audible conversation, anyway. But their eyes communicated, Natalie staring deep into the black vacuum of the lens, Hanif staring back through the viewfinder. The camera was like a shield between them; an excuse for Natalie to do something completely out of character and for Hanif to enjoy the nakedness in her eyes. The tension grew closer to boiling point with every sweep of the shutter.

Sitting there, naked, Natalie became intensely aware of herself. It was as if her clothes had muffled her senses, and, without them, everything was heightened. Her body felt more relaxed and, at the same time, more tense than it had ever been. Hanif's murmurs of encouragement were like butterflies on her skin. His gaze was like a satin sheet; it made her feel luxuriously sexy. Between her legs, she was starting to get wet. Her nipples stiffened. A surge of abandon ran though her.

Without realising what she was doing, she brushed her fingertips over her breast. Her fingernails gently grazed her sensitive nipple. The pleasure was faint, and so was her smile.

'That's lovely,' Hanif whispered, moving slightly closer. 'That look on your face. Oh, that's fantastic. Wonderful. So sensual.'

She turned her head, following her tiny reflection in the lens as Hanif moved around her. Lying back on the chaise longue, Natalie slowly unfurled her arms above her head, languidly stretching her body. She sighed.

'You're enjoying this, aren't you?' Hanif asked, appearing from behind the camera at last. 'Are you sure you haven't done anything like this before?'

'Never.' Feeling completely at ease, she didn't move as Hanif perched on the edge of the seat.

'You're a natural,' he said. 'I love working with women like you.'

Goosebumps rippled up her arms. 'And what sort of woman am I?'

He put his camera down and ran his fingers through his silky black hair. 'Sexy. Beautiful. Uninhibited. Surprising.'

'What's the surprise?'

'Like I said before, you seemed so . . . straight. And from what Chris had told me, I was expecting someone completely uptight. But you're not. Not at all.'

'Chris doesn't know me,' she said.

'Obviously not.' Watching his hand, he rested it on her foot. 'I think he's just frustrated. It drives him mad when women don't fall at his feet, like he's used to.'

Natalie watched him as he watched his hand. Her skin felt so warm under his palm. She longed to feel that warmth all over. 'I'm not really into falling at men's feet,' she said.

'What are you into?'

Their eyes met. Inexorably, Hanif's long fingers slid like silk up her shin. Natalie flung herself head first into the clear pools of his eyes. She answered him with a couple of slow, seductive blinks: I'm into this. I'm into you. If you want to fuck me, I'll let you. I want you to fuck me.

She sat up. Her hand moved downward to meet his, just as his reached her knee. Slowly, keeping her eyes locked on to his, she eased his touch to where she really wanted it. His fingers closed around the swell of her breast, tenderly moulding her shape into his hand. 'Natalie,' he said quietly. 'God, you're so . . .'

He leant forward, pressing his chest against her shins, and kissed her. Natalie slipped her fingers into his soft hair. Hanif's fingers were all over her. On her breasts, lightly pinching her stiff nipples, sliding round on to her shoulder blades, up to her neck. His tongue was like the rest of him: soft, languid, gentle.

'You're beautiful,' he whispered into her mouth. 'I want you. I want to make love to you.'

'Oh yes,' she breathed, less a reply to what he'd just said, more a reaction to his hungry lips moving down to her breasts. She didn't know what was going on. She barely knew this man. But she knew she needed him inside her. Delirious, she pushed his head down.

He slipped off the couch and knelt on the floor beside her. Gently, he eased her bent knees apart. Natalie lay down again as his supple mouth dipped to her pussy.

'Oh,' she gasped, any doubts and inhibitions gone as she let her legs flop open. 'Oh God.'

It was impossible to keep quiet. After the rancid

tension with Chris, and then the subtler tension of posing naked for Hanif, the pleasure was unbelievable. 'Oh Jesus,' she cried, arching her lower back, closing her legs round his head, squeezing his neck with her inner thighs, pushing on her heels; pushing her cunt further into his face.

'That feels so good,' she whispered, as his tongue flowed over her.

'Mmm,' he replied, lapping up the juices flowing from her. Sliding his hands around the tops of her legs, he poked his tongue far inside her pussy; so far in that he reached the part of her brain that was flooding with insane pleasure.

Her hips jerked as his long nose pressed against her clit. Her reaction stirred something in him. Breathing deeply, he stood up just long enough to shed his clothes. Natalie's desire poured all over his slender limbs. He was gorgeous. Just the colour of his skin alone would have been enough to make her salivate. But he was really beautiful. Slim, taut, with lots of dark hair wisping across his chest and down from his stomach. And his cock was long. And she wanted it buried inside her. And perhaps, perhaps, more than anything, she wanted to make Chris jealous by sleeping with his friend; by showing Hanif what Chris would never see – how sensual and uninhibited she really was beneath the business suit.

He lowered himself on top of her. Effortlessly, his prick slid into the heat between her legs. Natalie and Hanif groaned together as their bodies became one, and the pleasure flowed in a loop between them. Moving to the rhythm of her heartbeat, he started to slide in and out of her. Natalie wrapped her legs around his waist, urging him further and deeper. Her fingers didn't know what to do: she stroked his hair; touched his open lips; caressed her breasts, which made him moan. Squeezing one in her fingers, she eased her other hand down between their bodies. The tips of her forefinger and middle finger found the ache of her clit and rubbed until the painful need turned into ecstasy. Just as her breath caught in her throat, Hanif lost his slow, deliberate, measured pace and began to lose control. He pumped into Natalie's pussy. His slender hips jerked. Either side of her shoulders, his fingers dug into the velvet and all the muscles in his arms tensed as he thrust. His lips pulled back over his clenched teeth and grunts of effort escaped from his throat. His eyes full of need, he gazed down into her face.

Natalie closed her eyes as she came, heat rippling over her skin from beneath her fingers, and spreading inside her body from where his cock was buried, deep in her cunt. 'Jesus,' he cried, letting his breath out as his come spurted out of his body. 'Oh, Jesus.' He lowered himself on to her, resting his mouth in the crook of her shoulder.

After her climax came a wave of hot satisfaction. Can you see this, Chris? she asked silently. Can you see how straight-laced and conservative I am now? Still think I'm frigid? Can you see how your friend is lying with his cock between my legs, and emptying his come inside me? Can you imagine, Chris, how good it feels to be inside me?

They stayed like that for a while, as their breathing gradually slowed and their shared climax washed over them. Then, moaning as if it was a huge effort, Hanif raised himself back up on his arms and eased his prick out from between her trembling thighs. His hands were shaking slightly too, as he picked up his camera.

Kneeling, he pointed the lens at her flushed face. 'One more shot,' he said breathlessly, pressing the button one more time. Natalie heard the faint whirr of the motor as the film was rewound. 'There's nothing as beautiful as the look on a woman's face when she's just come.' He lowered the camera and stroked her cheek. 'You look stunning.'

She felt it. She felt like the most sexual, gorgeous, irresistible creature. All the tension had gone, pushed out of her body by the tension in his prick.

'It'll be the best portrait in the exhibition,' he said.

Natalie blinked sleepily, imagining a gallery full of people looking at her image. Anyone who saw that last photo would know what had happened moments before it was taken. They'd see it in her eyes: the after-effects of ecstasy. They'd see the telltale flush over her cheeks and neck, just as she'd seen it on the woman in his portfolio.

Somehow, she didn't like that idea. What they'd just done was private; not something for other people to whisper and snigger about. Not something for Paul, and Chris, and all the other members of the club to see.

'You can't show it to anyone,' she said, managing to get her brain to work through the sweet fog of her slowly abating ecstasy. Sitting up, she reached for Hanif's shoulder. 'Promise me you won't.'

'All right.' He shrugged. 'But it's a shame. It's going to be an amazing shot. It's not often you take a shot that you instinctively know is perfect. That was one of them.'

She pleaded with wide eyes. 'Please, Hanif. I don't want that photo in the exhibition. I don't want anyone to see it. Please.'

'Making love is the most natural thing in the world. Are you ashamed of what we just did?'

'No, of course not,' she said. But perhaps she'd just realised she wasn't quite as liberated as she'd thought. 'I just don't want anyone else to know that we . . . that I . . . Can't you use another shot?'

His expression changed. The admiration he'd had

for her suddenly dulled. 'I want to use this one. I know, as a photographer, when I've got it right. That last one was right.' His eyes narrowed. 'Look, I won't put you into the exhibition at all if you don't want.'

He was frustrated with her, and she felt like a fool. 'Perhaps that would be best,' she said, retrieving her clothes from the floor, and wondering why the look of annoyance on his face was making her feel so pathetic and guilty. 'I'm sorry,' she said, touching his arm. 'Maybe I should have thought about this a bit more. Maybe it wasn't such a good idea.'

'Yeah. Maybe you should. Maybe it was Chris you wanted to sleep with, not me.'

She winced. 'What do you mean?'

Hanif pursed his lips.

'Hanif, what are you talking about?'

'Oh, come on. The sexual tension between you two could be cut with a knife. I was here, remember? I've seen all the films where the woman slaps the man's face, and the next minute they're writhing around on the floor together. You and Chris are gagging for each other.'

'What we just did has nothing to do with me and Chris,' she insisted. 'I told you, I don't fancy him – at all.'

'Right. So the fact that you said his name as you were coming has no significance whatsoever.'

She trawled her memory. It was impossible. 'I didn't. You misheard me. I said "Christ". Christ, Jesus, God – I turn religious when I'm coming.' She laughed, trying to soften the sudden harshness in his eyes.

'You're sure you didn't say "Chris"? That's what it sounded like. Not very flattering, when you're fucking a girl and she starts to call out your best mate's name.'

'I didn't say his name. I said "Christ". Honestly.'

'Right.'

She did something she hadn't done for years; something she only did when she was nervous. She put her thumbnail between her teeth and nibbled on it. 'I think I'd better get back to work now,' she mumbled.

Natalie got a taxi back to the club. Her thoughts were as senseless as the driver's rambling conversation. She wondered what had possessed her to take off her clothes for Hanif. Whatever it was – anger at Chris; the flattering idea that she'd been good enough, and pretty enough, to be in Hanif's exhibition; an attempt to prove to herself that she wasn't straight-laced and conservative – it had backfired on her. She felt stupid now. She knew that, if she hadn't been prepared to let the camera into the secrets held in her eyes, she shouldn't have agreed to it. She wondered whether she should call Hanif and tell him he could use the shot he wanted, after all. Perhaps she would.

Then she arrived back at the club, and went up the stairs to her office. And all thoughts of Hanif, the prying eye of the camera and the exhibition, were squashed in the force of the shock that met her.

She heard his voice before she saw him. Pausing outside her open door, she listened.

'She did?' Chris's laugh rose into a screech. 'You're kidding, mate! You got her to take her clothes off?' There was a snigger so evil it sent shivers racing over her skin. 'How did you do it?' There was silence as Chris waited. 'You're joking,' he said at last. His voice was low, conspiratorial. He was like a teenager discussing his first fumble with his best mate. 'I don't believe it. You smooth-talking bastard. You really got Little Miss Frigid to take her clothes off? Has she got a horny body?' He made little leering noises as Natalie's body was described to him – in some detail, judging by the time it was taking. Trembling, Natalie put her hand to her mouth to stop herself from shouting out. She was furious, again, to hear them talking about her; she was curious, too, to hear what was said. And, although she didn't know it yet, she was inexplicably, fiercely turned on.

'What do you mean, "That's not all"?' Chris asked. Natalie heard him gasp. 'You bastard! You fucked her?' The salacious tone had gone; there was jealousy in his voice now. 'You smooth sod. What was she like, then?'

In the pause that followed, Natalie felt her body go weak. She should have known this would happen. She'd been given the warning sign: Hanif had admitted he was a good friend of Chris's. Men just couldn't resist boasting.

Chris whistled softly. 'You lucky, lucky bastard,' he sighed. 'I'll never speak to you again. Unless you make me copies of those photos.' His filthy laugh kicked in again, echoing in the marrow of her bones. 'You promise? Soon? Fantastic. I can't wait.'

As she heard the phone being put down, her mouth went dry. At the same time, sweat erupted in her palms and across her forehead. She heard Chris getting up, coming to the door, coming towards her – but she couldn't move.

'Oh! Hello, darlin'.' He smiled, as he saw her. 'Just got back?'

'A few minutes ago,' she managed, amazed her voice was still working.

'I've been hearing all about your session with Hanif.' He winked. 'Seems like you two got through quite a bit more film after I left.'

'Hanif asked me to pose for him. For his exhibition.'

'I know. He told me all about it. According to my mate Hanif, you not only wanted to take your clothes off, but you, er ... You – how shall I put this? You spread your legs for him.' His mouth leered lopsidedly. 'So much for your devotion to Paul.'

She bit her lip. She tried to burn holes in his skull with her eyes.

'He's making me a set of photos. I'm looking forward to seeing them,' he said.

'He can't do that. I asked him not to show them to anyone,' she said, her words coming out in a desperate rush.

'Yeah, but you don't always mean what you say, do you?' Chris put on a silly, whining, girly voice. 'You told him you "couldn't possibly" pose without your clothes on. But you did, didn't you? I think you often say things you don't mean, Miss Crawford. Besides, Hanif's my best mate. We share everything.' He patted her on the bottom as he squeezed past her and set off down the stairs. As Natalie realised what he'd just said, and that he wasn't only referring to the photos, he paused, turned, and winked at her again. 'Everything.'

That did it. She ran down the stairs towards him, almost tripping. Her ankles were weak. 'Look,' she said, spitting her words. They tasted like venom; like little flying fireballs laced with poison. 'I'm eternally grateful for what you're doing for this club. I realise I'm in the shit, and that without you this place is probably going to go under. But do not, for one minute, think that your helping me out gives you the right to treat me like this. Your constant sneering and innuendo – I can't take it.' That sounded wrong. 'I *won't* take it. Do you understand? This is the nineties, Christopher. Women expect to be treated with some respect. If I was employing you, I'd have sacked you on the spot for the way you spoke to me this afternoon. The way you talk to me – it's patronising and degrading and sexist. And if we're going to get on together, you'd better stop it, right now.'

Silence.

'What?' she asked, as a low, rumbling laugh bubbled up from his belly. 'What on earth are you laughing at?'

'You,' he said.

'Me?' Unlike his, her face was set hard. 'Why?'

He tutted, sighing loudly. 'Oh, Natalie. You've so much to learn.' Lifting a hand, he gently but patronisingly patted her cheek. 'You'd feel so much better if you just admitted how much you fancy me.'

'Chris, for once and for all, I don't –'

'Yes, you do. It's written all over your face. You blush every time we're near. Your voice goes up an octave with nerves.' His fingers slid down on to her neck, clasping her tightly. 'You wanted me from the very first minute you saw me. You enjoy the way I talk to you. It gets you hot. If only you'd admit it to yourself, Natalie.'

He was so powerful. His hand felt so strong, so big wrapped round her neck. Natalie was his prey. With a slow squeeze of his fingers, he could push the air out of her throat and have her gasping for mercy. She felt helpless in his clutches; trapped in the hypnotic darkness of his eyes. It was almost as if she was a bird, caught in his jaws, fluttering pathetically and willing the end to hurry up. Wanting him to take her. She faltered. She began to relish the sensation of being his, of being small and slender and vulnerable compared to his size, his strength – his mind. For a split second – a horrifying, exhilarating, gut-wrenching, terrifying second – her mind screamed YES.

'Didn't I tell you before? I don't want you touching me, ever again.'

Slowly, he took his hand away. He held it up. 'Fine,' he said. 'Don't admit it, then. It's your loss. But you and I know the truth.' Suddenly his smile was gone. 'You and I know that you only fucked Hanif to get back at me.' He licked his lips while he waited for her reaction.

113

She didn't give him the satisfaction. She swallowed hard. Her pussy clenched so tightly the sensation made her catch her breath. As she watched him turn away and walk off down the stairs, she cursed him. 'I hate you,' she hissed.

He didn't hear. But even if he had, he would have known it wasn't the truth. It seemed he knew Natalie better than she knew herself.

She waited until the last lesson of the day had finished, and the club was almost empty, before stalking down to the staff changing room. Her heart was racing again, and the fingernails of her left hand were badly bitten by now. But she had to do this. Not only to show Chris that, like she'd told him, she already had a wonderful boyfriend; but also to remind herself of the same thing. And to assuage her guilt for what she'd done with Hanif. She knew she shouldn't feel guilty. After all, she'd only known Paul for a fortnight. But she was living with him now, and she owed him her honesty in return. If she had timed this right, it would be perfect. Chris, just off court, would be getting into the shower just as Paul, who'd finished fifteen minutes earlier, would be getting out.

She was right. As she swung through the changing-room door, Paul was wrapping a towel round his slim hips. His bronzed body was glistening with water. His hair was wet. He looked so clean and fresh, so pleased to see her. So honest.

'Hello.' He grinned. 'I was just thinking about you. Fancy going for a pizza on the way home?'

'Paul, I've got something to tell you.' She walked across the floor towards him, her heels tapping loudly on the tiles. She slid her hands round his narrow, tight waist.

'Sounds serious,' he said.

114

'It needn't be. It's no big deal. Which is why I didn't want you to hear about it from anyone else.'

'Are you all right?'

She took a deep breath. 'Paul, I know we've only been seeing each other for a couple of weeks, and we haven't actually made any commitments to each other, but ... Well, what I'm trying to say is –' Her breath came rushing out again, heavy with guilt. Go on! Say it! 'You know the photographer, Hanif? I slept with him. This afternoon. After everyone had gone.'

'You did?'

She nodded.

'O ... K.'

'Is that it? OK?'

Paul nodded.

'You're not annoyed?'

'Why should I be? Like you said, we haven't made any commitments to each other. You're a free woman. I'm a free man.'

He dropped his eyes to the floor. He seemed odd, as if he was feeling slightly guilty, too. His calmness was confusing. 'You really don't mind?' she checked.

Raising his eyeline, he shook his head. 'I really don't mind.' Slowly, his wide mouth and blue eyes smiled. Somehow, although it was incomprehensible, he seemed to be pleased by Natalie's confession.

She was puzzled, but relieved. Now that she'd got that out of the way, and determined to do what she'd planned, she tugged at Paul's towel.

'What are you doing?'

'Making it up to you,' she said, cupping her hand to his crotch, which was still warm and damp from the shower. As she squeezed his balls, toying with their small, lopsided shape, she didn't have to look down to know his cock was beginning to stiffen.

'Chris is in the shower,' Paul warned. 'Why don't I

get dressed? Forget the pizza – we'll go straight home and you can make it up to me there.'

'No. I want to do this now, while I'm in the mood.'

'But Chris is in the –'

'I don't care.' She sank to her knees. The tiles were hard and cold, and slightly wet. Above her, Paul continued with his lame, half-hearted protests. 'Chris'll see. Natalie, don't. He's in the shower.' But he didn't try to stop her. Typical man, she thought. Weaker than any woman.

She sucked his beautiful, long, slightly curved cock into her mouth. Holding the hairy base in one hand, her other hand sneaked round his hips and grasped a wonderful, tight, taut buttock. She moaned at the feeling of his muscular, hard mound of flesh, just as he moaned at the pleasure of her strong lips. Savouring the taste, the clean warmth of his skin, the feeling of power despite kneeling at his feet, Natalie lavished his cock with attention. She licked and sucked, and massaged his balls. She poked the tip of her tongue into the tearful eye of his prick, making it weep, then flickered the silvery fluid away with her fast, darting strokes. She pulled on the swollen plum until it was purple with desire. She drew the juice from him as if her life depended on his salty, slimy come.

Out of the corner of her eye, Natalie could see the dark figure of Chris, watching from the row of showers. He'd been out of sight before. Now, as she'd hoped, he'd been drawn by the loud, undisguised sounds of Paul's building climax. Between her legs, her own juices flowed, making her knickers sticky for the third time that day. Her clitoris was as hard as a fist.

She swallowed Paul down, relishing the taste in her throat, gently holding his balls as he jerked into her mouth. When he'd finished shuddering, and a long, satisfied groan wafted from his mouth, Natalie got to her feet.

Paul looked at her through half-closed eyes. 'If that's what happens when you sleep with someone else . . .' His fingers absent-mindedly fiddled with his deflating prick. 'Mmmm.'

'Hurry up and get dressed,' she said, running her fingers through his hair, showing Chris. *Don't you wish this was you?* 'I want you to take me home now. We can continue this at home.'

'Anything you say.' Paul grinned. 'Oh! Chris . . .'

Chris stepped into the changing room. He was naked. Natalie suspected, by the look in his eyes, that he had an erection that was throbbing to get inside her knickers. But she didn't look. Forcing herself to keep her eyes steadfastly fixed to his, she smiled sweetly. 'Goodnight, Chris.'

He held her gaze. For the first time, Natalie could see something else in his expression; something lurking just behind the swaggering bravado, the leering and the patronising. There was tension there. Envy: a thin streak of pale green running through his dark-brown irises. 'Goodnight, Natalie.'

Two pairs of eyes followed the sway of her arse as she walked on air to the door.

Chapter Five

*T*he poster campaign was working, just as Chris had predicted. On the day the undeniably sexy images went up around town – in bus shelters, at the train station, at selected sites all over the place – the club had sixty-seven phone calls from potential new members. Not quite the hundred Chris had promised, but not far off. On the following day, when equally slick and sexy leaflets were received by those sixty-seven people, another forty-three called in response to the posters. By the first weekend after the campaign, Natalie had twenty fully paid-up new members. Every day brought more enquiries, more people and more money into the Crawford. There was some way to go yet, but, as she finished her meeting with the accountant and the bank manager, Natalie realised that the dire situation she'd inherited was on its way to being sorted. At this rate, the bank manager would soon be visiting *her*. And it was all thanks to Chris.

He was amazing. Everything he'd told her was right. The new, sexy image had sold the club, and brought more loaded women crawling out of the woodwork than she'd thought possible. This pocket of

Surrey was like a priceless antique riddled with wood-worm, and now, luckily, those worms were infesting her club. She didn't care much for them. They were all the same: shallow, as boring as they were bored, and far too concerned with what was on the surface – who was wearing what, and which tennis racquet so-and-so was favouring this season. But, as she stepped out of the taxi and back into her domain, and she saw their BMWs and Audis and Jags and Mercs crammed into her car park, she thanked her lucky stars that every one of those women had been born.

They were mainly women. A few had dragged their husbands along, but the posters and leaflets had naturally attracted more women than men. Chris was the most popular coach, and was constantly in demand, but the other coaches were each beginning to build up a loyal clientele too. And the change in the staff was unbelievable. They'd been half-asleep when Natalie had joined the club, working in sluggish slow motion, bored and tired and unable to raise any enthusiasm for their pupils. Now, they were brimming with enthusiasm, always smiling, always looking eager. This was the sort of business she'd always dreamt about. Rich customers, keen staff, challenges as satisfying as the profits.

If only Chris would calm down. His flirting was relentless. Despite Natalie's display with Paul in the changing room, Chris still insisted that it was him she really wanted. He could see it in her eyes, he said. He could tell, by the way she'd sucked Paul off, that she was more concerned with whether Chris was watching than with giving her boyfriend pleasure. 'You talk such crap,' she'd scoffed, when he'd told her his theory. 'You are so big-headed.'

But he was right. When she thought back to that evening, it was the blurred, dark image of Chris, seen out of the corner of her eye, that made her stomach lurch – not the remembrance of Paul's cock in her mouth and his groans of relief.

But she would never, ever, admit it to Chris. He was desperately, insanely attractive; but he was obnoxious, too, and so arrogant he deserved to be brought down a peg. For any woman to refuse him would be a shock, she thought; well, she would be the one to shock him. Her life was good now. She had Paul, and the club, and what more could a woman want?

And yet, as she pushed at the club's heavy oak door, her first thought was to tell Chris, not Paul, the good news that the business was out of the red for the first time in a year. Stopping at reception, she checked the roster to see where he would be. He had a session in the gym in twenty minutes. He'd probably be in his office.

Smiling to herself and singing softly, she strode down the long corridor. At Chris's office door she paused, hearing a noise inside and thinking he had someone with him. But there were no voices – only a low, moaning sigh. Silently, she pushed the open door a little further ajar.

Her smile slowly deflated, like a balloon that had been pricked. Chris was sitting with his back to the door, slightly side on to her, with his legs wide apart and his shoulders hunched over an open book on his desk in front of him. While one hand turned the pages, the other stroked up and down his swollen, turgid prick.

It was shocking to see him like that. Mesmerising, too. Her instinct told her to turn and go. He'd sense she was there; he'd look round any minute. But she couldn't go. Her feet were rooted to the spot. Her eyes were fixed to the place where his hand swept slowly up and down.

His prick was long, and thick, and dark. The muscle

was as hard as the rest of his body. The sight of it, looming from the pure whiteness of his shorts, made her mouth water and her pussy ooze juice. Her hands twitched as they longed to touch him; to feel just how hard he was. Her knees almost gave way as she imagined herself kneeling at his feet, gently pushing his hand away and enveloping as much of him as she could in her mouth. As his fingers grew faster, pumping harder, bringing him closer, she had to put her hand to her lips to stop the noise that almost came out. She wanted to gasp, to call out his name, to tell him she was there. She wondered what he'd do.

Then, all of a sudden, she realised that he already knew he was being watched. He turned himself slightly more towards the door, swivelling round in his chair. He moved his left hand out of the way, giving Natalie a better view of the hand on his cock. He didn't look at her, and he didn't hesitate for a second. But he knew she was there, and he loved it that she was watching, silently spellbound.

She didn't know what to do. She didn't do anything. She watched as he leant over his desk, flipping another page of the book he was masturbating over. The light reflected off the glossy pages, making it impossible for Natalie to see what was arousing him. She caught a glimpse of a woman's face, but that was all she could make out. Some girly magazine. Whatever, whoever it was, Chris was moaning louder now. As he reached the final page he slumped back in his seat and, keeping his eyes fixed on the image in front of him, he jerked his hand rapidly over the head of his erection. He shuddered as he came, and Natalie almost jumped in shock as she saw his white come spurting from the swollen end of his cock. Droplets landed like thick dew on his black leg, the colour making it all the more shocking, so pale against his skin.

He pushed right against his chair, tilting backward. His hand slowed to a sumptuous, post-orgasmic pace, stroking the last drops of come from the depths of his big, heavy balls. Then, in slow motion, he turned his head and looked at Natalie, who was standing shaking in the doorway.

'Hi,' she said immediately, wanting to fill that strained silence with something innocuous. Her attempt at a smile was as wobbly as raw egg white.

He didn't reply. He smiled crookedly, wickedly. In one swift movement, he slammed the book shut, stood up, pulled up his shorts, grabbed his towel and slunk past Natalie at the door.

'I came . . . to tell you –'

He grabbed her neck with his huge hand, and kissed her on the cheek. 'You are so goddamn sexy,' he said, and walked off towards the showers.

She watched him go. Then, still in shock at what she'd seen – and the fact that she'd stood like a Peeping Tom and watched him – she moved in a trance into his office. Stepping up to his desk, she looked down at the book he'd been wanking over.

It wasn't a book at all. It was a portfolio, the type that models use. But the photos inside were not of a model; they were of her. With trembling fingers, she turned the plastic pages.

The photos Hanif had taken were incredible. Like the ones he'd shown her, that day in his studio, they were so private they were voyeuristic. There was a sense of immediacy, of abandon, giving the images an intensity that practically radiated from the pages. They were incredibly sexy, too. Surprisingly so. Was this her? Did she really look like this?

He'd caught expressions she never realised she could make. There was an odd mix of nervousness and excitement as she'd posed first of all with her clothes on. There was a glint in her eyes as she'd got undressed, as if she was accepting a challenge. There was wickedness as she'd lain down on the chaise longue, luxuriating in her own abandon. And there was sleepy, sensual satisfaction in the last shot Hanif had taken, just after they'd made love.

He'd captured incredible eroticism in her eyes – latent in the first, tentative shots, burgeoning in the last ones. And the fact that her naked body couldn't be seen, apart from her throat and shoulders, made the images all the more tense and erotic. Only the photographer had enjoyed her nudity; anyone else looking at the photos had to imagine what was going on. The only clues they had were the expressions in her eyes.

It was more amazing then, that Chris had masturbated over these photos. They were revealing, in that Natalie had let her guard down and exposed her thoughts to the camera. But they weren't *revealing*. A stream of cold, fizzy surprise shot upward from her belly. Chris had looked at these and felt the need to jerk himself off. Chris, the sexist pig who never stopped commenting on women's bodies, had come just looking at her face. *Oh God.* That was the most flattering and arousing thing that had ever happened to her.

She turned the final page and looked at the last photo in the book. It was the first one Hanif had taken, seconds after Natalie had slapped Chris's face. Taken aback, she blinked slowly and swallowed hard. Chris, and Hanif, had been right. She did look amazing when she was angry. Her smooth skin was coloured with emotion; her lips were parted; her warm brown eyes had ignited and were on fire.

Chris cherished that image. He held it in his mind, languishing over it as he rubbed soap into his body. In his mind's eye, he stroked her fury-flushed cheeks as he rubbed himself dry. He looked deep into her fiery eyes as he looked into the mirror, into his own eyes, and another hard-on began to stir.

Jesus, how he'd love to extinguish the flames in Natalie's eyes. How he'd love to see gratitude in her expression instead; and desperate, undisguised need; and submission. The fact that she was resisting him was driving him wild. No woman had ever held out this long against Chris before; in fact, no woman had ever bothered holding out at all. Natalie was different. Natalie, he suspected, didn't yet know that the sweetest thrill of all was in giving in – in relinquishing control to another. Young, ambitious women were often like that. They didn't think they could enjoy anything unless they were in control of it. But Chris knew. He knew what women really wanted. And it was only a matter of time before Natalie realised it herself.

Putting on his shorts and trainers, leaving his upper half bare, he strolled into the gym. Picking up a pair of dumbbells, he absent-mindedly began to lift them with alternate hands, idly watching his reflection in the mirror. He had a good body. Shorter and meatier than Paul's, but more powerful. Did Natalie admire his body, like his clients did? Did she imagine running her fingers over his muscles, or being pinned down underneath his strength? She'd certainly given him a good look during the photo session. But what had she been thinking? He'd give anything to know.

He wondered what Natalie had thought as she'd watched him wanking. She'd been shocked; that had been obvious on her lovely face. But had she been turned on by the sight of his thick cock? Had her pussy got wet as she'd stood there? Had she wanted to touch him, and feel his hardness, and kneel at his feet and taste him on her tongue?

He put the dumbbells down and lay down on the

mat to do some sit-ups. The sound of his breathing and the sensation of his muscles tightening made him think of sex. And thinking of sex made him think of the fantasy he'd been cultivating ever since that tension-saturated day in the studio. The image was so overwhelming that he abandoned the sit-ups and just lay down on the mat, his eyes closed, his whole being focused on the image imprinted in his mind.

They were back in Hanif's studio. Natalie had just slapped him across the face. His cheek was still stinging from the venom in her palm. But instead of walking out, as he had done in reality, he stayed. Within a split second, a line of flames spread from her eyes to his. In that split second, he knew that she wanted him, and that she'd given in.

Hanif magically disappeared. (In his fantasies, anything was possible.) Chris moved towards Natalie and gripped the collar of her cream blouse. He ripped it open, and the mother-of-pearl buttons bounced across the floor. Dragging his attention away from her face, he looked down at her breasts. She was wearing a pretty, lacy, pale-cream bra that barely held her. Her breasts were full, ripe, heavy, and rising and falling with her shallow breathing. Snatching at the hook nestling in her sublime cleavage, he pushed the lacy cups aside and slid his fingers over her perfect, perfect shapes. He –

'Good afternoon, Christopher.'

Bugger. Was it that time already? He opened his eyes.

'Come along, darling, we're raring to go.'

He heaved himself back up on to his feet. 'Hello, ladies.' Carolyn Dubarrie and her pals, Felicia and Justine, smiled wickedly back at him. 'Ready for your session?'

'Ready and willing,' Carolyn said suggestively. Stepping up to him, she clasped her long, slender, perfectly manicured fingers to the bulge in his shorts. 'Seems you started without us.'

'I was thinking of you, Carolyn,' he lied.

'I should hope so, darling.'

She *was* quite lovely, but not his type. None of his clients were his type: they were all too perfect, too groomed, like prize 'best of breeds' at Crufts. Their hair was lacquered into perfection, their lipstick never smudged and they never seemed to sweat. Still, in the absence of Natalie, they'd do. And it was flattering that they wanted him, although he was under no illusions. He was their bit of rough, their bit on the side – their macho distraction from their insipid husbands and tedious lives. It was a tough job, but someone had to do it.

He set them to work, Carolyn on the rowing machine, Felicia (he couldn't say her name without thinking of fellatio,) on the inner-thigh machine, and Justine working on her upper legs. Not that any of these women needed working on. They were all so slim, with perfect proportions that could and would be adjusted with plastic surgery if necessary. But then, these women didn't come to the gym to tone their muscles. Not those muscles, anyway.

Chris moved Carolyn on to the bench. He sat her down astride it, with her back to the mirror, and pulled down the long steel bar behind her head until she could grip the handles. Putting the machine on to its lowest weight, he set her off. Sitting astride the bench, facing her, he gave her words of encouragement as she worked her shoulders and upper arms. Looking beyond her, into the mirror, he enjoyed the sight of her long, lean buttocks, encased in grey cotton lycra, and the pink G-string of her leotard separating her cheeks.

'What are you looking at, Christopher?' she asked.

He looked back into her eyes. There was a mischievous glint there: a sign of what these gym sessions were really about. 'I was looking at your arse, Carolyn,' he replied.

She tutted. 'Can't keep your attention on the job for a minute, can you, sweetheart?'

'Not when I'm surrounded by such loveliness,' he purred.

'Try and concentrate, darling. Am I doing this right?' Carolyn asked.

Chris shuffled closer to her along the padded bench. Resting his hands on her biceps, he felt her small muscles flexing as she pulled the bar up and down behind her head. 'That's perfect,' he said. 'This'll improve your upper arms, your shoulders and –' his big fingers slid around and down, on to the upper slopes of her breasts '– your chest muscles. Although you seem pretty pert around that region already.'

'How nice of you to notice.' Carolyn stopped pulling. Letting the weight drop and the bar slowly lift again, she brought her hands around to rest on top of Chris's. 'You don't think my chest needs more work, then?' she asked, pushing his hands down on to her slight mounds.

Chris squeezed. Beneath her thin leotard, her nipples were hard in his palms. 'Feels OK to me,' he said. 'Take your leotard off though – let's have a proper look.'

She did as she was told, as she always did. Slipping her arms out from the straps, she peeled down the material to expose her small white breasts. Chris admired them, taking his time, feeling them with businesslike fingers. After moulding her delicate shapes in the hugeness of his hands, he pinched her protruding nipples, hard.

'Well?' she asked, her breathlessness nothing to do with the exertions of the gym.

'Well, perhaps you do need to do a few more of

these,' he said, sliding even closer to her, lifting his legs over hers and wrapping them round her. With his feet on the bench behind her, he crossed his legs. Her pussy was now touching his cock, and beneath his shorts his erection twitched.

He pulled the bar down again until Carolyn could reach the handles. 'Ten more,' he commanded, and he held her tiny breasts in his hands as she did them.

'Am I doing this right?' called Felicia.

Chris looked over to Felicia. Lying on the mat, she was thrusting her pelvis up from the floor, clenching her buttocks and trying to strengthen her already muscular arse. Easing himself away from Carolyn, Chris crouched down by her side. He reached a hand beneath her bottom and rested his palm on one cheek. The thick muscle hardened as she pushed up from the floor. 'That's good,' he said. 'But you're being a bit lazy, aren't you, Felicia? Come on. You can work harder than that.' He stood up. Kneeling between her open feet, he positioned himself over her, with his body supported on his arms, his hands either side of her shoulders, his legs stretched out behind him – the position for press-ups. 'Reach your pussy up to my cock,' he said softly. 'Come on, girl, work for it.'

Looking up into his face, her eyes shining gratefully, Felicia did as she was told. She groaned, trying hard to lift her pelvis up to touch his. 'I can't,' she sighed, her voice squeezing with the effort.

'Try harder,' he said.

'I can't,' she insisted. 'I need more incentive. Perhaps if you . . .' Underneath his body, she reached forward and tugged at the waistband of his shorts. Pulling them down over his tensed buttocks, she rumpled them at the tops of his thighs. His cock sprung towards her. 'That's better,' she cooed, lying down again. 'I've something worth aiming for, now.'

She started again with her pelvic thrusts. Now,

every time she pushed, her pussy touched the weeping knob of Chris's prick. Felicia moaned quietly every time. Her hands began to slide up Chris's trembling forearms. Spots of dampness from his cock marked the crotch of her pale-blue leotard. She pushed up harder and faster until, 'I can't do any more,' she whispered.

'One more,' Chris insisted.

She protested but she did it, lifting her pelvis up from the mat. Shifting his weight on to one hand, Chris reached round her waist and held her up there. He pressed his cock towards her, prodding for entry at the tautness of her leotard. He held her there for a long moment, while her lips opened and her breathing grew shallow. She shuddered slightly as he rubbed his hard-on over her, then whimpered as he gently released her back on to the floor. 'Good girl,' he said, swiftly getting up and pulling his shorts back over his prick.

'Now, Justine, let's have a look at you.' He moved over to the inner-thigh machine. It was like a gynaecologist's chair, with footrests for the feet. Using two weights, Justine was opening and closing her legs. 'That's very good,' he soothed, standing beside her and leaning over to rest a palm on one inner thigh. 'You're very strong there.' Her muscles felt like cord, thin and taut. 'You must use these muscles a lot.'

'I do.' She smiled.

Chris inched his fingers higher as she squeezed her legs together once more. As her upper thighs closed over his hand, he pressed his middle fingertip into the damp warmth between her legs. 'Very good,' he murmured.

She opened her legs again. He inched fractionally higher. She closed her legs again. Beneath her leotard, he could feel her slit opening and closing too. He poked his finger just inside her. She mumbled something quiet and incomprehensible, and let the machine flop open. 'Don't stop,' Chris said, moving behind her and looking over her shoulder at their reflection in the mirror. 'Come on, don't be lazy, Justine. We're here to work.'

She carried on, but it was a struggle for her now. Chris was rubbing his thick finger over her gaping pussy, between her fleshy lips, over the tiny knob of her clit. Transfixed, she watched his hand at work between her legs, rubbing and teasing as her thighs opened and closed and effort mingled with enjoyment.

Then, just as he touched the spot that made her jerk, he took his hand away. That was the way to keep these sessions filled with tension; the way to keep these women coming back for more. Never let them have it until they were begging for it. That was his motto.

He swapped them around, moving them on to different pieces of equipment, exercising different muscles. He touched them, and let them touch him – but not too much. This session was an hour long. Desire had to build up slowly within those sixty minutes, until it reached bursting point. Then, and only then, would he do what they so desperately wanted.

So he talked to them, quietly and suggestively encouraging them. He touched them, sometimes reaching beneath their leotards to feel their breasts, sometimes just turning them on with his hands gripping their ankles or their wrists: showing them how strong he was, how he could take them at any moment if he wanted, and they'd be helpless. As he stood between their legs they reached out for him, fondling his buttocks, rubbing his cock or his balls through his shorts, and dribbling their fingers over his well-developed chest or stomach. Surrounded by mirrors, the women's eyes darted all over the place: their hands on his body, his hands on their bodies, the clock ticking interminably slowly towards the magic time.

Five to three. Fifty-five minutes of overt fondling, and all three women had damp patches in the crotches of their designer leotards. All three were dying for his cock, breathless in their need for him. Before any of them knew what was happening, Chris was manhandling the girls into position. Like synchronised swimmers, they slotted perfectly into the formation they'd practised many times before. Chris was almost exploding with anticipation when, out of the corner of his eye, something drew his attention.

He looked in the mirror. In the reflection, he saw the door. And, peeping through the window in the top of the door, he saw Natalie's face.

How long had she been there? Quite a while, judging by the mesmerised look on her face. And she stayed there, just as she'd done when she'd caught him wanking. And, just as he'd done when she'd caught him, he not only carried on but angled his body towards her, giving her a better view, showing her – playing for her. Like an actor, he felt his audience following his every move, and it made his performance better to feel her eyes on him.

Then, pretending he'd just noticed her standing there, Chris looked up. 'Hello, Natalie,' he said calmly, as if this sort of thing went on all the time in the gym – which it did. 'This is getting to be quite a habit of yours,' he said, going to the door and opening it. 'Why don't you join us, instead of just watching?'

She wanted to – he could tell. Watching his hands on someone else's soft flesh was torture; she wanted those hands on her flesh. She wanted him to give her what he gave those women. But the conservative streak that ran right through her – like 'Blackpool' running through a stick of rock – was telling her it was impossible; it was wrong. She looked beyond him, at the three women waiting in the gym. 'No, thank you,' she stammered.

'Oh go on,' he urged. 'Couldn't you do with a good . . . workout? Sitting in that office all day – don't you long for a good, hard . . . sweat?'

'I – I don't. No,' she muttered hesitantly. 'I came to . . . I thought . . .' Her attention slowly swivelled back to him. 'I think you'd better come and see me in my office when you've . . .' She blinked several times, clearly trying to compose herself. 'When you've finished here.'

'Sure. I'll be there in five minutes. Are you sure we can't tempt you?' He smirked.

She wasn't sure about anything any more. He could see the uncertainty in her eyes; hear it in her breathing; feel it shivering in the air. It made his hard-on jerk up towards his stomach.

'No,' she said quietly.

'Fine.' He strolled back into the room. 'Now, ladies. Where were we?'

Giggling, they showed him. Lying down on the bench, Chris let Carolyn pull off his shorts. As Felicia lowered her mouth on to his prick, kneeling on all fours on the bench, Justine knelt down at the end of the bench and pressed her lips to her friend's swollen pussy lips. Above him, Carolyn lowered her juicy cunt on to Chris's face.

'Shut the door behind you,' he called to Natalie, just before the faint, sweet taste of sex touched his lips.

It wasn't quite a slam, but there was anger in the way she shut that door. Could it be that she was jealous of these women – that, as he kept insisting to her, she wanted him for herself? Chris groaned as he felt his prick slip into something hot and wet and tight, and he imagined it was her.

* * *

132

Natalie's fingers were trembling slightly as she heard footsteps approaching her office, and she began to shuffle papers on her desk. She wanted to look nonchalant, as if she had other things on her mind, but it was impossible. She'd been able to think of nothing else since she'd come back up here from the gym. The image replaying over and over again, of those women, of Chris, lying down on that bench, enjoying all three at once – it made her feel dizzy. Her heart was jittery. Her mouth was dry. Deep inside her pussy, a mixture of rage and raging desire was throbbing powerfully.

Slowly, biting her lip, she looked up as Chris gave a cursory knock. Without waiting for her answer, he pushed at the door and stepped in. In three long strides he was in the seat opposite hers, his legs wide apart, his hands laced on top of his smooth bald head.

'You wanted to see me?' he said.

She glanced up at him but had to look straight back down at the desk. His chest was bare, and glistening with sweat. He'd come straight from the gym. The smell of sex was on his skin. The warmth of flattery she'd felt before, when she'd discovered what he'd been masturbating over, had turned into a heat which was spreading all over her body. She was envious of those women. She longed to lower her own pussy on to his waiting mouth; to feel his fingers digging into her flesh; to feel his cock touching the back of her throat. But above the envy were the usual emotions she felt in Chris's presence: anger and childish vulnerability.

'I have to ask you something.' Her voice was quivering as much as her inner thighs. She clenched them together under the desk, trying to calm the thrill swirling uncontrollably inside her. Take me, she thought.

'You can ask me anything,' he said.

She glanced up again, down again. Fixing her eyes

on the piece of paper in front of her, she steadied herself. 'Do you give sexual favours to all your clients?'

Silence. She had to look up. She found him grinning.

'I'm glad you find this funny, Chris.' Her voice ran away with itself, words tripping over each other. 'I was really shocked by what I saw in the gym, just now. I had no idea this sort of thing was going on here. Of course, it all makes sense now. The way your clients are mainly women. The way they rave about your "teaching methods". The way you wanted the most secluded court as your resident court, even though it's the poorest one in the club and has no windows.' She shook her head, bemused by the confidence shining in his dark eyes. 'Are you proud of what you do?'

He nodded slowly. 'I am, actually.'

His nonchalance was shocking, although Natalie couldn't quite distinguish where her jealousy ended and her professionalism began. 'If I had known what sort of coach you were, I'd have never let you come to this club,' she said.

He shrugged. 'Then that would have been your loss.'

'What you do is disgusting.'

'Sex isn't disgusting. It's natural. Don't be so fuckin' uptight.'

She started to speak but he interrupted.

'Listen, Natalie. I do what I do because I'm good at it. I'm good at teaching tennis, and I'm even better at knowing what women want. Women don't come to me just to improve their tennis and keep in shape – they come to indulge their fantasies. Women have far more kinky fantasies than men and, if their husbands won't help them realise those fantasies, who will? I'm providing a service.'

'How considerate of you,' Natalie snapped.

'No.' He jabbed a thick finger towards her face. 'Don't you dare take that attitude with me. You asked me to help you turn this club around, and I'm doing just what I promised. How many new members have joined since I arrived?'

'Well, almost eighty now, but –'

'But nothing. You didn't ask me how I was going to help. You were just happy to have me on board. Let's face it, you'd have been preparing for liquidation by now without me. So don't you dare get all pious on me now. My "teaching methods" have saved this place.'

He was right. 'But it's wrong,' she mumbled. 'I can't believe this sort of thing's going on in an exclusive tennis club.'

'Wake up and smell the bacon,' he scoffed. 'The people round here have got time to kill and money to burn. They don't join an extortionate and extremely exclusive club just to play tennis. They join expecting a haven from everyday life – a place where normal rules don't apply, where they can indulge themselves, play out their fantasies. I help them, that's all. And, Natalie, if you think what's going on here is shocking, you're more naïve than I thought. Suburbia's rife, believe me. It all happens behind closed doors. SM parties, wife-swapping, home-made porn movies. Mrs Spencer's got a dungeon, you know. She likes to be tied up and have groups of men come over her tits.'

It was Natalie's turn for silence. She tried to think about this rationally, but it was difficult, and it wasn't anything to do with naïveté. Her tennis club had been turned into an upmarket sex club, right under her nose. Women were paying her for the privilege of playing kinky games with Chris. Her ambition to run her own business – to make a success using intelligence and skill and determination – had been warped beyond repair. Sex sells. Chris's cock was saving the club. 'Don't fall out with that young man,' the bank manager had advised her.

'I don't like what's going on,' she said at last. 'But I suppose I haven't much choice. If you left now and went somewhere else, all your clients would follow you again, wouldn't they? I'd be in a worse position than I was before.'

'Yeah.'

'But I want you to know, I don't approve. This isn't the image I was hoping for, for the Crawford. I'll have to turn a blind eye to what you do with your pupils, until this club can run without you. But I'm not happy.'

He rubbed his palms over his chest. 'Can I ask you something?'

'What?'

'Are you unhappy because you think it's wrong, what's going on here? Or because you're jealous?'

She tried to swallow, but her mouth was dry as sandpaper. 'Jealous? Of what?'

'Of my clients.'

'I don't know what you mean,' she sniffed, knowing perfectly well what he meant, but lifting her chin defiantly anyway.

'Well, you insist you don't want me. But if you did . . .' He leant forward, resting his elbows on the edge of her desk. Lowering his forearms, he held her fidgeting fingers in his. 'If you did happen to want me, then it would be understandable that you were jealous of all those women. Those women who like me to touch them, and lick them out, and fuck them while their husbands watch –'

'That's enough,' she said, snatching her hands away and standing up. Flustered, she pushed back her chair and walked to the back of the office. Staring out of the sliding doors leading on to the balcony, she stopped herself from looking at his reflection in the glass. 'I don't want to know what you get up to. Just get on with your "work" and keep out of my way. I appreciate the money you're bringing in, but I don't want to hear the sordid details.'

'Because you want me.'

She closed her eyes. 'Chris. For the last time, I don't want you.'

Cold prickled the back of her neck as she heard him get up. He moved towards her. She felt his heavy, heady presence looming nearer. 'So, if I kissed you, you wouldn't kiss me back?'

'No.' Opening her eyes, she turned to him. He was standing so close. Her heart was beating so loudly in her ears, she was sure he'd hear it. 'I wouldn't.'

'Really.'

Before she knew what was happening, he'd dipped his mouth to hers. Natalie's gaze flickered uncertainly from his lips to his eyes. She couldn't move. His mouth was so close to hers she could feel his breath on her skin. Electricity sparked in the air. His lips moved inexorably closer. He was going to kiss her. This was it: he'd know. He'd know how desperately she needed him. She'd have to kiss him back, and then the pretence would be over. In a way, she was glad. She couldn't keep it going much longer.

He put his hand up to her neck. His fingers were so warm; so strong. With fear and desire mingling in her veins, she closed her eyes again and tilted her head in readiness.

His laughter hacked in the air as he walked away.

'Bastard,' she said through gritted teeth, slamming her fist against the glass.

Chapter Six

*S*o, that was it. He knew. All his taunting and teasing, his unsubtle provocation, his flirting – it had all been worth his while, because now he knew that she wanted him. Shit. He would make her life hell, now.

But he didn't. From that day on, Chris seemed to relax in Natalie's presence. He still teased and flirted, especially in front of Paul, but he didn't push it. It was as if, now he'd got her to admit, more or less, that she fancied him, he could bide his time. He could step back and wait for her, because sooner or later she'd be his. Sooner or later – when he decided – he would take her.

Natalie was almost disappointed by his new, laid-back attitude. It was strange, but she found herself missing his constant attention. She also cursed herself for giving in – for letting him know that he'd won, when she'd promised herself she never would. His smile had been full of lust; now it was full of infuriating self-satisfaction.

He was never more satisfied than after the tournament. It had been his idea – a tournament for the coaches, to sharpen up their skills and reawaken their competitive spirit, with all the members invited to watch. Afterwards there would be a black-tie party, and a collection for charity to assuage the middle-class guilt of those wealthy enough to belong to tennis clubs in the first place. It was important, Chris said, not only to keep the coaching staff motivated, but to develop the social side of the club.

Chris's grin was understandable. The tournament had been a success; the guests were now enjoying themselves loudly in the function room; and, most importantly, he had won. It had been Chris versus Paul in the final and, despite Paul's elegant, intelligent play, Chris had won through on sheer guts, determination and audacity. It had been a thrilling match, especially for the women watching. All that male aggression, testosterone lubricating their every move. Natalie had had to agree with Clarissa and Vivienne, the two friends she'd sat behind in the audience – she'd never seen such a sexy tennis match, either.

She felt sorry for Paul, though. From her vantage point in the corner of the room, she looked across the crowded party and watched him talking and laughing with some of his pupils. He was putting on a brave face, but she could tell he was devastated. To lose a match to anyone was a disgrace for Paul; to lose to Chris was unthinkable humiliation. She'd have to comfort him, later.

'What a loser.'

She went to turn round, but Chris's hand on her shoulder stopped her.

'Don't move,' he said quietly. 'I'm enjoying looking at your arse. You've got a fantastic arse. You're so fuckable in that dress.'

Fuckable. The word shot through her as if it had been injected into her spine. Thoughts of Paul were washed away with a sip of her champagne. Here it was, fuelled by his victory in the tournament – that aggression she craved and loathed in equal measures. Loud voices and laughter surrounded her, but it was silent in the bubble that encapsulated her with Chris. There were only the two of them, alone in the packed room; only the strength of his eyes on her body.

She had wondered, as she'd got changed earlier, what Chris would think of her in that dress. It was shorter than the skirts she normally wore for work; it was red; and it clung. Paul had told her she looked gorgeous, and she'd felt a spurt of cold guilt in her pussy as he'd kissed her, and she'd closed her eyes and imagined it was Chris she was kissing. Now, she basked in his attention again – the first time she'd had it all to herself since that day in her office.

'Hold this.' He stepped up closer behind her, and reached round to hand her his glass. She felt his hands spreading over her buttocks. Her skin crawled as the heat of his palms seeped through the thin, dark-scarlet material of her dress. 'Jeeezus,' he groaned into the back of her head, his voice muffling in her hair. Closer, and a finger travelled up her crack, following the line of the G-string separating her cheeks.

'Don't,' she said quietly, just as Paul glanced over towards her.

'Why not?' Chris asked.

'People will see,' she whispered.

'But I can't stop myself,' he said. And, as if he had no control over them, his fingers moved onward, tracing the waistband of her G-string round to the front, and then moving inexorably downward.

'Chris,' she breathed, mortified and insanely aroused. 'What are you doing?'

'Claiming my prize.'

Keeping her eyes firmly fixed on the back of Paul's head, she fervently hoped that no one was watching as Chris's touch moved down. 'Your prize?'

'The winner always gets a prize,' he said. 'I won the tournament; now I intend to claim my reward.'

Her hands full, Natalie was helpless as his middle finger pressed at the softness of her pussy. At the same time, he pushed his hips into her arse. She could feel his erection. It took all her concentration not to spill the champagne out of the glasses she was gripping on to.

'I want your pussy. Shall we do it here, or would you rather go somewhere?' Chris asked, relinquishing his hold on her, and taking the glasses out of her trembling fingers.

Quickly, she glanced across at Paul, then up at Chris, then down to her feet. This was it – she couldn't stop what was going to happen, couldn't fight it any more, even if she wanted to. 'My office,' she murmured, and she walked out of the party and into the unknown.

It was cold in her office, and silent apart from the hum of the air conditioning. She turned out the light and waited by the window for him to come up. He turned the light back on as he came in.

'What if someone sees?' she said, moving back towards the switch.

He grabbed her wrist, steering her backward. He was urgent, incensed, breathless. 'I don't give a toss. I need to be able to see you. To see that gorgeous arse of yours.'

'But –' What if Paul sees? The words disappeared soundlessly into the cool air as he slid one hand underneath her dress. He squeezed her buttock, grabbing greedy handfuls as if he was trying to break off a piece of her flesh to eat. As he mauled at her arse, he glared at her, disdain in his dark eyes.

She looked back at him, unnerved by his strength – and not just his physical strength. He was stronger

141

than her mentally, too. He had her exactly where he wanted her. And she couldn't think of anywhere else she'd rather be.

'Not thinking about Paul now, are you?'

She didn't answer; he didn't need her to. She let him turn her round and push her up to the window. He forced her head down until she was leaning forward. She spread her fingers on the glass and looked down at the empty courts below. In the far distance, the laughter of the party reached her through the thick tension clamping down on her senses. Without a kiss, a touch of her breast or another word, he pushed up the skirt of her dress and ripped her damp G-string down. Natalie felt it fall to her ankles, and felt it stretch as he kicked her feet further apart. His roughness stopped just short of hurting her. She whimpered with shock as he pushed her lower back further down, eased her pussy lips apart with his thumbs and thrust a finger deep inside her.

'Oh,' she pleaded, her voice thin and pathetic. She didn't know what she was pleading for – she didn't want him to be gentle. She wanted it hard; wanted his cock pounding remorselessly. Wanted him to fuck her until her brains imploded. 'Chris –'

'Shut up.' His finger slid out. His penis nudged at her hole. 'Shut up and take it. You know you want it. You've wanted it ever since we met.'

She braced herself as his fingers clutched at her waist.

'You've wanted this, you bitch, ever since that day. Haven't you? You were thinking about it when I caught you touching yourself up in the car park. You were thinking about it while you sucked Paul's cock and I watched from the showers. You were probably thinking about it last night, while Paul was fucking you.'

She groaned in surrender as his thick cock filled her.

He was so big, so long, there was no room for anything else in her body: no thought, no feeling, no sense. The only thing left was insanity; the insanity of submission; submission to mindless, mind-blowing pleasure. There was no love here, no affection, no laughter – just sex. Lust was what drove him to ram deep inside her. Lust was what made her spread her legs wider apart, until the elastic of her G-string dug into her ankles and her hamstrings screamed in protest. Lust was what made her close her eyes and shut down her senses, so she didn't hear the footsteps running up the stairs to the office.

'Bastard,' Paul shouted, launching himself across the room. His fist connected with Chris's cheekbone, landing with such force that Chris's body was separated from Natalie's and he was thrown sideways. He fell against a chair, stumbling clumsily with shock and momentum. It was the first time Natalie had ever seen him out of control.

'Are you all right?' Paul asked, his rage so honed towards Chris that he assumed Natalie was there against her will. She nodded, pulling up her wet G-string and straightening her dress.

'You disgust me,' he hissed, turning back to Chris. 'What the fuck do you think you're playing at? What's going on here?'

Chris struggled on to his feet. 'Why don't you ask Natalie?'

'Don't you try and pretend this has anything to do with her. I know how you operate, you pervert.' Paul rushed at him again. Another punch connected, although, as Chris calmly took it, there was laughter in his eyes which protected him from the pain.

'Do you really think Natalie would have come up here with me if she hadn't wanted to?' Chris smiled.

Natalie ran to Paul's side as he raised his arm again.

'Paul, please.' She clung to him. 'Please, don't. This was a mistake. Leave it. Let's go home.'

Wrestling his eyes away from Chris's, Paul turned to her. Slowly, his anger calmed as she soothed him. When he looked back at his enemy, determination had replaced rage.

'You did this to me once before,' he said. 'You're not going to do it again. Your month here is nearly up. You'll be gone soon. Leave my girlfriend alone. I won't warn you again.'

Chris held up his big hands. He was mocking Paul, but Paul didn't notice. He was too busy ushering Natalie out of the door with a proprietary arm tight round her waist.

'She's mine, Chris,' he said at the door.

I'm no one's, she thought, but she was unable to deny the thrill of having them come to blows over her.

'Think of me,' Chris mouthed to her, as she glanced up on her way down the stairs.

And that night, when Paul had been calmed down with a bath and a massage, and he was sliding fluently in and out of her body, she did. She closed her eyes, and thought of Chris, and came loudly. Later on, when Paul was snoring, she sneaked into the bathroom and lay down in the bath. She spread her legs and turned the shower spray on to her favourite setting. She pummelled her clit with the pulsing shaft of water, and she came again, and she thought of Chris.

144

Chapter Seven

The next morning, Chris came up to her office. 'Great party last night,' he said.

'Yes,' she said, trying to look busy, avoiding eye contact as if he were a mythical siren who could draw her in if she wasn't careful. 'It was a good idea of yours. Well done.'

'Everyone seemed to be enjoying themselves. The members had a great time.'

'That's good.'

'Shame you had to leave early.'

'Yes.'

He came up to the desk and leant over it, taking the pen out of her hand. She stopped what she was doing and looked up at him. He had a cut on his cheekbone where Paul's ring had sliced his face. His left cheek was slightly swollen.

'Did you think of me?'

The muscles in her pussy gripped with fear; the fear of being honest, of opening herself up to Chris – of admitting the truth to him. 'Yes,' she said quietly.

He nodded. 'I thought about you all night.' His hand closed over hers. 'I couldn't sleep,' he said.

'Neither could I.'

His skin slid away from hers as he sat down. 'Then why did you go home with Paul?'

She couldn't answer that; she didn't know.

'Why didn't you tell him that it's me you want?'

She looked down at the desk, hoping to find the answers written out for her somewhere in the pile of papers. 'I – it – It's not that easy,' she stammered.

'He caught me fucking you,' Chris said. 'How much easier could it have been?' He waved at an imaginary Paul. '"Hi, Paul, I'm sleeping with Chris tonight, OK? Catch you later."'

Natalie fidgeted in her seat. It felt uncomfortable all of a sudden, as if the cushions were filled with tiny, restless hands, pushing her in all directions. 'I like Paul,' she said. 'He's a lovely guy, and he's been kind to me. I don't want to hurt him.'

'You didn't think about hurting him last night, did you?' He reached across the desk and stopped her fidgeting hands, pressing them down flat on to the wood. 'You didn't think about anything except you, and me.'

He was right. Up here in her office, with the lights on and her knickers down round her ankles, thoughts of Paul had been quashed. Shame and anger and fear and guilt had been thrown aside like old clothes; all she'd wanted then was Chris's cock inside her. Now, guilt was seeping into her mind like a stain inching its way across a new carpet. And there was another flavour of guilt mingling with the first. It was her fault that Chris had been hit in the face. Paul's willingness to put the blame entirely on Chris's shoulders – a decision fuelled more by jealousy and humiliation than any rational thought – had been convenient for Natalie to go along with. She hadn't been honest with Paul, or with herself. 'I didn't want anyone to get hurt,' she said.

'I wouldn't be too concerned about Paul's feelings, if I were you.'

'Why not? What on earth do you mean by that?' she asked.

'Paul's a big boy now – he can look after himself.'

'What sort of answer is that?'

'How long have you known him?'

'Just over a month.'

He nodded slightly, knowingly. 'And do you think, if he was offered sex on a plate, that he'd refuse – because of you?'

She wasn't sure. She shrugged.

'You didn't refuse, did you? You were cheating on him last night, when he walked in. You've been cheating on him inside your head ever since we met.'

Right again.

'And why shouldn't you? Why shouldn't you let me fuck you, if that's what you want? What do you owe Paul?'

Nothing. She'd made no commitment to Paul. Was she feeling guilty purely because he'd given her a place to stay at a moment's notice? No. She did like him, and she felt sorry for him too. Chris, his old rival, had taken over his job and was now trying to steal his girlfriend from under his nose, for the second time in his life. Paul had confided in Natalie how much that had upset him the first time, and he'd sworn it would never happen again.

'It's time for you to decide, Natalie.'

'Decide what?'

'On Monday I'll have done a month here, as promised. The club's back on track, as promised. I'll have to tell the Shilton whether I'm going back there or not.'

'Do you want to go back there?'

'Of course not. I want to stay here.'

Thank God for that, she thought. The Crawford was

147

doing well, but she wasn't convinced it could stand on its own two feet without Chris at the reins. She didn't approve of his teaching methods, but she didn't disapprove of the money he brought in. Paul would be furious, but Paul would have to be placated, somehow. Natalie was just opening her mouth to bring up the subject of salary when Chris stopped her.

'If you want me to, I'll stay on. But I have one condition.'

She swallowed hard, trying to push the fear back down into her guts. She knew that, whatever Chris wanted, she would have to give it to him – not only for the sake of the club, but for the sake of her sanity. There was a challenge in his voice; a smile in his eyes. She'd seen that look before. 'What is it?' she asked, her voice hoarse with anticipation.

Chris paused, cruelly drawing out the moment. 'You.'

Her body deflated. 'Me?' she said, her lips moving but no sound coming out.

'You have to admit that you want me,' he leered.

'Never,' she whispered. But she knew it was a lie, and that she'd have to admit it sooner or later. After last night, they both knew it was a lie.

'I want you, Natalie. I want you to give yourself to me. Judging by the way you acted last night, I'd say you were ready to give yourself. I'd say you want to. You have to decide, Natalie. Me – or Paul.'

She hesitated, her lips apart, her lungs struggling for air. 'Chris . . . I do, but I have to think of Paul –'

'No, you don't. You're not thinking of Paul. You're just afraid.'

Indignant, she pulled herself together. 'Me? Afraid of what?'

'Of letting yourself go.' There was a sneer on his wide mouth as he stood up. 'You businesswomen – you think you're so clever, so independent, so fucking strong. But when it comes down to it you're all petrified of anything that doesn't fit neatly into your safe little lives. I don't fit in neatly anywhere. You're afraid to give yourself to me because you're afraid of what I'll do to you. You know exactly what Paul will do. He'll tell you you're gorgeous, and kiss you and fuck you, and then roll over and fall asleep. He's safe and controllable. And that's what you like. That's why you went home with Paul last night. Mr Predictable. Mr Boring.'

'Paul is not boring.'

'So why were you thinking about me all night?'

Because ... Why? Why should she think of Chris, when Paul's hard flesh was beside her, on top of her, inside her? What was it about Chris that dominated her thoughts?

'Admit you want me, Natalie. Admit you want to give yourself to me, and I'll stay on at the club. It's time to decide: Paul or me.' He strode to the door. 'But, if you choose me, you should know that it won't be safe, or predictable. I'll tell you you're gorgeous, and kiss you and fuck you. Then I'll fuck with your mind. Because your mind is the bit that really turns me on, Natalie. And if you think you can't handle that, then maybe you should stick with Paul.'

She tried to clear her mind, but her brains were as scrambled as the eggs she'd had for breakfast. Chris was right. Chris, it seemed, was always right.

She was afraid. 'Give yourself to me,' he'd said, and she knew that he didn't just mean giving him her body. He'd been fucking with her mind since the day she'd first caught sight of him: teasing, provoking, pushing her. He'd infiltrated her thoughts, creeping inside her head like a drug and making her do things which were completely out of character. All that, before he'd even so much as kissed her. If she gave in, and gave herself to him, she wouldn't be in control, she knew that. And that was frightening.

She'd always been in control. Her career, her men, her life – it had all been carefully choreographed to her own tune. And now here was Chris, threatening to ruin her careful, precise choreography.

He knew she had no choice. He knew, just as she did, that if she didn't give in soon she'd drive herself insane. She needed to keep him at the club; but above and beyond that there was something more, something secret and shameful. Something buried so deep inside her that she would never have known it was there, if she hadn't met Chris. But now it had been brought up it tasted bitter in the back of her throat, and it couldn't be ignored. There was a dark, infinitesimal part of her that longed to give control to someone else, just for once. It was terrifying, but it was the truth.

'OK,' she said, stepping inside the doorway of court number ten.

Alone, Chris was practising his serve. He hit one more ball, which bounced so hard against the wall it made Natalie jump. Then he stopped and turned to look at her. 'What did you say?'

'I said, OK,' she repeated, unsure of what she was agreeing to.

He came round the net, walking slowly towards her. 'OK what?'

'I've decided.'

He looked at her; she looked back at him. She told him, without words, what she'd decided.

'There's no turning back,' he said. 'Are you sure?'

She wasn't at all sure. She wasn't at all sure what any of this meant. The only thing she knew for certain was that nothing was certain. Choosing Chris meant choosing danger.

She nodded.

'Kneel down,' he said.

She did.

'Suck my cock,' he said.

Oh God. So this was what giving herself to Chris meant. As she eased his white shorts down over his heavy thighs, madness bubbled in her veins. She forgot to care whether anyone walked in on them; a fraction of her mind even hoped that someone would. She forgot to care about political correctness, or the fact that she was Chris's boss, or the fact that she'd promised herself never to give in to him. She imagined what she looked like, on her knees in her immaculate business suit, her skirt crumpled, her lipsticked lips opened wide to take his fat cock. Her hands were on his hard buttocks; his hands were in her hair, gripping her tight. She felt just like she'd felt the night before, at the party – as if it was a relief to give in, to give up.

It was a relief to Chris, too. He came quickly, like a virgin receiving his first blow job. Unlike a virgin, he held her head firm, making her drink in his come as it spurted inside her mouth. Then, with a violence that surprised her, he pushed her away. She fell back on to one hip, looking up at him, watching as he stroked his glorious cock.

'Are you wet?' He crouched down and reached between her sprawled legs. He touched her knickers. His breath shuddered in his throat as he slowly let it out. 'Your panties are soaking,' he said, delight in his rich brown voice but his face unmoved. 'I always knew this was what you wanted, Natalie. From the minute I saw you, I knew you needed this.'

She lifted her attention from his dark cock, from the white juice leaking from the tip of his prick, and looked up at him. Helpless, she ached to have his fingers inside her, not just brushing over the damp material between her legs. She longed for his cock in her cunt. 'Needed what?' she asked.

'Needed a man to take control of you.' He smirked. There was disdain in his eyes. 'You women are all the same, when it comes down to it.'

She couldn't help herself. She knew he was winding her up but she couldn't ignore a comment like that. 'We are, are we? And you men are such complex, sophisticated creatures compared to us.'

'Not at all. But at least we're honest.' He pushed a finger beneath the elastic of her white panties and into the wetness oozing from her pussy. 'We admit to what we like. We like great tits, great arses, and giving a girl a good seeing to. You postfeminist women are so fucking uptight about your jobs, and being in control of your politically correct lives, that you've lost track of what you really need.'

'Which is?'

'To lie back and open your legs and let the man take control.'

She gasped and pushed his hand away from her.

He laughed. 'See? You can't handle it, can you? That's why women like you go for men like Paul. They're safe. You can control them. But, when you close your eyes at night, it's men like me that are there –' he tapped her forehead '– inside your mind. You pretend you like being on top, being in command, when what you women dream about is this.'

His hands were big, powerful, like a tiger's paws. He pushed her down to the floor. As her back hit the ground she lifted her arms to hit back at him but he grabbed her wrists and pinned them down, either side of her head. With his knee he forced her legs wider apart, until her short, straight skirt rode up across her open thighs. He lowered his body over hers, supporting his weight on his muscular arms and holding himself just above her. His cock, so hard it made her gasp, pressed at the wet strip of material covering her pussy.

'Look at you,' he hissed, 'lying on the floor in your designer suit, so desperate for me to fuck you that you don't care whether your clothes get dirty. You realise my next clients will walk in any minute now, don't you?'

'Get off me,' she breathed, struggling for air under the weight of his chest and the uncomfortable pressure of her own lust bearing down on her.

'Admit that this is what you want.'

'Chris, get off. I can't breathe.'

'Admit it.'

She couldn't bring herself to admit it. Her body was screaming: every pore, every fibre, every nerve. Yes, this is what I want. Take me. Pin me down and fuck me. Hard. Show me your strength. Show me your lust. Make me feel helpless. This is what I want.

But it was frightening. His strength was frightening, and she struggled against it, trying to roll out from underneath him, pulling desperately to release her wrists from his grasp. She struggled with her mind, too. This went against everything she knew. And yet, deep in her bowels, fear and denial were turning themselves inside out, morphing into something else: a need, a lust that couldn't be denied.

Her body and mind gave up the fight. She lay still beneath him, meeting his gaze with eyes that were no longer sure. As if he'd got the answer he wanted, Chris let go of her and got to his feet. Holding out his hands, he helped her up. 'I've a lesson now,' he said, pulling up his shorts. 'I suggest you watch. I think this'll prove my point about women.' He smiled and waved as, right on cue, three immaculate ladies came through the door, laughing among themselves. 'These three have got everything,' he whispered to Natalie, steering her towards the umpire's chair. 'They're partners in a law firm. They're clever, attractive, and

153

stinking rich. And, unlike you, they're not afraid to admit to what they want. Watch and learn.'

Chris turned to his pupils. 'Morning, ladies. You've all met Natalie, haven't you? She's going to umpire for us today.'

The women nodded and smiled their agreement.

'What'll it be?' Chris asked.

They glanced at each other, excitement twitching suggestively at the corners of their mouths. 'Let's play forfeits,' one of them said.

'My favourite,' said Chris.

Natalie watched in amazement. As the doubles match progressed, she often forgot to give the score. No one noticed. Everyone was too busy playing another game. Not tennis; this was a match of shame and submission. It was the most exciting tennis match Natalie had ever seen.

At first, she found it incomprehensible that these women, who were intelligent and glossily good-looking, should choose to behave like this. But then, the more she thought about what Chris had said, the more it made sense. These women were lawyers; they spent their lives within the strictures of law practice, wearing the right clothes, saying the right things – being in control. This was their time off. So it wasn't so surprising that they chose to do the opposite of what they did at work – to give up control completely.

It was still shocking to see these fortysomething women doing what they were doing. It was shocking to see the barely disguised thrill on their faces; and for the thrill to echo inside Natalie's pussy, so strongly that she had to cross her legs and squeeze her inner thighs tightly together.

Judith and Larissa played together; Chris played with Patsy. Chris, being the best player by a mile, not only dominated the game but totally manipulated it, hitting gentle serves when he wanted the women to return, and smashing the ball past them when he wanted them to lose the point. The women playing opposite Chris and Patsy tried their guts out, but both knew it was hopeless. This match was in Chris's hands, and so were they.

Larissa hit the ball into the net, and the first game was Chris and Patsy's. 'Pathetic,' Chris said. 'You lost the game there, Larissa. You must pay a forfeit. Take off your panties, please.'

Larissa obeyed, blushing red as she slipped off her white knickers and ran over to put them in her bag. The others, including Natalie, watched as she bent over and her skirt lifted to show her bare behind. Then she ran back on to court. Apart from the flush of excitement on her cheeks, no one would tell by looking at her that anything was out of the ordinary. And yet, every time she served now, the others caught a glimpse of her dark triangle of pubic hair as she threw the ball up in the air; and a flash of white buttocks as she brought her racquet down behind the ball and the momentum flung her short skirt up. It was shocking to see instants of nakedness, and Natalie found her attention hooked on Larissa's skirt, following its swishing movements, and willing it to fly up. Chris told Larissa off for her poor service – 'I've taught you better than that,' he said – and he stopped the match and made her practise a few times. Natalie's attention switched to him; to the way his dark gaze attached itself to the hem of Larissa's skirt, and the way he leered slightly at the sight of her pussy. 'That's better,' he said, going back to the baseline with a hand on his groin. Natalie glanced back at Larissa, and she understood the naughty thrill that made the woman bite her lip. If she was feeling anything like Natalie was, she probably wanted to scream with the shame of it; to lie down and open her legs and let everyone look.

The match resumed. This time it was Patsy's poor attempt at a drop shot that lost the game. Her knickers came off; then, in the next game, Judith's were discarded. Now Natalie didn't know where to look. With every shot, every run into the net, every time one of them stooped to pick up a ball, there was a forbidden flash of hair or naked buttocks. But there was an unmistakable bulge inside Chris's shorts which was just as exciting. Perversely, it got envy stirring in Natalie's guts. She wanted to be the one giving him a hard-on. She wanted to be the one bending over, showing him her cunt, letting him look.

It was Larissa's turn for a forfeit once again. She served poorly, hitting the ball so weakly it didn't even trickle over the net, and she lost the game for her and her partner with a double fault. 'Larissa!' Chris shouted. 'I've told you before about that weak-willed serve of yours. You've lost the game now. Forfeit.' He brought her up to the net with a flick of his racquet. 'Kneel down,' he barked, producing his cock from his shorts like a threat. Pushing the net down with one hand, he held his thick penis in front of Larissa's open lips. 'Suck me,' he said.

The others held their breath as Larissa's small pout stretched to take in Chris's cock.

'So?'

Under the table, her inner thighs were trembling slightly. 'So what?'

He smiled, looking up as the waiter served him his lunch: a sandwich and a selection of fruit. Natalie had only ordered a drink. She didn't feel like eating. Her belly was full with anticipation.

'So,' he continued, 'do you understand now? Do you agree with my theory that what women really want, if only they'd admit it, is to let the man take control?'

'Maybe,' she said quietly, wishing he'd keep his voice down. The café was packed. 'Maybe some women enjoy it.'

'What about you?'

She swallowed hard, intensely aware of the waiter fussing around behind her. 'Maybe,' she said.

He leant across the table towards her. 'There's no need to be coy any more, Natalie. I saw your face when I made Judith lick Patsy out. You were wishing it was you, weren't you? You were praying I'd call you down from the umpire's chair and make you join in.'

The waiter left them alone, at last. 'Maybe I was,' she said, the faintest smile on her lips and a forced calmness in her voice.

'You were excited, weren't you? The most excited you've ever been.' He licked his lips, collecting a smear of butter that had oozed from his sandwich and was making them shine. 'I bet you were wet, sitting up there on your perch, watching us.'

She blinked a few times, nervously, in reply. She'd been so wet her fingers had itched to slide in the juice flowing from her pussy, and she'd had to wedge her hands under her thighs to stop herself.

'I bet you were dying to take your knickers off, too.'

She took a sip of her drink. Her mouth was dry. Her pulse was tripping over itself. This was insane. And unstoppable. She was afraid of it, and yet she wanted it – wanted to feel how those women had felt.

'Take them off now and give them to me.'

Natalie glanced around her. Oblivious, members and staff were tucking into their lunches, reading newspapers or watching the action on court number one. Paul was playing there with Lady Denhurst. No one was looking at Natalie and Chris.

'Do it,' Chris urged, ripping another bite out of his sandwich.

She wanted to, but still she hesitated.

'Natalie,' he snapped, making the couple on the next table look up from their meal, 'you wouldn't be here with me if you didn't want to do this. Take your knickers off and pass them to me, now.'

Still she couldn't move. She kept looking over to the court; to Paul. Mr Predictable. Mr Boring. Perhaps she was Mrs Boring, after all.

'Natalie.' He grabbed her jaw and turned her back to face him. 'You saw how those three loved it,' he whispered. 'I know you want to do this. Now, give yourself to me. Stop fighting. I promise you, you won't regret this. Just do everything I say.'

She couldn't help a huff of laughter. 'I'm supposed to be *your* boss, remember?'

He seemed angry and impatient. 'Shut up and do what I asked you to.'

She wasn't going to be spoken to like that. She got up to go, but Chris, without pausing in demolition of his sandwich, hooked her ankle under the table and brought her slamming back down into her seat.

'Now, Natalie. Before I make a scene.'

Keeping her eyes fixed on his, she reached underneath the tablecloth. Thank God it was long, reaching to the floor and hiding her hands as they pushed up her skirt. Thank God everyone around was too concerned with eating or watching Paul to notice what she was doing. Hooking her thumbs under the waist of her knickers and lifting her bum an inch from the seat, she eased them down over her hips. She pushed them down over her black hold-up stockings, over her calves and then over her shoes.

'Good girl,' he said, finishing his sandwich and wiping his mouth with the back of his hand. 'Now give them to me.'

Holding her hand out under the table, she reached for Chris.

'No. Pass them over the table,' he said.

Bastard. She looked down into her lap. Rumpling up the scrap of white lace, she hid it in her fist before sliding her closed hand towards his outstretched one.

'That's it,' he said, cupping his hand under hers. 'Good girl.'

Natalie slowly let go, making sure her damp knickers were pressed into his palm. Looking around, she took her hand away.

Mortified, she felt the colour drain from her cheeks as she looked back at him. Chris picked up her knickers with his finger and thumb. The scrap of white that might have been mistaken for a hanky was unmistakable as he held it up. 'Chris,' she hissed, glancing involuntarily towards Paul. 'Stop it, please.'

He obviously had no intention of stopping. His intention was to humiliate her, and he was succeeding. Holding her panties up, he pressed them to his face. Closing his eyes, he inhaled deeply.

'Mmmm,' he sighed. 'Pussy. Fantastic.'

'Chris . . .'

'Do you taste as good as you smell?'

'Chris, please.'

He leered at her for a long moment, feeding off her discomfort. Then he seemed to forget what he was doing, and he put her knickers in his pocket and focused on the plate of fruit in front of him. Grateful that he'd stopped his torment, and that no one had seen, Natalie watched his big fingers as he sliced an apple and peeled a banana. His hands were mesmerising, and she was almost lulled into submission.

'Let me taste your cunt,' he said, passing her the banana.

She woke up. 'What?'

'You heard. I want to taste you.'

Her hand flew to her mouth. She looked from him, to the banana being offered, back up at him. 'Chris,' she whispered urgently. 'Don't be disgusting. Put that down before someone looks over.'

He stood up. Moving round to her side, he draped an arm round her shoulder and bowed his head down to hers. 'If you don't take this banana and put it inside you now, I'll do it for you. And believe me, people will look.'

She turned to plead with him but he pushed her head back round. 'This is what it's all about,' he breathed. 'Time to stop playing safe, Natalie. Living by your rules is boring. Live by mine for a while. Go on. Do it.' His lips touched her ear. 'Be dirty for me, Natalie. Be a filthy, dirty girl. For me.'

Filthy. Dirty. When he said them, those words sounded like the most disgusting, depraved words in the language. Filthy. Dirty. She wanted to be. She wanted this. She took the phallic fruit from his fingers and surreptitiously moved it into her lap.

Chris sat back down again. He was glowing with triumph, high on her submission. A slow smile appeared on his face as Natalie opened her legs and moved the banana underneath the tablecloth. Almost imperceptibly, Chris nodded encouragement at her. She had to close her eyes for a second as she brought the tip of the fruit to her open lips. It felt a little like a penis, hard but yielding, and as it touched her pussy she wanted to push it right inside her.

Instead, breathing deeply, hoping against hope that no one was watching the visible tension hovering in the air between her and Chris, she rubbed the banana over her swollen pussy lips. Her juices flowed; longing filled her cunt and made her want to cry out – to beg for him to take her to his office and fuck her. She bit down hard on her lip, keeping her emotions inside. She knew in that instant, surrounded by customers, feet away from her 'boyfriend', acting dirty in the clean whiteness of the café, that she was his. She'd do almost anything he asked. Even though they might try to, neither her mind nor her body could resist. The inevitability of it all – knowing that she was in his hands now, like his clients were – was disturbingly thrilling.

He held his hand out and she passed the banana back to him. Her juice was invisible against the colour of the fruit, but she could see it shining on the tip. There was a glint of approval in Chris's eyes as he sucked on the thick flesh before biting off the first inch. He murmured his enjoyment, pushing the plate across the table at her. She looked down at the thick slices of red-skinned apple, and without another word from Chris she did what he wanted.

The apple had been in the fridge, and it made her jump to feel the chill sliding inside her. Her buttocks gripped and she gasped, but she fought the shock and poked the slice right into her moistness. Her inner muscles clenched and then pushed, repelling the small, cold intruder. Her hand was there to catch it, and she passed it across to Chris's waiting fingers. He popped it straight in his mouth, sucking on it hard before chewing it. Natalie reached for another slice and then another, feeding Chris with her juice. He savoured the taste, smiling at her; or perhaps it was her surrender that was making him smile. Tentatively, Natalie smiled back.

'You have that one,' Chris said, pushing the last slice back towards her. Eager, he leant on his elbows and watched as she bit off a chunk. The taste of her pussy was barely discernible but it was there: a different sweetness to that of the apple; a stickiness coating the firm-textured flesh. But the real sweetness was her shame – the pure filthiness of sticking fruit into her soaking-wet pussy underneath the clean white tablecloth.

And she no longer cared whether anyone saw.

When Paul caught her eye, and scowled to see her sitting with Chris, she felt nothing but pity for him – Mr Boring. Mr Predictable. She followed Paul's gaze back to Chris, and asked him, 'What now?'

'My, my,' he said. 'You are a hungry girl today, Miss Crawford.'

She was. Hungry for more. Ravenous for his cock. So thirsty she would have licked the sweat from his chest.

'You're enjoying this, aren't you?' Chris asked.

'You know I am,' she murmured.

'Ohhhh,' he sighed quietly, his eyes flickering over her face, her throat, her cleavage. 'You are so fucking gorgeous,' he said slowly, lavishing her with his words. 'You dirty, dirty girl.' He stood up, dabbing at his mouth with her knickers. He held out his hand. 'Come with me.'

'Where are we going?' she asked. But she didn't care.

Out in the corridor, Chris bent down and lifted Natalie up into his arms.

'What are you doing?'

'Just play along,' he said. 'You'll enjoy this, I promise. Just relax.'

It was hard to relax, not knowing what he had in store for her now. The sharp thrill of the unknown was heightened by the closeness of his body; by his hands around her knees and waist. He was strong, and hard; there was fierce determination in his expression, a complete contrast to the mush inside her mind. His masculinity was frightening. As she put her arm round his neck, like he told her to, she looked at the smallness of her hand against the thick bunch of muscle at his shoulder. She realised her frailty, both mentally and physically, compared to him. And she realised with a stab of surprise that this was arousing.

Knowing that he could pin her down, like he'd done before on court; knowing that he could fuck with her mind – could, quite easily, make her do things she thought she didn't want to do. What is it about you, she wondered, looking at his face. How do you know what I want? How do you know how far I'll go?

They went as far as the staff room. Chris kicked at the door. Inside, he put Natalie down on one of the sofas and told her to keep still. He left the room, leaving Natalie to smile uncertainly at the three coaches who were in there, watching the first match of Wimbledon on the TV. A minute later, he returned with the physio.

'Natalie's hurt her ankle,' he said, ushering Dave towards her. 'She was umpiring for me and she fell as she got down from the chair. Have a look at her, will you?'

Dave sat down by her feet. 'Which ankle?'

Chris pointed at her left one. Dave held it gently in his highly trained fingers, bending her leg until her foot was flat on the sofa. He slipped off her shoe. Tenderly, he pressed all round her ankle. 'Tell me where it hurts,' he said.

Natalie couldn't: apart from the fact that it didn't, she was distracted. Chris was kneeling down beside her. Watching her reaction, he pulled at her right leg, easing it apart from her left. Natalie looked anxiously from him to Dave, realising what Chris was doing and hoping against hope that Dave wouldn't notice. But he did. With her thighs apart and her left leg bent up, her tight skirt was gaping invitingly, and Dave couldn't resist a glance up into the darkness of her stockinged inner thighs. He flinched, obviously taken aback to find she had no panties on. His gaze jerked up to Natalie, then across at Chris, then into the shock of her naked pussy again before returning to his fingers on her ankle. His eyebrows slowly lifted.

What must he think of her? Jesus, this was humiliating. Almost as embarrassing as his double-take at
her pussy was his valiant attempt, now, not to look
again. Natalie could sense the tension in his neck as
he struggled to concentrate on her ankle. He blinked a
hundred times, disguising quick glimpses up her
thighs with his eyelids' rapid fluttering. Natalie felt
her cheeks heat up. There was more heat where
Chris's hand was holding on to her right leg, keeping
her from closing the gap and hiding her shame.

She looked down at Chris, silently pleading with
him to end this. But he just stared back at her, silently
telling her it wouldn't end until he decided it was
over. He dug his fingers further into her calf and he
smiled, snaring her in the intensity of his dark eyes.

'Please,' she mouthed at him, but he didn't take any
notice. At the same moment, Dave stood up.

'Your ankle isn't swollen,' he said. 'I don't think
you've done any damage but, if it does feel tender
later, come and get a support bandage.' He took
another look up her skirt, as if he still couldn't quite
believe it, before turning to Chris. 'Can I have a quick
word, mate?'

'Sure.' Chris winked at Natalie before joining Dave
outside. She could hear their mumbling, but couldn't
make out what they were mumbling about. Still, it
wasn't hard to guess.

Chris returned to the sofa carrying a satisfied smirk.
'Lads,' he said, talking to the three watching telly,
'Dave wants a word with you in the changing room.'
Grumbling, the three left Chris and Natalie alone.
Sitting in Dave's place at Natalie's feet, Chris put her
'injured' ankle in his lap and gently held on to it.
'They'll all be along to have a look in a minute,' he
said.

'Who will?'

'All the other coaches. Dave's the biggest gossip in

the club. Right now he's telling the others to come and have a look at our kinky manager, lying here with no knickers on.'

'Oh my God. What did he say to you?'

'He said he was pretty sure you weren't wearing anything under your skirt. He said he couldn't believe it at first, but he'd taken a good look and he'd swear you didn't have any knickers on.'

'Jesus,' she sighed, pulling her foot away from his hand.

'No, you don't.' He held on to her. 'You're going to stay right here and take this.'

'Chris, please let go, I can't do this –'

'Just relax.'

'How can I?' she hissed, glancing quickly at the door, expecting someone to appear there. 'I'm the manager here, Chris. How is anyone going to have any respect for me if I let them see me like this?'

'You don't have a choice.' He put a finger to her lips, pushing her away until she sat back against the armrest again. Dropping his gaze, he took a good look at the view. 'Believe me,' he said, 'they'll have more than respect for you, after this.'

As if to confirm what he was saying, a face appeared in the doorway. It was Mark, one of the younger coaches. 'Hi, Natalie,' he beamed, with a false brightness that hid what he'd really come for. His smile faltered as his eyes dipped into the darkness between her thighs. He paused, losing control of his features as the shock registered on his face. Then he was gone.

Natalie glared at Chris. Further down the corridor outside, she heard the door of the coaches' changing room slam. She heard Mark's voice, faint but clear.

'Fuck!' he shouted. 'Dave was right! I think I've just seen Natalie's pussy!'

An intermittent procession of voyeurs traipsed down the hall, each one pausing at the door to the staff room. Some were more blatant than others, drifting inside the room and delaying while they pretended to check the tennis score on the telly. One even stopped at the end of the sofa to chat to Chris for a while, giving a quick, lascivious lift of his eyebrows to show Chris that he'd seen. Then he was gone, and another pair of prying eyes appeared. The three who'd been watching telly before returned slowly, one by one, with schoolboy smiles on their faces. But by that time Natalie had been pushed too far to care. By that time she was barely aware of the way their attention trailed up the silky insides of her thighs, and into the darkness of her cunt; or of the way their expressions changed as they met her eyes again. She was fiercely aware of a handful of things: Chris's fingers around her ankle; his eyes full of perverse pride; his prick, hard underneath the stockinged sole of her foot; and the way her clit was pulsing with shame.

'How do you feel?' he asked, when the last Peeping Tom had shuffled out, leaving them alone.

'Weird,' she said, slightly out of breath.

'Weird how?' he asked. 'I want to know exactly how you feel. Tell me.'

She thought about it for a while, trying to make sense of it. 'I feel so humiliated,' she confessed. 'They'll all be talking about me. They've all seen my ... the most private, secret part of my body. I'll never be able to look any of them in the eye again. I feel angry with you for doing this to me, but I know I could have stopped it if I'd wanted to. It made me feel dirty, and ... and ...'

'Yes?' He sat up, eager and evil, like a dog waiting for the command to kill.

'I can't understand it,' she said, her voice and fingers quivering. 'It turned me on.'

'How much?' he asked, his fingers letting go of her ankle, at last, and sliding up towards her stocking top.

'A lot.'

The door was wide open. Someone could have been standing there, for all she knew. Right now, she knew nothing except him: his eyes, his mouth, his touch against the soft hair covering her pussy. His fingertips in her wetness. His thumb, easing between her curling lips, easing inside her, making her gasp. At last. At last.

She grabbed at his wrist as he pushed in and out. It was only his thumb, but she wanted to keep it inside her; had to have something to fill the yearning hole. He spread his fingers up into her pubic hair, rubbing her clit as his palm moved over her, up and down, in and out, rubbing the nerve endings until her body jerked.

'Fuck me,' she said, under her breath.

'What did you say?' he asked, his hand still, his eyes shining.

'You heard me.'

'Say it again.'

'Fuck me,' she whispered.

'Say it again,' he teased.

'Fuck me, you bastard.'

'Again.'

'Oh.' His thumb slipped out of her and on to her burning clit. His skin was slimy with her juice. He spread it over her clitoris and she felt herself falling; sinking into the sofa's cushions. Losing control of herself. 'Fuck me,' she murmured.

'Say it again,' he said, his voice soaking wet, just like her.

'Fuck me,' she whispered, lying back, her body flooded with desire. 'Fuck me,' as her knees fell apart. 'Fuck me,' as his thumb rubbed her clit into a pleasure that was almost painful.

'Say please,' he demanded.

'Aahhhh.' His whole palm rubbed her open pussy. 'Please, please, Chris. Fuck me. Fuck me. Please . . .'

'Beg me.' Two of his fingers slipped inside her. 'I want to hear you beg.'

She took in a sharp breath, jolted by the sensation of his thick fingers stretching her; shocked by his cruelty. 'Haven't you humiliated me enough for one day?'

His laughter went through her skin and bone and curled around her innards. 'I haven't even started with you yet, Natalie.'

He jerked his fingers hard into her. Her spine twitched in involuntary response. His thumb flickered evilly over her hard clit, making her close her eyes and moan uncontrollably.

'Beg me,' he said.

Slowly, she opened her eyes. 'Never.'

He was gone. The air supply was cut off as his fingers left her pussy empty and clasping.

'Chris,' she gasped, leaning forward to grab his hand. He caught both her wrists before she could, and turned with hateful lust in his eyes.

'Chris . . .'

'I want to hear you beg me,' he said.

She swallowed hard and tried to breathe. She knew she'd have to give in. He was stronger. He knew what he wanted. She couldn't have what she wanted unless she did this. 'Please.' Her voice was so faint she tried again. 'Please. I beg you. Fuck me.'

He went to get up. For a second, she thought he was leaving; leaving her alone, like this.

'Oh, please, Chris, please, I'm begging you.'

Pushing her leg aside, he stood up, his body moving with urgency now that he'd heard what he wanted. Now that he'd got her lying there, moaning and gasping like a wild thing; wet and ready and open and begging for his cock.

He slammed the door shut with his foot, then leant over to grasp her ankles. He pulled her effortlessly towards him, as if she was a doll, bringing her hips up to his. Her lower back was on the sofa's high armrest, her legs dangling over the edge. Her skirt was crumpled up over her hipbones, exposing her pussy. Helpless, waiting, holding her breath, she watched him push down his shorts. His cock pointed aggressively towards her. She wanted that aggression sheathed inside her so badly she was almost in tears.

Then he hooked his hands round her legs, lifting her pussy an inch or two higher to bring her up to his prick. Bowing his head, he concentrated for an agonising moment as he brought himself to the entrance of her cunt, then –

The shame and humiliation and anticipation were mashed into one. One irrational, incomprehensible thought. Not even a thought – just a feeling, washing through her, sliding over her skin, filling her up. She was cushioned in a fog, and it was dense and weightless and filthy and pure all at the same time.

Then it was nothing. It was just his cock, ramming hard between her thighs, reaching the neck of her womb. Her pussy, thick with the juice of desire and with him.

Natalie looked up at him, his neck bent as he looked down at the place where their bodies met. His mouth was open, his teeth bared. His fingers were clawing so tightly around her thighs that it was hurting, but the pain was just a part of the pleasure. They were animals, him grunting and thrusting, her rocking her head around and whimpering. She followed his gaze, looking down her body, watching as his black cock pumped in and out of her. His skin was covered in her juice. The sight was hypnotic, pushing her not into a trance but into desperation.

Deeper, harder. Fuck with my head like you promised. Wrapping her lower legs round his back, she levered herself further towards him, trying to tell him she wanted more. He read her body language and gave her more, thrusting slower but harder, withdrawing until only the head of his prick was left inside her and then pounding in again with the whole force of his body behind him. Someone chanted, 'Oh, oh, oh,' in the distance, and it was a while before she realised it was her.

Everything stopped as he came. Holding on tightly, he jerked violently into her. Heat gushed into her pussy as a long, low sound came from his lips.

'Jeeeesusfuck,' he said. 'God, I needed that.'

So had she. She hadn't come, but that didn't matter. She was satisfied. His ferocious lust had satisfied her mind. No doubt she'd get her climax later.

Chris's watch beeped. Letting go of her legs, he turned it off. 'Got a lesson in ten minutes,' he said. 'I'll have to go – I need a shower.'

With that, he withdrew his cock. Natalie felt a stream of warmth trickle down her inner thighs. 'Don't go.'

'I have to. Some of us have work to do.'

'Ooohhh.' She groaned in exasperation. 'What time do you finish?' she asked, wishing it was now. Wanting him inside her all afternoon. All night.

'Not till late,' he grumbled. 'Think my last lesson's at eight.'

'I'll wait for you,' she said.

'Don't bother. I'm going out with the lads tonight.'

'Tonight?' She moaned seductively, rolling her hips. 'Don't. You can't. Stay with me tonight.'

'I don't want to. I want to see my mates.'

His coldness killed her desire. She sat up, swinging her legs off the armrest and pulling her skirt back down.

'Don't sulk about it,' he laughed. 'We've got the

whole weekend ahead of us. I finish at twelve on Saturday.'

'And what am I supposed to do tonight?'

He shrugged. 'I don't know. Fuck Paul again, for all I care.'

So this was what he meant by fucking with her mind. Well, two could play at that. 'I will,' she said. 'I'll go home with Paul.'

'Fine. Have fun.' He turned at the door. 'And here –' He threw his T-shirt at her. 'Clean yourself up. You've got come on your stockings, you dirty girl.'

She looked down. There were telltale dribbles on her sheer black stockings. She dabbed at them with his T-shirt for a moment before giving up. Holding the soft white cotton up to her face, she breathed him in. She could smell his aftershave. His sweat. His skin.

'Hi.'

She looked up: it was Paul.

He sat down beside her. Natalie saw the confusion in his eyes as his gaze fell quickly over her. She imagined what she must look like: dishevelled, flushed, glistening with sweat. Skirt creased. Blouse half out. One shoe on; the other lying on the floor.

'What the hell have you been doing?'

She looked at him, at the suspicion on his face, and for a moment she was tempted to unravel the puzzle in his eyes. I was fucking Chris, she would say. Or rather, he was fucking me. I want him, Paul. I thought I wanted you, but I don't.

'Did you hurt your ankle, or something?'

'Erm, yeah. I think I twisted it. It's nothing.'

'There's a rumour going round about you,' Paul said, looking down at her thighs. 'The other guys are saying you were lying here without any –'

She burst into tears, throwing herself at Paul, partly to shut him up but mainly because of what Chris had just done.

'What's the matter?' Paul purred, folding her in his long arms. 'Natalie, darling, calm down. Calm down. Whatever it is, it can't be that bad.'

She closed her eyes as he rubbed her back. It felt safe there, huddled against his chest. She stayed there for ages, until her sobbing stopped.

'Are you going to tell me what's wrong?'

'I've just had a bad day, that's all,' she mumbled into his shoulder. 'I want to go home. What time do you finish?'

'I've just had a cancellation. I've finished now, that's why I came to look for you. Can you bunk off early?'

She had loads of work to do, but there was no way her mind would be able to focus on it now. 'Sure,' she said.

'You deserve the rest of the day off; you've been working too hard.' Paul stroked her hair. 'Is that what's wrong? Have you tired yourself out with all the stress of running this place?'

'Maybe.'

Gently, he lifted her shoulders away from his. Gently, he smiled. 'Come on. Let's go home. We'll get a takeaway and watch a video. I'll run you a bath and give you a long massage.'

'That sounds good,' she said, managing a watery smile.

Paul's blue gaze fluttered over her hair. When it returned to her eyes, there was a different smile on his face.

'What?' she asked.

'You. You look really sexy with your hair like that.'

'Like what?'

'Have a look.'

She retrieved her other shoe and got up, hoping he wouldn't notice the trembling in her thighs. She went to the mirror. Her hair was a mess. She'd started the day with it up in a smooth French pleat, but now it was falling out all over the place, like her inhibitions. Soft strands framed her face and wisped down the back of her neck. She looked like the wanton, carefree sister of her usual sleek, slicked-back self.

Paul appeared in the reflection behind her. Sliding his arms round her waist, he cuddled her close. 'You should wear your hair like that more often. You look all wild and sexy.'

'Hmm.' Ignoring his approval, she started pinning her hair back into its usual neatness. 'I'm supposed to look like a manager.'

'Come on,' he said, taking her hand. 'Let's go home. I want to mess up your hair again.'

Lying awake that night, with Paul softly snoring beside her, she fought with herself. Her thoughts were a mess, muddled beyond repair by the soft, slowly seeping orgasm Paul had given her. They'd had a nice evening together – but 'nice' was a word she didn't like. A Chinese, a bath, a massage, a slow, comfortable screw – it was nice. But was it what she wanted?

Did Chris have what she wanted? She'd tasted shame, feeding from his fingers, and it had been bittersweet. She wanted more. But did she really want to put herself in his hands – to be used and dropped according to his wishes? And would she be able to exorcise him from her mind now, if she decided she wanted to?

There was the club to think about, too. It wouldn't survive without Chris and his customers, and he wouldn't stay on without her. It was impossible. The only option would be for her to leave and find another manager to take her place. But then she'd have to start again, looking for a job, with her parents whining, 'I told you so,' down the phone at her.

Of course, she knew now that, club or no club, she had no choice. She'd already given a piece of her mind to Chris, and it was too late to turn back. She wanted to carry on, but she was frightened, just as he'd said. She was looking for a way out, without wanting to find one.

Her mobile rang at half-three. She answered it before it woke Paul, and took it into the living room, softly closing the door behind her. She knew who it was before she put the phone to her ear.

'Still thinking about me?'

Still angry with him for what he'd done, making her beg and then dropping her. 'What do you want, Chris? It's late.'

'It isn't late – it's early. It's Saturday morning, and I'm ringing to remind you that you're mine this weekend.'

'You're drunk. Go to bed. You've got a lesson at eight.'

'I'm not drunk,' he said calmly. 'I can't sleep. I'm thinking about what I'm going to do to you tomorrow, and it's getting me hard.'

She was silent, apart from her heartbeat. The menace in his voice was making it race.

'I want you to wear something pretty. Not that usual frigid, tight-arsed, no-nonsense stuff you wear. Put on a summer dress. High heels.'

'Where are we going?'

'To help a good friend of mine celebrate his birthday.'

'Oh.'

'You'll enjoy it, I promise.'

She had no doubt that she would.

'Bring a few clothes. You're staying at my place for the whole weekend.'

'Am I? You've got this all planned out, then. What am I supposed to tell Paul?'

'Tell him something's come up and you have to go away for the weekend. He won't mind.'

* * *

And he didn't. When she woke him up at seven with a cup of tea, and broke the news that she was going away, he pulled a very odd face.

'You don't mind?' she asked, surprised by his nonchalance.

'Not at all.' He looked distant, thoughtful. 'I've a few things I need to do, myself.'

'OK then.'

'OK.'

She showered and packed, unsure of what to take. As instructed, she put on a pretty summer dress, one with thin straps, low cut to show a hint of cleavage. It was short and black, with tiny dark-red roses and oak-green leaves rambling all over the floaty material. She couldn't wear a bra underneath it, and she felt more naked than naked with her breasts bouncing and just her silky black knickers on beneath. Her strappy black sandals were high enough to make her have to concentrate on walking; but they did what everyone always said high heels did. They tightened her calves, made her hips swing slightly, and made her back arch provocatively. 'You look like sex on a stick,' Paul said, as she got into the car beside him. 'Who is it you're spending the weekend with?'

'Just a friend,' she said casually.

'Male or female?'

'Male.' She looked out of the corner of her eye, waiting for a reaction. But she didn't get one.

They were both going mad – that was the only explanation. Paul wasn't jealous; she wasn't guilty. She should have been miffed at his complete lack of envy, but she wasn't. By the time they arrived at the club she had one thought on her mind.

Chapter Eight

*H*e looked her up and down, nodding to himself. 'Fucking lovely,' he muttered. 'Good enough to eat.' He emphasised the 'eat'. She wished he wouldn't speak to her like that – it got her wet, and made her want to do dirty things for him.

'You look . . .'

He looked good enough to make her mouth water. It was the first time she'd seen him in normal clothes. He was wearing dark jeans, tight around his huge thighs and his gorgeous arse. His shirt was black and fairly close-fitting as well – the type of shirt that either made a man look gay or pussy-clenchingly, achingly, aggressively masculine. It had short sleeves that showed off the muscles in his arms, and was open at his wide neck. It was a hot day, and he was wearing sandals – the type of sandals that either make a man look like a washed-up old hippy or a laid-back film star.

'Let's go,' he said.

'You go on ahead,' she said. 'I'll meet you in the car park.'

'Afraid Paul will see us together?'

'No, I've just got a couple of things to finish off.'

'He won't see us. He's on court ten with Mrs Spencer.'

'I thought that was your court. I thought Mrs Spencer was your pupil.'

'Paul's a good coach. There's no reason why we can't share some of our clients.'

She was slightly taken aback by this new, professional attitude. 'Are you being nice to him because you're feeling guilty?'

'What have I got to feel guilty about?' He moved round her desk. Opening the top drawer, he swept all her papers away inside it. 'Come on.'

He took her small bag in one hand, her small hand in the other, and led her outside to his car.

It was like him: big and black, heavy but fast, and reeking of sex. He put the roof down, and, as they crawled through the traffic on its way out of town, people looked at them. Natalie smiled at a young woman who pulled up in the lane beside them looking enviously at the car – and at Chris. If only you knew, she thought. You wouldn't be jealous if you could feel what I'm feeling – pure, sickening, ferocious fear, clawing and slavering rabidly in the pit of my stomach.

They drove out of town, on to the dual carriageway and into the outskirts of London. Somehow, Chris managed to find a parking space within walking distance of the All England Club, and for the first time ever Natalie strolled into Wimbledon.

Chris had some sort of VIP pass, and they were met by someone he seemed to know and escorted through the crowds towards one of the outside courts. At the changing rooms, Natalie was made to stand outside while Chris went in to wish his friend good luck. The excitement of being at Wimbledon was doubled by the glances of the people looking at her, wondering who she was and why she had been brought to the locker room. For a moment, her fear began to blur and fade, and she almost allowed herself to relax. Perhaps this afternoon was just going to be a pleasant one spent watching tennis, eating strawberries, drinking champagne – doing the things normal couples did at Wimbledon. But then she heard Chris's sniggering and she turned to find him and another man at the door of the changing room. They were both looking her up and down, as if she was an object – their object, an ornament put on the earth for their pleasure. Her apprehension tightened its grip again.

'Hi,' she said, waving at Chris's friend, hoping Chris would act normally and introduce her. But he didn't. He just whispered and laughed – a low, hacking, wicked laugh – and told his friend God knows what about her. The other guy – tall, tanned, long wavy hair and a stubbly goatee – laughed along with Chris and leered unashamedly at Natalie. His grey eyes drank her in, from her fuck-me sandals to her glossed lips. Natalie folded her arms across her breasts and wished there was somewhere to hide.

'I'll see you later, Sam.' Chris slapped his friend on the back. 'Happy birthday, mate. Enjoy the match.'

'I will.' Sam winked at Natalie. 'Catch you later, darlin'.'

'Who's he?' she asked.

'Sam. Used to be my best mate when I played on the circuit.'

'How come he's still playing and you're not? Weren't you good enough?' It was a dig – she wanted to get back at him for sniggering laddishly at her.

'I got badly injured,' he said. 'Crushed all the ligaments in my knee. I couldn't carry on. Didn't want to move into coaching so early but I had to.'

'Oh. Sorry, I didn't . . .'

'Don't be. I injured myself fucking an acrobatic little blonde and her twin sister. It was worth it.'

'Oh.'

'Sam's too old to make it now. He only carries on for the money – and the pussy. This'll be his last year before he becomes a veteran.'

She was hovering between discomfort and pride as she and Chris were taken to their seats. It wasn't one of the main courts, but it was still good to be there, and several people waved and called to Chris. It made her feel special to be with someone who was recognised. Pathetic, she knew – but true.

'Do you think Sam'll win?'

Chris shrugged, scanning the small crowd for other people who might know him. 'Doubt it. He never wins. His mind's on other things.'

She huffed, finding it hard to believe that someone playing at Wimbledon could have his mind elsewhere. 'Such as?'

'Such as what I've promised him for his birthday.'

'Which is?'

Pausing in his selfish search of the audience, he turned to her. For the first time that day, he really looked at her. Putting his arm round her shoulders, he drew her closer.

For the first time, he kissed her. Natalie forgot the annoyance she'd felt as he'd leered at her. She forgot about the crowd around her. His kissing was like his fucking – urgent, no messing. Desperate. Flattering. He poked his tongue on to hers, crushing their lips together, opening his mouth wide and wetting her skin.

'You're so horny,' he said, loudly enough for the woman sitting in front to look round.

She forgot about the question she'd asked. By the time she remembered it was too late – the players were trooping out on to court.

Sam looked arrogantly attractive as he swaggered out to his seat. In many ways he was the opposite of Chris. Chris was bald and his skin was luscious; Sam's hair was lank and straggly, and with his messy beard he somehow looked a little grubby. But in other ways he was just like Chris: macho, confident, bursting with lazy charisma. As he put his tennis bag down by his seat, he looked up for Chris and Natalie. They were sitting two rows up, directly in line with his chair. Chris waved, and Sam grinned.

'What's he doing?' Natalie asked.

He was turning his chair round so it faced into the audience, instead of facing into the court as usual.

'Some players like to look into the crowd,' Chris whispered, resting his hand on her thigh. 'Sam likes to look for pretty girls.'

Natalie suspected Sam had no trouble finding them. He may not have been a big tennis star, but he had something a lot of the big stars lacked. She watched him warm up, his long legs and arms moving effortlessly, his lazy strides covering the court while his opponent's short legs had to move at twice the speed. His serve was fluent and powerful, and he won the first game with an ace. She could imagine girls wanting him – he looked like he didn't give a toss. She could imagine herself wanting him. As she watched him slope back to his chair, she felt Chris's envy.

'You fancy him, don't you? All the girls fancy him.'

At last, a chance to tease Chris. 'I wouldn't say no,' she said, watching Sam put on a headband. 'He's very sexy.'

'That's just what he said about you.'

Natalie looked up at Chris. He wasn't envious at all of her admiration of his friend. He was calm, proprietorial, as if she could admire anyone she wanted, but it was up to him whom Natalie slept with. She gripped

180

her inner thighs together as he curled his fingers round her knee.

'What are you doing?' Her whisper was urgent, and the woman in front turned round again.

Chris put his lips to her ear. 'Open your legs. Let him see.'

'No way,' she mouthed. 'Stop it, Chris.' Ineffectually, she pushed at his hand.

He tightened his grip. 'Open your legs, or I will cause such a scene you'll wish you'd never been born.'

She closed her eyes. She tried to calm her breathing. Her heartbeat was so loud she could feel it echoing in her lungs. In the orange darkness behind her eyelids, she pretended this wasn't happening.

Her inner thighs relaxed and Chris eased her left leg away from her right. Mortified, furious with herself for thinking, even for a moment, that this would be a normal day, she ground her teeth. When she opened her eyes again, Chris was grinning down at Sam. Sam was looking straight ahead with a lopsided smirk on his wide lips.

Somehow, this was even worse than yesterday. Today she still had her knickers on, but in the sedate atmosphere of Wimbledon it seemed dirtier, more depraved, to sit there with her legs apart. It made her feel weak to realise that Chris and Sam had prearranged this, and dread swirled icily down her spine as she wondered what other humiliation was coming.

It couldn't be much worse than this. Every time the players took a break, Sam stared blatantly up her skirt. He sat with such a nasty smirk on his face that a man in the front row noticed and turned round, obviously trying to find out what Sam was looking at. Natalie tried to close her legs but Chris wouldn't let her, digging his fingernails into her flesh and warning her not to move.

As the match went on, Chris even pulled her thighs

further apart, until her dress was stretched tight above her knees and her legs were almost as wide open as his. It was a mean thing to do, but, just like the previous afternoon when she'd been positioned on the sofa, the shame had a double edge. On the flip side was irrepressible, insane arousal. Sam's eyes were like fingers; she felt her clit pulsating and her juices flowing, again.

Sam lost the match through laziness, but he didn't look disappointed. He grinned wildly up at Chris, and applauded Natalie with his racquet.

'Come on,' Chris said, pulling her to her feet before the audience had stopped clapping. 'Time to give him the rest of his birthday present.'

'What have you got him?'

He didn't answer, putting a hand on her arse instead and squeezing her buttock. Natalie kept her eyes straight ahead, ignoring the looks and tuts of the people they were disturbing as they sidled along the row. It wasn't until she got inside the changing rooms that she realised Chris had given her an answer.

He flashed his pass at the attendant guarding the door. The grey-suited man opened the door for him but stopped him from pulling Natalie inside. 'I'm sorry, sir. Ladies aren't allowed in here while the players are getting changed.'

Chris snorted and pulled Natalie in after him. 'She's no lady.'

He bundled her down the short corridor and kicked open the door. Sam's short, victorious opponent looked up, startled to see two people barging in.

'Hop it,' Chris said, jerking his head towards the door.

The little man looked at Chris for a moment before deciding to do as he was told. Chris locked the door behind him.

'You lost again, you lazy shit.'

Slumped on the bench, Sam emerged from beneath the shroud of his towel. Looking past Chris, he leered at Natalie.

'Your girlfriend put me off,' he said.

Chris shrugged. 'Only doing what you asked. You're the birthday boy.'

'Aren't I lucky.'

Sam held out a hand. Natalie looked at his long, grubby fingers and squirmed inside. But still she didn't realise what was going on until Chris moved behind her. With his hands on her shoulders, he manoeuvred her until she was standing right in front of Sam.

'Happy birthday,' he said.

Oh God. This was why she was here. She watched in horror as Sam lifted his hand.

'Chris,' she pleaded, pushing back against him; trying to edge away from the filth in Sam's smile. But she should have known by now that Chris was there to grip on to her – to force her to fight her natural desire to run away. She was made to stand still as Sam's fingers slipped under the hem of her dress and on to her bare thigh.

'What do you think?'

Sam looked her up and down. 'Very nice,' he murmured. 'Has she got nice tits?'

She didn't know where to look as Chris pushed the thin straps off her shoulders and down her arms. Involuntarily, Sam's hand clenched into her thigh as her breasts were revealed. His skin was clammy and cold. His eyes were greedy.

'Oh yes,' he concurred. 'Lovely, lovely tits.'

'I told you,' Chris said. Reaching round, he squeezed her breasts in his big hands. He pushed them together so her wide nipples peered obscenely at Sam. Unable to resist, Sam sat forward on the edge of the bench and sucked one between his lips.

Her body tensed as Sam's teeth bit down on her sensitive skin. Chris held her tight, absorbing the shock in his body, so thick and solid compared to hers. She was weak; ready to crumple at the slightest touch.

She looked down at Sam's greasy hair. His head rolled between her full breasts, his lips nibbling and sucking on each nipple in turn until the tips protruded and the soft skin surrounding them turned hard. He smelt of sweat. His fingers, clutching like talons round the curve of her breast, were stained with the rancid yellow of a smoker. The fingers hidden underneath her dress inched slimily upward. She was repulsed by him; loathed him almost as much as she loathed Chris for treating her like this. And yet – and yet –

As he bit down hard on her nipple, his hand flew up her inner thigh and delved between her legs. She sucked in air as he rubbed her pussy, sliding his hand backward and forward over her knickers. Her panties were wet. Her fleshy lips began to swell at his touch. Her clit, already throbbing, began to burn.

It was happening again. Her feelings were twisting; shedding their skins; exposing the raw blood and guts just beneath the surface. And writhing in her blood and guts was something incomprehensible – something Chris had somehow seen the moment they'd met.

She surrendered, allowing herself to be manhandled until she had her back to Sam – allowing herself to enjoy their clumsy, urgent male hands and the way they pushed and pulled at her body. 'Look at that arse,' Chris urged, lifting up her dress. Behind her, Sam ripped down her knickers. His cold touch spread like slime over her buttocks, and she felt her skin crawling.

'What an arse,' Sam agreed, before his voice was swallowed up between her cheeks. Natalie jumped to feel his nose pressing into her cleft. She was shocked to feel herself opening her legs wider and arching her lower back, urging him further into her most secret place.

His tongue, which was as slimy as the rest of him, ran the length of her cleft. She shuddered with embarrassment: a stranger's face pressed to her arse, his tongue poking at her anus. The way her back ached as she arched it further, wanting more – she was as bad as them, if not worse. They were bound to be enjoying this. She shouldn't be. She should have been struggling; fighting with them; demanding for this to stop.

All she did was whimper as Sam's tongue forced its way into the tightness of her arsehole. Steadying herself, she held on to Chris's thick forearms. She looked up at him. She could feel his breath on her face and could hear its urgency. His eyes were full of depraved admiration for her. He was as turned on as she was.

'Why are you doing this to me?' she whispered, fighting to find the energy to form the words.

He smiled slightly. 'Why are you letting me?'

She didn't know. She didn't have time to think about it now. Her mouth opened wide as Sam replaced his tongue with a long, probing finger. The nerve endings inside her secret passage squealed with the shock and her whole body froze in terror. The pleasure of a finger in the arse was so different from a finger in the pussy. Her inner muscles clutched, trying to repel the finger sliding slowly in and out. Her body, her nerve endings, her common sense said, No! Get out! You're not supposed to be in there! It was frightening, allowing a man inside that most private place; petrifying when she had no choice but to let him in. But her mind, addled with dark, addictive shame, said, Yes. Touch every inch of me. I'm yours. Do what you want with me.

'She likes it up the arse,' Sam said.

'She likes it any way,' Chris said. 'She's a dirty, dirty girl.'

'I love dirty girls.' Sam's finger pulled out and he kissed her gasping arsehole, gripping on to her buttocks and holding them apart. One hand moved between her legs and closed over her mound. Slipping back and forward, he pressed with the tip of his middle finger, prising open her swollen lips. He found the opening he was blindly searching for and slid his finger into her pussy. It was so easy compared to her arsehole; so wet and yielding and ready.

'Oh God, she's soaking wet,' Sam mumbled. 'I've got to fuck her, now.'

'How do you want her?'

'On her hands and knees. I want to take her from behind,' Sam grunted, from somewhere far away. 'I want to look at that gorgeous fucking arse while I fuck her senseless.'

Natalie was lowered on to all fours. Her dress was pulled off over her head, while, behind her, her knickers were disentangled from her shoes and thrown aside. She waited there, naked and panting like a dog, her breasts dangling to the floor, her inner self open and exposed. Ready for a man she barely knew.

Sweat wafted in the air as Sam knelt down behind her. Sweat and the smell of sex, salty and warm, and the smell of shameful fear, dark and bitter. Chris moved round to her side and watched as Sam parted her pussy lips with his thumbs, readying her for his assault. Then – breath pushed out of her, all sense of self swallowed up and she became an animal – he was inside her. His cock felt long and thin, like him. His fingers were sharp and cruel, twitching at her waist and then up to her breasts. Leaning over her, Sam used his tight grasp on her tits to keep her still while he pumped into her. Natalie let her head fall forward and she looked at his nicotine-stained fingers on her soft flesh; beyond, at the neat stripe of her dark pussy hair; and beyond to his hairy thighs rocking into hers. She heard herself grunting loudly and unstoppably. She felt herself spreading her knees wider apart and bending her elbows to dip her upper body towards the floor. She was opening herself wider to him; letting him in deeper. Giving herself. What the hell was happening to her?

With Natalie in that position, Sam's cock was let in so deep the pleasure was more intense than normal fucking. So deep, it felt like the knob of his cock was pushing into the soft tissue at the base of her brain. This wasn't sex; it was torture. The pleasure was so raw it was almost pain. If only it would stop. If only it would never stop.

The torture increased and, as it did, the volume of her cries grew out of control. She was vaguely aware of his fingers twitching around her pussy, catching the juice spilling out as his cock dived inside her, and then she felt those fingers pressing at her arsehole again. Lubricated by her quim, one finger poked easily between her open cheeks. Immediately, her muscles closed round it; but already he was pushing with another. Two fingers inside her arse. Along with his prick, pumping hard into her pussy, and his other fingers pinching her engorged nipple; it was too much. She couldn't move. Her mind shut down. Her body dissolved. She ceased being human and became a simple creature made of cunt and cock, arse and breast, ecstasy and despair. Impaled on Sam's lust, she couldn't even make a sound when there was a knock at the door and Chris's footsteps moved across the floor towards it. Summoning all her energy, she turned her head to look as he unlocked the door and got rid of whoever was out there trying to come in.

'You'll have to hurry up, mate,' Chris said. 'They want to get changed for the next match.'

As if he'd been half-hearted before, Sam began in earnest. He slammed into her with such force she had to push back against him to stop herself being flung across the floor. With every thrust his fingers followed his cock inside her, pushing into the depths of her arsehole and bringing tears to her eyes. Her angry clit was the only part of her being ignored, and yet she felt the rush of orgasm building inside her. It wasn't just a mental rush. She felt her innards giving way. Her vital organs surrendered to the pressure and, as Sam gave a series of rapid, doglike jerks inside her, everything let go. Her elbows collapsed to the floor. The lights went out in her head. Her thoughts turned black. Something that had only happened once before, after she'd spent three glorious, selfish, self-indulgent hours masturbating, happened again. A gushing stream of heat trickled down the backs of her legs and into a puddle on the floor.

'Jesus.'

'Fuck.'

She closed her eyes in shame. There was silence apart from the sound of heavy breathing and the occasional obscenity from one of the men. Someone knocked insistently on the door again.

A hand smoothed her cheek. 'You're amazing.'

It was Chris, crouching down beside her. He eased her face up from the floor. Through suddenly sleepy eyes, she looked at him. 'Help me,' she said. 'I haven't got the strength to move.'

He hooked his hands under her arms, gently lifting her on to her feet. Her legs were shaking ridiculously. There was an uncontrollable tremor in her inner thighs.

'Here.' Sam threw a towel. Chris caught it. Kneeling at her feet, he dabbed at her pussy. Natalie steadied herself on his shoulder and looked down at him, her humiliation at wetting herself slightly cushioned by the reverence with which he was cleaning her.

'That was incredible,' he whispered in awe. 'That was the most amazing thing I've ever seen.' He glanced towards the small damp patch on the floor, admiring it as if it was liquid gold that had spilt from her cunt.

She'd explain later; explain that Sam had managed to find that magic spot, buried somewhere far inside her, that she'd found only once before with the help of a state-of-the-art, pulsing, throbbing, swivelling, ridged vibrator and a grim determination. Then, she'd wet the bed with her pleasure. Now her ecstasy was on the floor of a Wimbledon locker room. Sam, a complete stranger, a man as repulsive as he was sexy, had given her the most complete orgasm she'd had in ages.

The men were impressed by her total physical abandon. No doubt it stroked their egos. As Chris slid her dress back on over her head, his touch was tender on her skin. Pulling on his own clothes, Sam stared at her with undisguised admiration. 'You're the best birthday present I've ever had,' he said. He stooped to retrieve her crumpled knickers from the floor. 'Can I keep these?'

She nodded weakly.

'You're a lucky, lucky sod, Chris,' he said, still looking at her.

'I know.' Chris steered her towards the door. It was even harder to walk in her heels now, since her legs seemed to have lost the will to walk and her three-inch heels seemed to have grown into stilts.

'Natalie.'

She turned.

'If you ever get sick of Chris, give me a call.'

He blew her a kiss from his dirty fingers. She caught it inside her dirty mind.

'What are you thinking?'

She finished her mouthful and put down her knife and fork. She looked round the Harvey Nichol's restaurant, laughing inside at the freshly blow-dried, heavily made-up beauties delicately picking at their food. 'I was just wondering how many of these women have been to Wimbledon.'

'Loads.'

'And how many d'you reckon have ended up on all fours on the locker-room floor?'

His eyebrows flickered. 'You'd be surprised.'

'So I'm not the first?' She felt a strange twinge of jealousy at the thought of him smuggling other women into the changing rooms. Why she should feel like that, she didn't know. He wasn't hers, and, no matter how many times he said it, she wasn't his. But, strangely, his giving her to one of his friends had sparked something inside her. A piece of her belonged to him now – the most important piece. Her mind. She wanted his in return. She wanted every second of his attention. She wanted monopoly on every thought. Knowing that she'd never get it made her feel empty inside.

'I think you're probably the first to wet herself,' he said.

She looked down at her plate, embarrassed again. 'I told you before. He found my G-spot. God knows how: I can't find it myself. Only managed it once.'

'I'll help you find it again.'

She looked up. His expression was odd. Hiding behind the usual aggression, barely discernible, was the faintest wash of green. There was sad envy in his eyes. She wondered if it was possible that he'd watched Sam, and watched her losing control over her own body, and wished it had been him making her feel like that? Was there a tinge of regret that he'd allowed another man to taste her – that he'd ever started this game?

'What were you thinking?'

He studied her for a long time before answering. His liquid brown gaze, thick as treacle, dripped over her throat, across her shoulders, down into her cleavage and along her bare arms. 'I was wondering whether Sam will give me something as beautiful for my birthday.'

Their eyes met. They looked into each other. Peering behind what was visible, Natalie searched for the truth. There was a change in Chris, and it was telling. His voice was softer. His touch was tender as he reached for her across the table. Clasping her fingers in his, he lifted her hand to his mouth. He sucked on her middle finger, slowly rolling his tongue over her skin. If she was right, then this mad, dangerous game they were playing was no longer completely in his control. Jealousy was a sign. If he was jealous of the mindlessness of her pleasure, then there was a chance he was starting to need her as much as she needed him.

And she knew now that she did need him. Not only did she need his hands, his mouth, his cock inside her: she needed him to push her into places she'd never been before. She wanted him to push her over the edge. She wanted to take him with her.

'Did you enjoy watching Sam fuck me?'

He lowered his eyeline to his empty plate. 'It's always amazing to watch a woman come,' he said quietly. 'You looked so . . . so . . .' His voice trailed off into nothing. He sighed almost silently. His eyes glazed.

She waited for him to return from his thoughts.

When he did, he seemed colder; more determined than ever before.

'Eat up. We've got some shopping to do. You need something special to wear tonight.'

'Why? Where are we going?'

'You'll find out tonight,' he said.

She finished her late lunch and followed Chris out of the restaurant. Suddenly he was back to his old self, pulling her along by the hand as if she was a doll he was dragging behind him. As they found the lingerie department, Natalie realised that the 'something special' she'd imagined to be a dress was going to be something to wear under a dress. She smiled nervously at the sales assistants as he pushed her around the rails.

'May I help you, madam?'

Chris butted in before Natalie could answer. She winced at his rudeness – he didn't even look the grey-haired assistant in the eye. 'I want something really sexy for her. Black. Skimpy. See-through, if possible.' He flicked his hand at Natalie. 'Tell her what size you are.'

Natalie told the woman. She was obviously used to being ordered around by boorish, ill-mannered customers, because she went off obediently, without a word, selecting items from the various displays.

'The fitting rooms are over here,' she said, beckoning Natalie to follow her. Chris followed too. 'I'm sorry, sir,' she said. 'Gentlemen are not allowed inside the fitting rooms.'

Natalie glanced at Chris. He was at least a foot taller than the assistant, and he was glaring down at her with a look that would have withered most women. 'I'm no gentleman,' he said.

She wasn't going to be beaten that easily. As Natalie slipped away from the tension, into the cocoon of a white-curtained cubicle, the woman put her arm up to block Chris's path.

Alone, Natalie slipped off her dress and looked at herself for a moment in the mirror. Standing there in only her heels, she studied her body, imagining what Sam had thought of her. She did have a good body, more by default than by diet and exercise. She had high, full tits with big, dark nipples; a small waist; wide, womanly hips. She liked the way her legs looked so much longer in her high heels; and the way she'd trimmed her pussy hair last night, in the bath. Her fingers drifted over the narrow strip of curls and then down. Sliding her middle finger between her lips, she found herself wet, again. Unable to stop herself, she slipped her finger inside, closing her eyes as she felt what Sam had felt: tight, ridged flesh. Soft. Clutching. Warm. Soaking.

'Is everything all right, madam?'

The voice from just outside the curtain woke her up. 'Fine, thanks,' she said, hoping to God the woman didn't come in. Somehow it was fine to be fucked like a dog, but not to be seen in the nude by a middle-aged shop assistant.

She fiddled with one of the bra's catches and straps and then pulled on a matching G-string. The material was gorgeous: black, and silky as Chris's cock. She touched herself again, sliding her fingertips all over her hidden pussy and under the swell of her breasts. The bra was beautiful, and it pushed up her breasts and plunged deep into her cleavage. The soft, dark circles around her nipples were so big that slivers of brown flesh peered above the edge of the material. She looked naughtier with this stuff on than when she was naked.

'Your husband would like you to try these on, too.'

A hand pushed through the curtain. Natalie took the sheer stockings and suspender belt from the woman's hand, laughing at the thought of Chris being her husband. Kicking off her shoes, she unfurled the fine nylons over her thighs, and clipped the lacy tops into the suspenders. She slipped her shoes back on and admired herself again. Naughtier still. What was it about stockings?

She heard an argument going on outside: Chris's low voice pitted against the high shrill of the assistant. Chris obviously lost, again, because a moment later the woman was at the curtain once more. 'Your husband wonders if you'd step outside to show him your outfit,' she said. As Natalie emerged she pursed her lips and raised her eyebrows, telling Natalie she didn't approve one bit of her 'husband'.

Natalie peered out of the entrance to the fitting rooms. Chris was standing in the middle of the department, several feet away. 'Chris,' she hissed. 'Chris!'

He turned to look at her but didn't move. 'Come and show me,' he said, waving his huge hand.

'I can't.' She looked out at the other people browsing around. 'You'll have to come here.'

'Come here. Now.' His voice boomed across the room. All the other assistants, and several customers, stopped what they were doing and looked with pity at Natalie and revulsion at Chris.

They didn't know that this was part of their game. They didn't know that the falter in her step, as she walked across the floor, was because of the thrill shooting down from her mind into her knickers. They didn't know Chris.

She stood in front of him, posing for his approval like a slave. He looked her up and down, batting at her with his hand, making her turn round and show him the rear view. 'Nice,' he said, patting her bare buttocks. Natalie could almost hear the feminist movement drawing in its breath.

He turned her back round to face him. Lifting his

194

hand, slicing through the thick tension filling the conditioned air, he touched the upper curve of her cleavage. Natalie was transfixed by his open mouth and his lowered eyes; his concentration; the way he was doing it again – making her feel helpless in front of all these people. The way he exposed her, and brought her inner self crawling and blinking out into the open, was incredible. If he had told her to get to her knees, right there, in Harvey Nichol's lingerie department, she would have done.

Chris was transfixed by her cleavage and by the way his fingertips followed the path of her exaggerated curves. 'I can see your nipples,' he said, touching the tender brown skin. 'You're so beautiful.'

There it was again: that hint of a different side of Chris. For a moment, he seemed to forget about pushing her to new levels of humiliation, and about the people watching. There was only him and her. Her body. Her mind. His body.

Then all of a sudden that side of him was gone. 'I'll help you try on some more,' he said, grabbing her hand. She teetered behind, trying to keep up with his long strides.

He held up his hand, stopped the changing-room guard before she could speak. 'I know it's not allowed, Ms Frigid, but I'm going to do it, anyway.' And he bundled Natalie past the woman's beady glare and outraged sucking in of breath and back into the cubicle.

'Try them all on,' he said, grabbing the mass of black lace and satin hanging up on the wall. He sat down on the floor, facing the full-length mirror. There wasn't much room left with his big body in there and his thighs sprawled in the way. Natalie stood in the only space, between his legs, with her back to the mirror.

Chris's eyes darted between Natalie and her reflec-

195

tion as he threw items up at her, enjoying every angle of the view. She tried on one outfit after another, having to fiddle with her suspenders every time she changed her knickers. Chris gave his comments, muttering his approval as she tried on see-through lacy things that showed her nipples and pubic hair. In particular he liked the G-strings, mumbling that 'Sam was right. Your arse is fantastic.' But most of all he liked to see her touching herself as she arranged her breasts in the various bras and pulled the thin strips of material up between her cheeks.

'Jesus,' he said. 'You're a wet dream.'

She looked at him. He was fidgeting uncomfortably, fumbling with the erection in his jeans.

'Come here. No, closer.'

She stepped right up to him. He wanted her nearer. He grabbed her arse and pulled her crotch into his face. Off-balance, she reached for the wall and planted her feet either side of his hips. 'Look at that,' he groaned, and she looked over her shoulder.

It was like a scene from a soft-porn film. Her all in black, dressed in the pseudo-bondage trappings of male fantasy; him, fully dressed, with his dark hands all over her pale arse. He left the image behind and put his mouth to her pussy, nibbling at the thin material hiding her from his hungry eyes. 'Jesus,' he said, biting at her lips.

'Is everything all right, madam?'

'Ye–es,' she managed, before her voice tightened into a knot. He was licking her, holding her arse and pushing his mouth into her panties. Through the damp fabric, she could feel his tongue lapping and her lips swelling and opening. She wanted to feel more, and he did, too. He slid a hand under one thigh and lifted it up. There was a stool conveniently waiting in the corner and Natalie put her foot up on it. With her legs wide open for him, she moaned at the sensation of his tongue rasping over her panties. She wanted more. She had to have more.

Reaching down, she pulled at the thin strip of material. Holding it aside, she showed him her pussy. He was still for a moment, breathing deeply, drinking in the sight. 'You want me, don't you?' he asked, bowing his head again, and kissing the fingers that were holding her knickers for him. 'You want me to lick you till you come. You filthy slut. You want me to do it to you, right here. God, you're bad. Say please.'

'Please.'

His tongue poked between her open lips. Her bones turned to jelly as he licked deep inside her; deep, deep inside her mind.

'I'm fine.' She screamed at the woman who coughed and asked, again, whether madam was all right. 'Leave us alone, for God's sake.'

She was coming. Her whole being quivered as she waited for it to happen. He licked and licked, dipping right inside her; sucking on her succulent, fleshy lips; nibbling on the engorged anger of her clit. Her inner thighs twitched as he found the right spot – the spot that sent sighs of mindless ecstasy curling from her mouth. 'Oh God,' she gasped. 'Oh God, oh God, don't stop, oh God, that feels . . . oh, so good . . .'

Before her climax had even begun to flow his mouth was gone. Fiddling frantically, Chris freed his cock and pulled her down into his lap. Open, wet, willing, she slid her body easily on to his. Oh God. Now she felt complete. The heat of climax seeping inside her; the force of his cock engulfed in her cunt.

Urged on by his hands at her waist, she began to slide up and down. The friction caused more heat to sear her skin. She threw her head back and groaned. His hands slid up to her breasts and pressed them together. Hooking under the edges of her bra, his fingertips pulled at the cups, revealing her swollen, bouncing breasts. His saliva coated her skin, his tongue swirling over her tits as they jerked in front of his face. Reaching for a nipple, he bit down, and she gasped as the spasm of pain travelled down her spine and into the core of her inside her hips. But she didn't stop. She carried on, pumping his thick cock; clenching her pussy as tightly as she could round his hard, hard flesh.

Oh God. His fingers reached down and found her clit again. Her first climax mingled with the second, growing into something bigger, something stronger, something as hard as a fist in the guts and as soft as syrup being poured over her skin. 'Ohhhh,' she said, slamming herself on to him and hearing his desperation.

His groan was so loud as he came that Natalie couldn't help laughing at the thought of the shoppers on the other side of the curtain trying to remain poker-faced. Chris was oblivious – or rather, he didn't care. He cared only about her, and she felt pride mush-rooming inside her as she realised that, at this moment, he was hers. Every part of him belonged to her. His eyes blind to everything except her body; his body emptying into hers; his mind focusing so intently on her flesh. His thighs juddered with the aftershock of his climax and then he bent his legs up behind her. Gently pushing her backward, he made her lean on his powerful thighs as he smoothed his hands up over her torso. Natalie stretched out, letting her arms fling back, jutting her naked breasts towards him as if she was a figurehead. She relished his touch. His fingers were all over her, stroking her skin, smoothing over her belly and rubbing her stiff nipples. She watched him, and his worship of her body excited her so much her pussy clenched round his prick.

He wriggled as he felt it. His eyes fell to her pussy. His fingers traced the edge of the G-string that had been pulled aside to let him in. 'I'll have to buy these,' he said. 'They're wet.'

'You'll have to buy them all,' she said. 'They're all wet.'

He looked up at her, admiration burning in his eyes as it had done in Sam's. 'You're so dirty.'

'Would you want me any other way?'

Chapter Nine

*H*e cooked her dinner and watched as she ate it.
He loved watching women eat. He could tell a
lot about women by the way they ate. He could tell
whether he liked a woman or not, and what sort of
lover she was. He hated women who picked at their
meals, and refused second helpings when really they
were still hungry, and whined about cheating on their
diets while they were stuffing their faces. They were
never good in bed. He loved women who enjoyed
their food; who tucked in as Natalie did, without any
hint of self-consciousness.

She ate all her pasta, washing it down with good
red wine. She wiped up the sauce with her bread and
then accepted when he offered her more. He didn't
have more himself – he just sat and watched, feeling
his admiration for this woman billowing inside him.
Of all the women he'd fucked, none had affected him
like Natalie was doing. Her resistance to him at first
had turned him on. Her willingness now, to go where
he led her, was driving him insane. If there was such
a thing as his perfect woman, then Natalie was probably it.

He'd never admit that to her, though. It pained him to admit it to himself. Women were toys; food for his hungry libido. Something for his aggression to gnaw on. Creatures to be played with until he decided it was time for the kill. Natalie was creeping her way inside his mind, and he couldn't afford for that to happen. There were millions of girls out there he hadn't yet fucked. He couldn't possibly become attached to one. She would slow him down.

And yet, as he watched her, he felt pangs of something that went deeper than the domineering game he was playing with her. His heartbeat quickened just looking at her lips, which were shiny with olive oil. Her hair was straggling down her back, still wet and messy from the shower. She had no make-up on, and she didn't realise it but, without her usual lipstick and eyeliner and mascara, and with her hair unruly and damp, she looked fragile and sexy, and desperately fuckable. Her pure, pale-olive skin was delicious. Her eyes. Jesus, those eyes. He'd never forget the look in her eyes after Sam had made her come like that – absolute surrender to pleasure.

He realised with a jolt that the pangs he felt were jealousy. Giving her to Sam had seemed a good idea at the time: a way to push her beyond belief; a way to show her beyond all doubt that he was in command and she was his to do with as he wanted. And it had certainly seemed worth it when he'd watched her mind clouding with shame and her body unable to resist. He'd almost heard the struggle taking place inside her mind, and when the struggle was lost her moans of abandon had been deeply satisfying. Using her like that, seeing her on all fours on the floor, wanton and wet, had given him a cruel thrill. But seeing her come so completely, her body ravaged by the pleasure Sam had given her, had been difficult. He hadn't expected to feel anything but powerful. Instead, he'd felt weak. At the moment when her orgasm had taken hold, he'd wanted to push Sam out of the way and hold her tight, absorbing her cries and her shaking. He'd wanted her to take him with her as she fell over the edge.

He rubbed his bald head thoughtfully, trying to stimulate his brain. This wasn't right. This wasn't how it was supposed to work. He was the one in command here. He was the one pulling her strings. So why did she seem so relaxed? She'd come with him, not knowing what this weekend had in store for her, while he'd had it all planned out. So how come she was the one tucking into her meal, and he was the one who couldn't eat?

All he knew was that tonight would put him back where he belonged – in command. Tonight she was going to be given to another of Chris's friends. But this time it would be for his pleasure, not another man's.

He let her relax in the living room while he cleared up the dinner, then had a shower and a shave. He took his time, knowing he had plenty of it before his appointment, and wanting to lull her into a false sense of security. He'd promised her a treat tonight, and she'd get one. But she didn't yet know that she'd have to wait for it, and wait a very long time.

He wrapped a towel round his waist and summoned her into his bedroom. Lying on the bed, he told her to choose a bra and panties from the lingerie he'd bought her. With one hand behind his head, and another reaching beneath the towel, he savoured the sight of her getting ready for sex. There was something about watching a woman getting dressed that made him hard. It was perverse, but seeing her breasts and pussy being covered was more of a turn-on than seeing her naked. And seeing her touching herself, even though her fingers were businesslike, was incredible. Half the time, he thought, women had no idea that what they were doing was gut-wrenchingly sensual.

'Does it turn you on, to touch yourself like that?' he asked, as she eased her G-string into the luscious crack of her arse.

She looked up. It was dark in his bedroom, with only the lamp on, but he could still see the glint in her eyes. 'The truth?'

He nodded.

'Yes, it does.'

'Really?'

She nodded, glancing over her shoulder at the mirror. 'I often have to masturbate while I'm getting dressed in the mornings.' She looked casually over her shoulder at him. 'Sometimes I get my panties so wet I have to change them before I leave the house.'

Jesus. His erection jumped beneath his hand. He pushed the towel aside and stroked his heavy balls as she carried on.

She ignored him, but he could tell she was intensely aware of him. Every movement was for him; every movement was designed to make his cock harder and his lust sharper.

Bitch, he thought, as she reached inside her bra to push her breasts up even further. She knows exactly what she's doing. She's teasing me. Trying to take control.

Standing by the bed, she used his bedside table to rest her foot on while she slowly unfurled a stocking. Her hands smoothed upward over her calf and thigh, gently pulling the sheer, sexy nylon up to her suspender belt. She fastened the stocking then changed legs and began again. Her bare arse was so close to his face he longed to grab it; to pull her on top of him. Her legs were so sexy, so slender and shapely compared to the thickly bunched muscles in his thighs, that he longed to feel them wrapped round his back. He clasped on to his cock and kept hold of his self-control.

'Well?' She slipped her high heels on and turned to face him.

'Well what?'

'Well, how do I look?'

He ignored her, looking down at his cock.

'Do you want me to do that?' She knelt by the bed. Her delicate fingers pushed at his, urging them away. 'Let me,' she purred.

He pushed her away. 'I haven't got time for this. I've got things to prepare.'

'For my surprise?' She sat back on her heels and watched him.

'Yeah.' He got dressed, slipping on some trousers and a shirt.

'What is it?'

'It wouldn't be a surprise if I told you, would it?'

'Am I going to like it?'

'I don't know.' He stepped behind her, rummaging in the bedside-table drawer by her side. 'You're probably not going to enjoy this bit, much.'

Her shoulders twisted as he pulled her hands together behind her back and clicked the handcuffs on her wrists.

'What are you doing?'

'Making sure you don't go anywhere.' He pulled her up by one arm and marched her back into the living room. 'I have to go out for a while,' he explained, pulling a chair out from the dining table and pushing her down on to it. Before she had time to protest, he'd opened her legs and cuffed each ankle to a chair leg.

'Don't leave me like this,' she pleaded as he strode to the door. 'Chris! These handcuffs are too tight. Chris!'

He shut the door, shutting out the sound of her voice, and went out to meet his date for the evening.

By the time Chris returned home, he was high on whisky chasers, Vivienne, and a sense of power. The look on Natalie's face as he kicked open the door was almost enough to give him a hard-on, again.

She looked hurt and angry. 'You bastard.' She spat fury. 'What the fuck do you think you're playing at, leaving me like this? Let me out. Now.'

He just smiled and let his eyes lazily drift over her body once again. Absence made the heart grow fonder: two hours apart certainly made the sight of her all the sweeter. He'd almost forgotten how sexy she looked.

Vivienne looked sexy too, although in a different way from Natalie. Vivienne was pushing fifty, and her sensuality lay not in smooth skin and young, firm flesh, but in experience and the fact that she no longer cared what anyone thought of her.

Vivienne was drunk. Her lipstick was smudged and her usually perfect, dyed-blonde hair was skewwhiff, falling out of its French pleat. Her mascara had run slightly from crying with laughter, which was one of her most endearing habits, and her clothes were rumpled from their fumble in the taxi. Her skin was slightly sagging, slightly wrinkled, but there was attractiveness in the laughter lines on her face, and in the filth in her laugh. Vivienne was one of the naughtiest women Chris knew. Perfect for this; perfect for tonight.

She tripped as she followed Chris into the living room, and giggled raucously. The high, bubbling sound stirred Natalie's anger, and she glared at Chris with hatred in her eyes.

'Who's she?'

'You remember Vivienne? You should do. She's a member of the club.'

Natalie couldn't even raise a smile in acknowledgement. 'What's she doing here?'

'Oh dear,' Vivienne cackled. 'What rattled her cage?'

'I think you did,' Chris said in a stage whisper. 'I think she was hoping to have me to herself tonight.'

'Greedy girl. She'll have to learn to share.'

He watched as Vivienne slunk over to Natalie's chair. While the prisoner seethed in Chris's direction, Vivienne draped her red-tipped fingers through Natalie's hair. 'She's a pretty little thing,' she murmured.

In a rage at being spoken about as if she wasn't there, Natalie jerked her head away from Viv's hand. 'Chris,' she said quietly – the voice of a mother who'd finally had enough of her delinquent children – 'If this is a joke, it isn't funny. Let me out of here, now.'

Vivienne put a finger to Natalie's lips. 'But the fun hasn't started yet, darling.'

Natalie looked up at her. 'I've been sitting like this for the last two hours. My wrists are hurting; I've had cramp in both calves; and I'm fucking furious. Fun is the last thing on my mind right now.'

Viv tutted patronisingly at her. 'Don't get worked up, sweetheart. This is for your own good, believe me.'

Natalie huffed and turned to Chris again. 'Let me out of here, you bastard. I don't want to spend another minute in your company.'

Chris smiled to himself and sloped across the room to stand behind Vivienne. This was more like it: this was how he wanted Natalie. Angry. Hating him. Helpless. Her fury would make this even better, because she'd be fighting herself.

'I'm sorry, Natalie. I can't let you go yet,' he said,

holding Vivienne close to his body. 'I promised you a surprise. And I never renege on a promise. Do I?'

He kissed Viv's long, perfume-soaked neck, sliding his hands on to her breasts. She sighed in reply, pressing her cool hands down on top of his. 'You've never let me down, darling,' she said.

Natalie let out a long, frustrated sigh. 'I'm not interested in your surprises,' she said. 'If you're not going to let me go, at least get me a drink. It's so hot in here.' She looked up at him accusingly. 'It's so humid. You could have left a window open.'

'Ooh, poor love,' Vivienne cooed in sympathy. 'It is very warm in here. Look at her, Chris. She's dripping.' She leant forward and trailed a finger from Natalie's chin, over her throat, into her cleavage. When Chris returned from the kitchen with a glass of water, her touch had reached the taut curve of Natalie's belly. Chris watched with bated breath as Viv's fingertip continued downward, over the thin strip of material stretched tight across Natalie's pussy.

Natalie's inner thighs jerked and her breath sucked in. Now, when she looked at Chris, there was confusion in her eyes as well as anger. 'Tell her not to touch me,' she said.

'But that would spoil your surprise.' He smiled, handing Vivienne the tall glass. She took a sip before bending over Natalie and raising it to her lips.

Natalie drank the water, gulping down greedily. But Vivienne tipped the glass quicker than she could swallow, and the water began to trickle down Natalie's chin. She managed a sound of protest before all sound was washed away, and she could only gasp as the rest of the icy water was tipped down her front. Her body shivered with the shock. Her stomach muscles clenched. She looked down, just as Chris did, at the way her soaking-wet bra now clung to her pointed nipples and the thin gauze of her G-string stuck to her wet pubic hair.

'You bitch,' she whispered, when she'd recovered her breath.

'My goodness.' Vivienne slapped her hand to her own face in mock horror. 'Such a filthy mouth on such a pretty girl. Are you going to let her speak to me like that, Christopher? I was only trying to cool her down.'

'I know.' Chris's hands returned to Vivienne's tits. Looking over her shoulder, he unbuttoned her silk blouse and opened it. 'She's an ungrateful girl,' he said, sliding his fingers over the generous white cups of Vivienne's bra.

'Not like me,' Vivienne purred, turning her head up to his.

'Not like you.' Chris stuck out his tongue to touch hers. He banged their lips together, thrashing around inside Vivienne's mouth and tasting the whisky they'd got drunk on.

'I always show my gratitude, don't I, darling?' Vivienne swivelled round within his arms to face him. She undid his shirt, pushing the material aside and lightly scratching his tight chest before dipping her lips. She kissed him, softly biting his nipples, working her way down until she was on her knees. Smiling up at him, she unfastened his belt and eased his trousers down.

'Sweetheart,' she soothed, at the sight of his bulging shorts. 'Oh, sweetheart.' She pushed her hand up over his erection and hooked her fingers beneath the elastic. Tugging at his pants, she pulled them down until they were crumpled round his ankles. 'Oh, my darling,' she sighed, kissing his balls. 'I think I'm going to have to show you my gratitude again.'

He watched her bottled-blonde head bobbing at his cock for a while, savouring the feeling of being inside her mouth again. Then he looked up at Natalie, and the sight of her made his prick twitch between Viv's lips.

She was struggling pathetically with her cuffs, and scowling fiercely at him. If looks could kill, he thought. 'What's the matter?' He smirked. 'Jealous?'

Her expression was hard. 'Do you think this is funny?'

He didn't answer. He groaned as Vivienne's tongue ran the length of his prick, and smoothed his hands in a self-satisfied way over his stomach.

'You're sick,' she hissed. She tugged again at her ankle restraints, but, realising she'd look foolish trying to move with a chair attached to her, she gave up. 'As soon as I get out of these, I'm leaving,' she threatened.

'No, you're not.'

Incensed, she was breathless. 'You can't keep me like this for ever. I'll scream for help. The neighbours will think you're a pervert – if they don't already. They'll call the police, and then you'll have some explaining to do.'

You'll be screaming later, he thought. But not for help. 'You won't be going anywhere,' he promised. 'Once you've had the surprise I promised, you won't want to leave. Believe me.'

She closed her eyes, as if she had to escape his infuriating, knowing smile. She muttered something vicious.

'What did you say?'

Eyes open; fire spitting. 'I said, you're a cunt.'

'Aaaaaahh.' The sound of that word on her lips. The feeling of Vivienne's lips on his cock. His head fell back as he came on Viv's tongue.

'Did you hear that, Viv?'

Viv finished lapping his salty come and looked at him. 'Did she say the C word?'

'She called me a cunt.'

'That's it,' Viv said, unsteadily getting to her feet.

209

'I've had enough of her ungrateful behaviour.' Reaching under her skirt, she slipped off her panties. 'If you can't watch your mouth, young lady, you will have to be taught a lesson. Christopher's my friend. You don't speak to him like that, no matter how pretty you are.'

She pulled her white panties into a long, thin strip and put it between Natalie's lips. Natalie struggled, flicking her head from side to side, but Chris grabbed her and held her still. Vivienne's knickers were generous, like her hips, and pulled taut they were the perfect length for a gag.

It was the shock, rather than the gag, that silenced Natalie. There was bitter realisation in her eyes now. She knew, as she looked up at Chris, that there was no escape. She seemed tired of being angry, and resigned to her fate.

Seeing her broken brought a wave of tenderness rushing over him. He reached out for her, delicately brushing his fingertips over her fury-flushed cheek. Don't worry, he wanted to say. I don't want to hurt you. I just want you to find the absolute extremities of your pleasure – and to do that you have to find anger and helplessness and submission. I'll be there with you, every step of the way.

Then Vivienne laughed shrilly and he came to, awakened by her excitement. Viv had been delighted when he'd asked for her help. But then Viv, like Natalie, was a very dirty girl.

'Can we give Natalie her surprise now?' she asked.

Chris nodded. Going over to the sofa, he sat down to watch.

Vivienne attacked her task with enthusiasm. Like most of his friends, Chris loved watching two women going at it, and he stuck firm to his theory that most women would, given half the chance. But this thrill was sweeter than ever, because, as much as Viv relished this, Natalie was repulsed by it. For now.

He placed a bet with himself over how long it would take for her to give in. Right now, her whole body was tense, pushing back in her chair, desperately trying to move herself out of Vivienne's reach. But she couldn't hold out – no woman could. He glanced at the clock. Three minutes top, he reckoned.

But barely a minute had passed before the first sign showed. As her breasts were exposed, the satin cups of her bra pulled down over the swollen curves, Natalie bowed her head to watch. As another woman's hands gently squeezed and moulded her flesh, she blinked slowly. And as another woman's fingers first circled her nipples tenderly, then pinched the reddened tips, hard, she met Chris's eyes. For a split second it was there, humming in the sticky air, written clear across her face: submission. Then, embarrassed by her own weakness, tormented by the way she'd been manipulated into this, her eyelids fluttered nervously and she looked away.

But it was over. Natalie had lost out, her fury and humiliation crushed again by the force of her own lust. She couldn't resist the sensation of a woman's touch; a woman's mouth. The cuffs were pointless – she was a prisoner to her own body.

Vivienne sucked on Natalie's beautiful tits, coating them in glistening saliva and pulling on Natalie's skin as if she was feeding from her. She bit down on the pointed tips until Natalie's body stiffened with the pain, then she moved down, licking her way over the sweetness of her prisoner's belly. On her knees – purposely, if he knew Vivienne at all, giving Chris a view up her skirt, between her cream stockings, into her pussy – Vivienne buried her head between Natalie's open thighs. Holding aside her wet, see-through G-string with one hand, and holding on to the poor girl's trembling leg with the other, Vivienne nibbled and lapped and poked with her tongue until

211

Natalie's body bucked uncontrollably. All the time the victim kept looking back at Chris, as if she couldn't stop herself.

He moved towards her as she came, slipping the gag from her mouth to let the sound of her ecstasy out. She looked gratefully up at him as her head dropped back. He looked in awe down at her.

'You look so beautiful when you come,' he said, touching her open mouth. Her moans were warm on his skin. He wanted to be smothered in her warmth.

He wanted her. He realised, in an instant that turned him cold, that he couldn't resist any longer either. What had started as a challenge, to get her to admit to her desires, had twisted on itself. He was the one who had an admission to make now. Beneath the cruelty and the mind games there was something growing inside him; something so dangerous he had to reach inside and pull it out, before it crushed his lungs and heart and brain. He had to tell her. Tell her that he was hers, if she wanted him.

But it was too late. When he knelt down behind her and unlocked her wrists and ankles, it was Vivienne's arms she fell into, not his. They lay on the floor together, writhing and gasping into each other's bodies, pleasuring each other as only women can – taking for ever. Vivienne's classy designer clothes were pulled off and they rolled together like yin and yang, one all in black, one all in white. They twisted themselves until Vivienne's mouth was on Natalie's pussy, and Natalie's lips were fastened between Vivienne's milky thighs. They gave each other quick, violent orgasms, and slow, rolling ones that rippled through their soft bodies and out into the air; and into his head. It was torture. She didn't need him. She didn't want him. She wanted lips and teeth and fingers at her clit, inside her pussy, on her breasts and between her perfect cheeks. It didn't matter whose. Her pleasure wasn't selective; just demanding.

He watched them for an hour, before they sleepily decided to retire to his bedroom. Only then did they remember he was there, and Vivienne held out a hand in invitation. 'Come to bed,' she said, and he followed them in. And in lots of ways he enjoyed having two women in his bed sighing softly and touching each other and him. But they were tired from so many orgasms, and when they went to sleep it was with Vivienne in the middle, and him left on the end without enough covers.

Tomorrow, he promised. Tomorrow he'd end this. He'd drive her to the edge and push her over, and hold her hand and jump with her. Tomorrow, he'd claim her as his own.

Tomorrow came quickly. Vivienne left early to go to church with her husband. Natalie got up for a hot bath, which made her feel tired again, and she got back into bed and fell asleep until noon. Chris read the papers while he waited for her, afraid somehow to wake her up and do what he wanted to do to her. Best to save himself for this evening, he thought. Best to let it all build up inside him, and then show her how he felt in one unstoppable, undeniable burst of lust.

He looked up as she came, blinking lazily, into the living room. 'I'm starving,' she mumbled.

'Well get dressed,' he said. 'We've been invited to a tea party. You can eat there.'

'A tea party?' She wrinkled her nose in disbelief. 'Who's invited us?'

'The vicar.'

Her eyes narrowed while her smile widened. 'We're going to tea with the vicar?'

He nodded. 'You'll enjoy it, I promise.'

She studied him; spotted the latent excitement in his face. 'What have you got planned?'

'Something very special.'

The vicar's garden parties were always well attended, but today there seemed to be more people than ever milling around his huge garden. Chris stood on the patio, talking to some of his pupils, watching Natalie as she mingled. A few of the club's members were there, as well as about half the coaches, who were talking shop with the Shilton Club's staff. Unaware of the real reason everyone was there – the dark thing that lurked behind the façade of cucumber sandwiches and Pimms – she switched into manager mode and set about doing some PR. He watched her laughing politely at someone's joke; saw how the sun shone through her summer dress; saw the innocence of her smile. She turned her back, and a dark, blistering flame ignited inside him. Later, he warned her, addressing his thoughts to the back of her head. You won't be smiling later.

It was agony waiting for later to arrive, knowing what was coming while she had no idea. His throat felt dry as he longed for the words of surrender to fly from her mouth into his and slide down his neck and soothe away the rasping ache inside his lungs. His guts were gripped so tightly it was painful, and he had to down a gin and tonic to try to relax his coiled insides. He had to relax. There was a long time to wait.

It would be worth it in the end, he thought, looking away again from the conversation he was half-heart-edly involved in. He found her instantly, right at the edge of the garden, radiant among the dullness of the crowd. His eyes took in everything about her, as if it was the first time he was seeing her. And, just as he'd done the first time he'd seen her, he swore he'd have her. Later.

Later, wrapped in the heightened tension of these Sunday gatherings, her submission would be absolute. She'd beg for mercy, and he'd give it, and give himself, and give anything she wanted, in return for her. Alone together, in the darkness, they'd be complete. He would admit he didn't want anyone but her. Couldn't have anyone but her, not any more – not now that she was in his head, imprinted on his thoughts and waiting for him behind his eyelids whenever he shut his eyes.

Jesus Christ. What had happened to him? Why did he feel like this was the end of the world?

Eventually, teasing him with its slowness, the sky turned a darker blue and a chill sent a few people indoors. Natalie drifted back to his side, tipsy and slightly flushed. 'Shall we go?'

'Go where?'

'Back to your place?'

'No. Not yet. The party hasn't started yet.'

He filled the confused silence with a kiss, gently sucking on her lower lip.

The familiar bell rang. Natalie looked around as the guests began to make their way indoors. 'What's going on?'

'Why don't you go inside and see?'

He offered his hand. She took it, and followed the others inside; into another world.

She looked confused as the vicar's wife greeted her. 'Natalie. You've not been to one of our parties before. Come with me.' And she glanced over her shoulder, her brow creased, as she was led away from Chris.

While she was upstairs with the women being prepared for her ordeal, Chris had a cigarette and enclosed himself in an impenetrable 'don't talk to me' smog. He couldn't be bothered with the other blokes today; with their fussing and fiddling, their talk of equipment and paraphernalia. He didn't want to talk to anyone but her, about anything but the two of them. For once he found this slow build-up tedious and infuriating; not thrilling.

The doorbell rang, and the rest of the coaches from the club were shown into the room. Paul was one of them, and, after he'd been introduced to everyone who didn't already know him, he sidled up to Chris with silly grin on his silly face.

'All right, mate?'

Chris jerked his head in reply.

'So this is where it all happens. Jesus.' Paul whistled, looking around. 'I still can't believe all of this.'

Chris glared at him, wishing he'd piss off and take his eagerness with him. 'What can't you believe?'

'Well, I've lived round here for nearly three years now. I had no idea.' He turned back to Chris. 'Did you come alone?'

He shook his head. 'I brought Natalie.'

Paul paused for a minute before laughing nervously. 'Ha! Thought you were serious for a minute there. Good one. Can't quite see Natalie getting into this stuff, can you?'

'Can't you?' He shrugged. 'Well, you probably know her better than I do.' He walked away, leaving a puff of bitter smoke behind him.

At last, the curtains were shut, the lights dimmed, and Margaret, the vicar's wife, reappeared.

'Gentlemen,' she said, cracking her whip on the floor. 'Silence as the meeting of the Sunday worshippers is brought to order.'

Chris rolled his eyes. 'Get on with it,' he muttered.

The men took their seats around the room. Those who were newer converts, and hadn't yet earnt the right to sit, stood behind the circle of chairs. Silence fell quickly, smothered by the impatient male anticipation in the stale air.

'Now, gentlemen, may I present to you the ladies of the congregation.'

Margaret stalked back to the door, struggling slightly in her thigh-length boots. She cracked her whip again and the usual procession of rubber-, leather- and PVC-clad women trooped in, in single file.

They formed a circle facing their waiting audience. As they staggered around on their stiletto heels, their plastic catsuits creaking, rubber squeaking, Chris found his attention waning. The sight of all these women, dressed in straps and thongs and chains, had been exciting at first. Now, it wasn't even enough to give him a hard-on. It was strange, but this highly organised kinkiness was one of the least kinky things he could imagine. And these people, with their shared penchant for leather and bondage and the wicked, secret twinkles in their eyes, were some of the most boring people he'd ever met. He'd been coming here for years for the casual sex and the suburban depravity, but all of a sudden it seemed so dull. The thrill had gone. He got more pleasure from watching Paul's vacant panting.

And then – and then she appeared, and the thrill returned, shooting up the back of his neck like the poison from a sting. She looked so incredible, her easy beauty encased in cheap black rubber. The shock of seeing her like that, a stranger in that familiar gathering, made him close his eyes.

'Gentlemen,' Margaret announced, a quiver in her well-spoken voice, 'May I introduce to you the newest member of our flock.'

He opened his eyes again. His cock hardened at the sight of her, and at the admiring murmurs of the other men. She's mine, he warned, his pride thickening as she was paraded around the room.

For now, she was everyone's. Her body belonged to the group. Her body looked amazing – all in black, the tight rubber following every curve. The catsuit went right up to a high neck, and right down to her ankles, where high-heeled, pointy ankle boots cheapened the effect even more. There was only one way in and out of that rubber: a zip running from her pussy, between her legs, and up between her cheeks. The zip was padlocked to a gold ring set into the catsuit at her navel.

She was blindfold and her lips were painted in dark red. Her hair had gone, hidden beneath a wig that matched her lipstick: a deep, dangerous auburn cut into a sharp bob – a harsh shape and cut that made him long for the softness of her all the more. Chris glanced across the room at Paul, wondering whether he'd recognise her, but he didn't. His eyes were blank, his mouth open. He saw what the others saw: a body. You stupid sod, Chris thought, aching to punch his ignorant, handsome face.

Natalie was introduced to the group the way all new members were. Blind, and unsteady on her pinpoint heels, she was guided around the room by the women, who passed her along the outside of their circle. When a man wanted her – and every man in that room wanted her – he held up his hand and Natalie was stopped. Then whoever it was asked for whatever he wanted. The only thing they couldn't do was get inside that zip. That came later. That was what the padlock was for. Tonight, Chris would be the one to get the key.

He accepted a joint that was passed to him and watched. Detaching himself from the situation, he pitied the poor men who were mauling her. They could do what they liked, but they couldn't have her.

They could leer, and drool, and discuss her among themselves for weeks to come, but she wasn't theirs.

Some touched her, running their ravenous hands over her body. Some asked for her on her knees, and guided her head over their pricks. One or two wanted her arse, and she was turned round and made to bend over, and spanked or whipped on the buttocks. The shock of the pain opened her lips and sent small sounds flying out into the room; sounds that flew to him. She was his. He was hers. She knew, from behind her blindfold, that he was watching her. He knew that, after these men had finished and she was taken upstairs, it would be him who claimed her. Him who took her away from all this, and into the despair of infinite ecstasy.

Patiently he waited, letting the dope waft around his thoughts. When she came round the circle to him he waved her away, not wanting to be part of this. But then he changed his mind, and he held her jaw and pressed his lips to hers, showing her he was there. 'Chris?' she whispered, gasping for breath, and he answered her with another passionate kiss. She did what she hadn't done to any of the men around the room: she reached for him. She put her hands on his shoulders and threw herself into his kissing, forcing her tongue into his mouth and showing him that she, too, was waiting for him. Then she was moved on, and someone's cock filled her mouth, and Chris took a deep drag and closed his eyes and waited.

After Natalie's introduction, the other women joined her in pleasuring the men. Crawling around on all fours, they were at the beck and call of the male members of the congregation. There were no restrictions placed on these women – no padlocks keeping their pussies away from fingers, mouths and cocks. It wasn't long before one woman was sliding up and down on someone's lap; another with her fishnet-stockinged thigh hooked over someone's shoulder, her pussy naked and in his face. Handcuffs and collars and blindfolds and gags were clicked and buckled and knotted into place. Whips were brandished on bare flesh. Butt plugs were inserted between flabby cheeks. Paddles were used on bottoms and clamps on nipples. Every kink that festered deep in middle-class suburbia was on show, glinting in the darkness like the horse brasses on the fireplace.

Chris stood alone with his lust as the room merged from twosomes and threesomes into a long chain: a mess of hands and legs and moaning and sighing. He was happy to be left out of this mass of shared perversion, for once. Happy to know that he belonged to her.

He closed his eyes again as the joint slowed his brain. He thought of how she would look, tied to the bed the way all new converts were tied. Up in that room within a room, there was no sound; no sense of reality; no reason not to let go. Her cries would go unanswered by everyone but him. He'd be there with her, holding her shaking body, muffling her pleading with pleas of his own.

He drifted off into his dreams.

The next thing he knew, he was jerked awake again, suddenly being hit by the strong sensation of being alone. He panicked as he realised she'd gone. Squinting in the dim, smoky light, he searched the room full of people again but she definitely wasn't there. She must have been taken upstairs already. He pushed his way through the seething, sweating tangle of limbs and out into the hall.

Margaret was there, checking her painted reflection in the mirror.

'Where's Natalie?'

'Mmmm? What, love?'

'Is Natalie upstairs?'

'Yes, dear, but there's someone with her, I'm afraid.'

Everything went cold. 'Someone with her?'

'Yes, dear. Oh, I'm sorry. Did you want . . . I didn't know. You should have said. A nice young man asked me about her and I sent him upstairs.'

He swallowed hard, trying to stop himself from smashing her sweet face into the glass. 'You knew that I came with Natalie.'

'Ye–es, come to think of it, I do remember seeing you two together. But, my dear Chris, these evenings are for sharing. You know that by now. She's such a lovely girl, you can't possibly expect to keep her all to yourself.'

He took a deep breath. 'I've got to go up there. I've got to stop them.'

Margaret placed a determined hand on his chest. Her voice changed. 'Christopher, you've been coming here long enough now. You know the rules. Besides, they're in the safe room and the door's locked. They can't hear a sound in there. You could stand there and shout for a week, and they wouldn't know you were there.' She studied Chris's worried face. 'She went up quite willingly, you know. Quite happy, even when I told her it could be any one of us who got to open her padlock.'

Was that supposed to be a comfort to him? He looked up the long staircase, straining to hear a telltale sound. 'Who is it?'

'You know I'm not allowed to tell you that.'

He barged past her, back into the room. He looked around the ring of familiar faces and tried to recall the one that wasn't there.

'Oh Jesus,' he said, going back into the coldness of the hall. 'Jesus Christ. You stupid woman. Why didn't you tell me you were taking her upstairs?'

Margaret gave him a little smile. 'You stupid boy. Why didn't you tell me you wanted the key?'

With that, she rejoined the group. Alone, Chris banged his head against the wall and closed his eyes. He felt sick. It could have been the mixture of sherry, gin, Pimms, nicotine – when he hadn't smoked for over a year – and dope.

It could have been the sensation of his life slipping through his fingers.

Chapter Ten

*A*lone, with only the infinite darkness and her heartbeat for company, Natalie waited. Her body was tied in an X, her wrists and ankles fixed in fur-lined cuffs to the corners of the bed. Her pulse was strong in her pussy. She'd been told that someone among the crowd downstairs would be given the key – the key to unlock her pleasure.

She knew it would be Chris. She knew he'd brought her here for the ultimate humiliation, and, now that she'd endured being passed around the room like a spliff, she knew he would come for her. His kiss had told her everything. I'm here, it had said. These men want you, but you're mine. We understand each other.

She wanted to be his. This game he'd played with her had been delicious, delirious torture, but now she was ready to give up. She didn't want to be given to others any more. She wanted to give herself to Chris, and for him to give himself to her. She thought she'd read that in his kiss, but she couldn't be sure.

She would read it in his body when he came up. She'd know then. But, for now, all she could do was wait, and think about the things that had happened to her since she'd known him.

The things she'd done – God, if someone had told her a month ago, she'd have thought they were out of their minds. Sucking Paul's cock while Chris watched, posing naked for Hanif, letting her male staff have a glimpse of her pussy, allowing herself to be given to Sam. Parading around Harvey Nichol's in her underwear. Vivienne had almost been the biggest shock. Already fuming at Chris for leaving her alone like that, she'd been desperately angry that he'd brought another woman home to fulfil his clichéd male fantasy. But it had become her fantasy. She'd thought of being with a woman before, but had managed to pass it off as just another dream she didn't want to turn into reality. Faced with the reality – the unbelievably sweet reality – of another woman kneeling between her thighs, she'd abandoned herself to the truth.

All those people; all those dark and dirty acts she'd done. And now, tonight, the most shameful thing of all. Blindfold, anonymous, she'd been treated as just a body. A mouth to suck, breasts to squeeze, an arse to spank. Every moment she'd spent with Chris had been manipulated to show her she was helpless in all this. Hiding behind her shame, her body in other people's hands, she'd tasted the bittersweet thrill of submission and found the mindlessness of pleasure. Tonight, she shouldn't care who came upstairs and took her.

But she did. She didn't know if he'd meant it to happen, but everything he'd done had sharpened her need for him. He'd been behind everything. Even her fucking Hanif had been because of him. He was like the shadows in her mind – always there. His treating her like a toy should have made her relish the anonymity of sex. But it had just made her yearn more for him.

It seemed like an eternity she waited. She thought

of him and her heart pounded so quickly she heard it in her throat. 'Please,' she begged into the silent nothingness. 'I can't wait much longer.'

Just as desire was making her feel claustrophobic – making the cuffs tighten round her wrists and ankles – she heard something. She turned her head on the pillow, looking towards the sound. Deprived of her sight, she strained every cell to hear. Then, the door to her room opened and closed, and she heard a key in the lock.

He was in the room. She could feel his presence. She felt as if she was sinking into the bed with relief. He was here. She tried to call his name, wanting confirmation, but she was gagged again and it just came out as a strangulated sound.

But it was him. She heard his heavy breathing; felt his heavy footsteps reverberating through the bed, into her soul. Felt the heaviness of his lust bearing down on her.

The bed dipped under his weight. Fingers. The clink of keys. A low, satisfied grunt. The sound of metal on metal as the zip was pulled open. The feeling of the rubber parting and the air touching her skin.

The long, loud groan of his appreciation.

She squirmed, wishing she could see his face. A group of women, including some she knew from the club, had been waiting upstairs for her. As they'd explained what happened at these Sunday-night gatherings, they'd bathed her, soaped her pussy and shaved her clean. The sensation of busy female fingers on her had been almost as mind-blowing as this – him seeing her nakedness for the first time. She hadn't been allowed to touch herself before her body was encased in rubber, but he touched her now. His cool fingers felt every inch of her, reverently exploring the shocking smoothness. His fingertips discovered her as if he was blind, too. He was soft and searching, wanting to feel everything. And then he felt every-thing all over again, with his mouth.

A cushion was pushed under her hips, raising her up. The bed bounced as he climbed on and knelt over her prone body, his knees by her waist and his face between her legs. With long, sweeping strokes he lapped all over her bare mound and then snaked between her lips. He opened her up with the tip of his tongue and then ran his wet touch over the inner surfaces of her pouting lips. Natalie groaned and pulled on her ties, trying to push herself further into his face. Her desperation spurred him on and he unfurled his tongue inside her, opening his hot, wet mouth over her hot, wet cunt.

I'm yours. Take me.

He did, drawing her pleasure out with his mouth, sucking hard on her clit and flickering rapidly with his tongue until she began to jerk and writhe beneath him. Then, making the bed bounce again as he turned round, he slid his cock inside her gasping pussy lips. In the madness it didn't feel like Chris; but the urgency was definitely his. He was like an animal, panting and growling and pounding relentlessly. His lust was like rage; the tension of the time they'd spent together condensed into pure white sexual energy that lit up the darkness. He rammed himself hard inside her, banging their hips together, forcing himself into the depths of her consciousness. Every muscle in his body was harnessed; every aggressive ounce of his weight was thrown into fucking her. The insides of her eyelids pricked with tiny, multicoloured sparks of light as a different orgasm grew inside her belly and then burst and seeped all over her, finding its way beneath her rubber skin and turning her cold and then hot.

I'm yours, she promised, as his cock stabbed into her infinite softness.

I'm yours, as her hips bucked uncontrollably.

I'm yours, as the sounds of her submission pushed their way through the silk gag in her mouth.

'You're incredible,' he said, pulling the gag out so her voice was free at last. 'You're gorgeous. What's your name?' And the heat left her.

It wasn't him.

'It's Natalie,' she whispered faintly. With his cock still inside her, he tentatively pushed at her blindfold. She waited for her eyes to adjust to the candlelight; waited for the impossible to materialise.

She looked. It was impossible, but it wasn't him. She called for him, but the shock in her throat strangulated the sound.

'Hello, Natalie,' said Paul. 'I – I – your hair. I thought – I thought you'd gone away.' His voice was panicked and pathetic.

She didn't know what to say. 'Have you got the key to these handcuffs?'

He nodded.

'Undo them, please.'

Avoiding her eyes, he did.

She sat up, rubbing her wrists. He sat on the edge of the bed with his head bowed. At that moment, she felt no guilt at being dishonest with him, or at cheating on him. She just despised him for not being Chris. Hated him for ruining this night and making her have to speak about things she didn't want to discuss, here and now. Like the fact that their relationship was over.

'God, this is embarrassing.'

'It needn't be,' she said softly. 'We're both adults.'

'I . . . er . . .' He turned to her, struggling to control his face and find an excuse. He was mortified and confused – she could see the thoughts as they crossed his brain. She'd said she was going away; he'd said he had things to do; he'd fucked her without knowing it was her.

'Oh, God.' His hand flew to his mouth. 'Chris said he came here with you, but I didn't believe him. I didn't know it was you. I'm sorry, Natalie.'

She almost laughed with the absurdity of his guilt. Paul was apologising – for sleeping with her.

'You don't need to be sorry,' she said. 'Neither of us have been faithful from the start, have we?'

His face overtaken by nerves, he gave her a totally inappropriate smile.

'That's why you weren't bothered when I told you about me and Hanif.' A tiny bud of pity made her touch his shoulder. 'It's all right. We never said we were going to be faithful. Why should we have done? We hardly know each other. I should never have moved in with you.'

Another momentary smile flickered across his lips. He thought for a long time. 'So ... where were you this weekend?'

'With Chris.'

He nodded, biting his lip. 'I was with Antonia – Mrs Spencer. She invited me. Well, all of us. We're all here. It's like a club outing.'

She laughed, her hatred softening slightly. 'I'm sorry, Paul.'

They looked at each other. He shrugged. 'What can I say? Except that was incredible.'

'Yeah. It was.' But only because I thought you were Chris. 'Why haven't you fucked me like that before?'

'I don't know.' Guilt clouded his pure blue eyes again. 'You've never been tied to the bed wearing rubber before.' His head bowed under the weight of his embarrassment. 'Sometimes it's easier to let yourself go with a stranger. I thought...' He reached across the sheet for her hand. 'Natalie, I mean ... That was great, wasn't it? Maybe we could ...'

But she was already at the door.

* * *

'Margaret? Margaret!'

The vicar's wife stopped whipping the bank manager's buttocks and peered through the gloom at Natalie. 'Oh, you've finished, darling. Did you have a nice time?'

'Where's Chris? I can't find him.'

'Chris?' She thought for a minute, looking around the heaving throng. 'I've seen him somewhere.'

'Think,' Natalie demanded, grabbing her fat arm. 'Please,' she added.

'No, what am I talking about? That's right. Chris left a while ago.'

'He did? Oh. Can I call a taxi?'

'Left with those nice girls who run a law practice. Clever girls. Do you know them? Three of them. Judith, Larissa . . .'

She shuddered. 'You mean he didn't leave alone?'

She tutted and rolled her eyes. 'Does he ever, dear?'

It was then that it hit her. Paul's sleeping with her hadn't been an accident. It had all been part of Chris's deviant plan. The 'something special' he'd promised was the embarrassment of being confronted with her own boyfriend. Chris didn't want her, after all. He just wanted her to want him – and to tear apart the relationship she'd had with Paul. She clapped a hand over her mouth, suddenly feeling nauseous.

Chapter Eleven

She walked slowly past the courts on the way up to her office. Glancing inside each one, she saw what she'd never had time to notice before. Each of her coaches had been turned into a watered-down version of Chris. Each one was flirting with his pupils; touching them up; helping them live out their sordid little fantasies. Even Paul, who'd been so incensed when Chris had come to the club, had taken on his teaching methods. He glanced at her nervously as she passed, giving her a wan and apologetic smile.

She climbed the steep staircase to her office and threw down her briefcase. She was exhausted by the walk from the car park up to her office, and she rested for a moment with her head on the glass overlooking her domain. It was a different picture she looked down on now. Full courts; plenty of people milling around in the shop, in the café, and all of them spending money. Even at this time on a Monday morning, the place was busy. And it was all thanks to Chris.

Chris. The coldness that had kept her awake all night returned like a bad dream. She rubbed away the goosebumps stippling her arms but the coldness wouldn't go. It had wrapped round her last night like a blanket and her skin seemed to be soaked in it. She wondered if she'd ever feel warm again.

If only she'd kept her promise to never get involved with men she worked with. She'd managed it until she'd come to the club. Here, she'd got involved with two of them at the same time. It had been a disaster waiting to happen. What the hell had she been thinking of?

Paul was understandable. Paul was sweet and considerate, a little bland perhaps, but he was safe. Handsome. A good lover.

How ironic, she thought, that, of all the great sex they'd had, the best had been last night, when he'd thought she was a stranger and she'd thought he was Chris. And how telling that they'd both been dishonest with each other. They'd had some good times, but they clearly weren't supposed to be together. How sad, that what could have been a long and satisfying affair had fizzled out, dampened by the dark, looming presence of Chris.

Chris. He wasn't such an understandable choice. He wasn't her type at all. Domineering. Aggressive. Cruel.

She'd tried all night to work it out. Why, whenever she closed her eyes, did she see him? Why, when she'd almost fallen asleep and she'd rolled over in bed, had she reached out for him and woken with a jolt at the realisation that he wasn't there? Why, when Paul had fucked her so ferociously, had she been so bitterly disappointed to find out it wasn't Chris?

He didn't deserve a minute of her thoughts, let alone a whole sleepless nightful. Of all the things he'd done to her, taking her to that party last night had been the worst, most devastating humiliation. He'd spent the weekend breaking her, grinding her down until she was weak, and all for this. He'd spent a month prising her away from the simple pleasures of Paul, only to have her shaved and bound and given back to him as a writhing, rubber-clad wanton, changed beyond all recognition. What a vindictive thing to do. What viciousness. He was sick – that was the only explanation.

And then, high on his achievement, he'd left her alone with her embarrassment. Apart from the inconvenience of having to call a taxi, collect her things from Paul's, and then spend the night in a hotel with the couple in the adjoining room banging away for hours – and she could still hear the pounding in her head – there'd been the agony of knowing she'd made a mistake. 'You stupid, stupid bitch,' she muttered, turning hot at last as the embarrassment flared over her, again. She'd thought, somehow, that she and Chris had found something; something other than the pleasure they both got from his kinky mind games. She'd been sure. She'd read it in his kiss. She'd felt his tongue, his lips, his whole being clasping at hers. She'd waited in that room, gagged, cuffed and blindfold; waiting for him to suffocate her with his lust. And all the time, his sick, disgusting plan had been to give her back to Paul, soiled and scarred, her thoughts tainted for ever. He'd callously set her up and then gone home with three of his cronies. He'd left her feeling so alone she'd cried that night.

'I want you to give yourself to me,' he'd said. And she had done. He'd taken everything. All she'd got in return was her shame.

She hoped he'd had a good time with Larissa, and Judith and Patsy. She hoped he'd found what he was looking for in their well-toned bodies and their filthy minds. She hoped he dropped down dead of a long, protracted and extremely painful illness.

As she picked up her briefcase the catch fell open and all her papers dropped out on to the floor. She crouched down, feeling tears welling up inside her again. Blinking them back, she picked up the mess and moved it over to her desk. But her hands were shaking and she dropped the lot again. She left it on the carpet, putting a clammy hand to her clammy forehead. It didn't help that she was hung over, too. Hangovers didn't mix well with sleepless nights and complete devastation.

She slapped her own cheek, trying to wake herself up. 'You stupid bitch,' she spat. To think she'd wasted time craving someone so breathtakingly, mind-blowingly cruel.

She couldn't believe it. It still shocked her to the core that he'd taken her to that party and then left her. It didn't seem right, and the memory of how she'd felt when she'd found out he'd gone kept coming back to her and striking her hard. What had this weekend been about, then? About pushing her into insanity? Because that's where she was. About breaking her link with Paul beyond repair? Did he hate Paul that much? Did he hate her? Was it all women he despised, or just her? What had she done to him to make him treat her like that?

She sighed, her whole being deflating. She just had to face up to it. She'd made a big mistake. She should have trusted her common sense and never admitted to Chris that she wanted him. She'd made a fool of herself. She'd bared her inner self to him; let him pick over all the dark and dirty bits of her psyche. He had stories about her he could dine off for life. 'Did you hear about when Natalie went to Wimbledon?' She shuddered as she heard the crowing, sniggering voices. 'She really went for it with Vivienne. Did you hear the one about Natalie and the banana?'

And rumbling along beneath was the reason all this had happened – the reason she'd have to face up to this situation every single hour of every day. The club.

She cursed the place. Without it, she'd never have met Chris. Without its imminent failure she'd never have needed him. Without the pressure of keeping it afloat she could ask him to leave, today.

Her breath grew shallow and quick as panic set in. What was she going to do? Was the club strong enough to grow without him? Probably not. Was she strong enough to stay, with him still there, fucking his pupils in the gym, wanking in his office and laughing at her behind her back?

She opened the French windows leading on to her balcony. Stepping outside, she tried to breathe. The sunshine was warm on her skin but she felt colder than ever. Beneath her thin silk blouse, she felt her nipples stiffen.

She heard laughter and looked down. The builders were working on the outside courts. Or, at least, they should have been. The pair of them were staring up at her.

'Phwoar. Wouldn't mind giving her one,' one of them muttered, probably thinking she couldn't hear – or maybe, knowing builders, hoping she could. 'Classy bit of stuff, that is. Like to give her a bloody good seeing to.'

She gritted her teeth. She wasn't in the mood for this today.

'Step out a bit further, darlin', and we'll be able to see right up your skirt.' They sniggered like schoolboys. 'Show us your tits, love. Get 'em out for the boys.'

That was it. Fired up by a rage that was nothing to do with the builders, she lost it. 'Come up here and say that to my face,' she shouted down at them. 'Come on!' She pointed at the older one. 'You. Come up to my office, now.' Stunned, he didn't move. She screamed at him, surprising herself with the power of her voice. 'Now!'

She waited, arms folded, her heart racing out of control. Pure evil was pumping through her veins. The unsuspecting builder had pushed her too far and he was going to get the full force of her wrath.

'Come here,' she said as he appeared at the door, pointing at a piece of floor just in front of her feet. He obeyed, despite the fact he was older and bigger than her – probably frightened by the headmistress tone in her voice. 'Now, say that again.'

'Say what?'

'What you just said to me, outside.'

He smiled stupidly, shaking his head. 'I can't remember, miss.'

'Did you think I couldn't hear you?' She pierced his grey eyes with hers. Her voice tightened. 'Did you? Did you really think I couldn't hear? Or did you do it on purpose? Did you hope that I could hear you? Because men like you do that to women all the time, don't you? Shout out at them, embarrass them, leer at them when you should be getting on with your work.'

'I'm sorry.'

'Shut up. I've had enough of ignorant pigs like you. You're so fucking brave, aren't you, up on your scaffolding and out on your building sites. It's such fun for you, isn't it, looking down girls' tops and up their skirts. Do you ever think of how we feel? Ever?'

'I –'

She wouldn't be stopped. It was all coming out. 'You're such a bunch of fucking wimps as well, aren't you? That's what gets me really angry. I bet, if a woman did what you asked her to, you'd die of fright. You probably wouldn't be able to get it up. You're not a man: you're a schoolboy, with your brain in your pants.'

'I . . . don't –'

'Let's see, shall we? Let's see how confident you are when a woman talks back at you. Ask me again.'

'Ask what?'

'Say exactly what you said when I was standing on the balcony.' He faltered, his mouth opening and closing, his eyes looking anywhere but at her. 'Say it, now, or I'll call your boss and get you sacked.'

He met her eyes. He was petrified. In his forties, with forearms that could crush bricks and LOVE and HATE tattooed on his knuckles. Petrified of this small, screaming, rabid woman who was paying his wages.

'I . . . well, I said . . . But I didn't mean it – it's just how we talk on the job, you know, amongst the lads. Just a bit of banter. No offence.'

'Say it again. Now.'

He swallowed his disbelief that this was happening. 'Show us your tits.' He tensed, waiting. 'Love,' he added, as if that would soften it.

Power surged inside her. Her breath was long and slow now; controlled. She was in control. Fixing him with her eyes, she slowly unbuttoned her blouse. 'Like this?' she asked, opening it up. Unable to stop himself, his eyes dropped. 'Or like this?' She undid the hook in her cleavage and exposed her breasts.

His jaw dropped. He swayed from foot to foot, as if he'd lost his balance. His brow creased and he gulped again. 'Fuck,' he whispered.

'So.' She was calm. Intensely, eerily calm. All her rage had been wiped away. 'What are you going to do now? Now that I've shown you my tits.'

His thick eyebrows lifted. 'I – I – I –'

'Why don't you lick them?'

His gaze lifted to hers. 'What?'

'Lick them,' she demanded. 'Don't you want to?' He hesitated. 'Come on. You don't ask to see a girl's tits and then not do anything about it. Lick my tits.'

He smiled, an unsteady smile that had loose threads of fear sewn into it.

'What's your name?'

'B–B–Bob.'

'Come here, Bob.' Bob came. She put her hand to the back of his close-cropped, dusty brown hair. 'You got what you wanted. You've seen my tits. Now be a man and lick them.'

She pulled his head down.

He fought against her but she reached down with her free hand and gripped his balls, so tight he froze. 'Lick them, Bob.'

To begin with, Bob's licking was as watery as his smile. This was, quite clearly, a first for him. But then, as her worrying grip on his groin loosened, and the more primitive side of him took over, he forgot about his disbelief and began to get stuck in. His nicotine-and-coffee breath soaked her skin as he licked all over her breasts. His lips were dry and they tickled her as he sucked on a nipple. His grunts were laced with gratitude.

'Enjoying yourself, Bob?'

He groaned and opened his big mouth wide, trying to suck on as much of her breast as he could.

'That's it, Bob. That's nice. Oh, yes. Harder, Bob. Bite me.'

She gripped her sharp fingernails into his scalp as he inflicted pain on her. He bit the protruding tips of her nipples; bit them hard, encouraged by the way she arched her back and held her own breasts and pushed them further into his face.

He stood up for air, looking at her with suspicion in his eyes.

'What are you stopping for, Bob?'

'You're mad,' he whispered, fiddling with the crotch of his filthy, faded jeans.

'Don't get mad, get even,' she laughed.

'What?'

'I've been mucked about by men, Bob. Luckily for you, you're paying for it.'

Bob was none the wiser. 'Right,' he said. 'You're the boss. Whatever you say, miss.'

'Were you the one who wanted to "give me one"?'

It took a moment for Bob's slow mind to catch up. 'Er, that was my mate. Ken.'

'Do any of you have names longer than single syllables?'

'Hmm?'

'Forget it.' She laughed again. Inside, she was full of laughter. She went out on to the balcony and summoned Ken. 'Hello, Ken,' she said, as he scuffed into her office. 'I believe you want to give me one.'

Ken looked uncertainly at Bob; Bob shrugged.

'Isn't that what you said? You wouldn't mind giving me one?'

Ken's wide eyes were staring at her naked breasts. 'Huh?'

'Have you got a big one, Ken?'

He looked up at her. He was much younger than his mate. He had scruffy tufts of dark-blond, dust-dulled hair sticking up at all angles, blue eyes, and a look of panic stretched across his mouth. 'Huh?'

She slinked towards him, pushing her breasts out like weapons. 'Have you got a big one, darlin'?' She trailed a wicked fingertip down from his bottom lip, over his bare chest, through the soft hair wisping over his stomach, lulling him – then she snatched at his crotch and made him jump. 'Come on then, big boy. Give me one.' She winked and blew him a kiss. 'I'm ready for you, you charming little piece of rough.'

'Huh?'

'Not very intelligent, are you, Ken? Lucky you're good with your tools.' She almost made herself laugh out loud with her schoolboy smuttiness. Fuck, this was liberating. 'How are you with this tool, Ken?' She slid her hand over his stomach and into his jeans. 'Oh, Ken. Dear me. What a sad, pathetic man you are.'

Standing close to him, she stroked up and down inside his boxer shorts, rubbing a response out of his flaccid little prick. Her other hand strayed up to her breast and she squeezed herself, smiling as Ken's gaze fell. She circled her fingertips round and round her nipple and then pinched the engorged tip between finger and thumb. Beneath her other palm, Ken began to stir.

'That's better.' She sighed encouragement. 'Oh yes. That's much better. Oh . . .'

The miracle of an erection. His limp prick transformed beneath her fingers into something far more promising. 'Come on, Ken. Get your cock out for the girls.'

Ken didn't move.

'Shy all of a sudden? Shall I help you?' She unfastened his jeans, ripping at the button fly. Pulling him by the elastic of his shorts, she led him over to her desk. She perched on the edge, lifting one foot up on to her chair. 'Come on, love. Give me one. You know you want to.'

The poor boy looked round at his mate for help. Natalie brought his face back to hers. 'Don't look at your friend. Look at me. Look.' Her hand flew between her open legs and she rubbed her middle finger over her panties. She felt her lips swell. She felt Ken's attention and his disbelief, and she felt the joy of teasing and humiliating someone the way she'd been teased and humiliated.

She caught his hand and pulled it to her panties. She moved his fingers up and down over the white satin, knowing he could see the outline of her lips against the material; knowing he could feel the dampness soaking her; knowing he was falling.

Sure enough, when she stopped moving his hand it carried on on its own. 'That's it,' she said. 'That's lovely. Now finger me, Ken.'

Hypnotised by her insistent voice, he did what he

239

was told. Slipping his fingers underneath the elastic, he fumbled for a second, shocked by her wetness, before poking a finger inside her. 'More,' she said, and he obediently pushed another one in alongside the first, gently stretching her. Whether he knew it or not, the heel of his hand aroused her clit, and her pussy and mind flooded.

She pushed his grubby hand away. Holding her panties aside with one hand, she delved for his prick with the other. She pulled on him, bringing him shuffling forward and almost making him trip over his jeans. Moving the head of his penis between her fleshy lips, she reached behind him and held on to his buttocks. 'Give me one,' she urged. 'Give me a bloody good seeing to, Ken.'

Using all her strength, she pulled him into her. Her cry clawed its way out of her throat as he filled her – more with the thrill than his cock. He wasn't exactly huge, but the release was enormous. This is it, she thought. This is where I belong. In control. Look at me, Chris. Look at what you've lost.

'Harder,' she commanded. Shuffling back an inch on the desk, she lifted her other foot and hooked both of them round his waist, leaning back on her hands. 'Harder. Harder, Ken. Come on. You can do better than that.'

At last, his unstoppable male urges took over from his inhibitions. He thrust so hard she was pushed back on to the desk. Lying down, she brought her legs back through his arms and rested them on his chest. She crossed her feet around his thick, straining neck and urged him harder, faster.

But it still wasn't enough. She needed more; needed an orgasm so strong it would wash away all her shame. Clinging on to the edge of the desk, she reached down with her other hand. Her fingers found her tender, throbbing clit and she began to rub. The feeling was so intense it was a fight with herself to keep going, but she knew she had to. Had to exorcise the demons; force them out with the rush of a fresh climax. Even before Ken had begun to grimace, her pelvis was rocking and jerking under the strain of the pleasure. She closed her eyes and opened her mouth and just cried out with relief.

Look at me now, Chris. I don't need you. This is what I need. It's filthy and mindless and it has nothing to do with you. It belongs to me.

'Oh, Ken,' she moaned, throwing her arms back over her head. 'Good boy.'

She watched, smiling uncontrollably, as his thrusting stopped and it was his turn to hold still while his body was emptied of pleasure. Feeling full of herself – feeling a hint of the invincibility she'd had before she'd met Chris – she stroked her breasts as he recovered. Slowly, watching her carefully, as if she was a wild and unpredictable and bloodthirsty beast, he withdrew his prick and pulled up his shorts. As he moved away, and Natalie's legs dangled over the edge of the desk, Bob reappeared in her view. He had a tight-lipped grin on his face and was fiddling with his trousers.

'What the fuck are you smiling at?' she asked.

'I'm going to give you one now,' he said, unzipping his cock. 'It's my turn.'

'No, it isn't.' She sat up and slid off the desk, drawing herself up to her full height. 'Who the hell do you think you are? Get out of my office and get back to work at once. And this counts as your tea break, by the way. Don't let me catch you slacking or I'll report you to your boss.'

The builders looked at each other, completely non-plussed by this mad woman who, a moment earlier, had been writhing around like a wanton.

'But –'

'But what, Bob? What, exactly?'

He couldn't answer.

'Thought so. Now get back to work, the pair of you. And breathe a word of this to anyone and I'll make sure you never work again.'

'Fucking crazy bitch,' he muttered.

Disdain curled her lip as she watched them shuffle out. She sat down behind her desk and rearranged her clothes, then leant back in her chair with her hands behind her head.

This was more like it. This was good. If only Chris could have seen her, taking command like that. She hoped the builders couldn't keep their mouths shut, and that he got to hear about it. She hoped he'd be jealous and have to go and sit in his office and masturbate again. She hoped with all her being that he lived to regret what he'd done to her.

Her train of thought stopped at a dead end. She realised Chris was still there, lurking like a dark cloud over everything. Even this had been because of him – some cock-eyed, twisted way of getting back at him for the way he'd used her. Of making her feel in control again. Of convincing herself that it was better to take than to be taken.

But she knew now, as the inexorable chill crept back over her skin, that the sweetest thrill of all was in giving herself completely. She'd been ready to give herself to him – to let him take her wherever he wanted to.

The phone rang. It was the bank manager. She spoke without knowing how to form the words. She didn't know anything any more.

At least she didn't feel cold any more. Now she just felt numb.

Somehow, she got through the day. Closeted away in her office, she got her head down and got on with the paperwork. In the back of her mind, like an itch she couldn't reach, was the worry about what she was going to do. Ask Chris to leave? Leave herself? Carry on as if nothing had happened?

She ignored the itch and concentrated on her work. That was the most important thing now, and she had to throw herself back into it. Finding some energy from underneath the heavy layers of her exhaustion, she caught up on the stuff she should have done on Saturday and ploughed straight through Monday's agenda without a break. Her secretary brought her coffee and a sandwich but she didn't touch the food. In situations like this she existed off caffeine and her nerves.

It was a good job they were strong. It was lucky her father had patronised her all her life, because she'd built up defences that got her through times like these. Be strong, she urged herself. Forget about Chris now, and think of yourself. You're a strong woman.

But her strength, her determination to carry on, and all her promises not to think of him again were thrown into question at seven o'clock that evening. She was leaving the office, setting off back to the hotel, when the phone rang. Going back to her desk, she leant over it and snatched at the phone. It was her Uncle Justin, calling from Sao Paolo. With her back to the window, and Justin's overexcited shrill in her ear, she didn't see or hear him come into the room.

Was it Paul, or Chris? It could have been either one.

The backs of her legs shuddered as he wrapped his heavy body round hers. Natalie's thoughts blurred as she tried to work out which man it was behind her. Distancing herself from the violent pressure on her senses, she picked up the clues: the hungry fingers, the urgent sounds, the desperation. There was only one man it could be. It was Chris, come to torture her again. She was sure this time. She could tell. Chris's hands sliding on to her waist. His presence filling up her senses with sticky longing.

Fight it, she told herself. Fight it. You don't want this; don't want him to dominate your every thought. Cut it dead, now. Don't let him treat you as if he owns you.

But she didn't move. Bent over the desk, telling Justin the club was now in the black, no thanks to him, she just stood there and waited. Her tiredness took over and suddenly, soothed by Chris's palms sliding over her arse, she felt like closing her eyes and drifting off. His touch was so smooth, so warm and so what she needed.

I don't need him, she insisted. You do, her body said.

The backs of her legs tingled as his palms moved over her skirt, down to the hem, and then up again under her skirt. Creeping up over her bare thighs, his fingers caressed her into an admission. I do need him. I don't want to, but I do. He repulses me, and yet I need him inside me, for ever. His desire is my oxygen. His lust is my food. His cock makes me feel whole.

As his touch went higher, he knelt down behind her. She gasped, and had to make an excuse to Justin to explain the sound. Behind her, Chris's lips were pressed to her panties. His breath was hot through the flimsy material. His hands were on her arse and then round the front of her, on her thighs, pulling her towards him. He gulped at her pussy. He licked her through her knickers and inhaled deep, yearning lungfuls of her.

She needed this. She couldn't stop herself. She hated him for what he'd done but her body was willing to forgive. Her body told the truth.

She listened to Justin's news. He pulled her knickers down. She spoke to Sinbad. He kissed her pussy lips. She said goodbye, don't worry about the club. He stood up and held her hips and prised open the centre of her self with his thick, hard cock.

The phone fell out of her hand and banged down on to the desk. Her upper body, drained of energy, lay down, and she rested her forehead on the back of her hand and closed her eyes. She shook, literally shook, as he lowered his torso down on to hers. He wrapped his arms round her waist to hold her still, as if she might escape. As if she had the strength to do anything but nothing.

He started slowly, easing himself in and out of her with long, luscious strokes. As she moaned he began to thrust harder. As she squirmed in his arms, half-heartedly trying to free herself from the torment of the pleasure, he started to pound with his usual aggression, grunting with the effort. He came quickly, and as she cried out for release his fingers rubbed at her clit and she quickly followed him. Like the death throes of some delicate trapped insect, quivers fluttered down her legs as she came.

'Oh, Chris,' she sighed, groaning for him with every cell in her body. It was good to have his name on her tongue again, not just inside her head. It tasted rich and intoxicating. 'Chris.' It was like breathing. It was like the soothing caress of his fingers as he stroked her hair.

But he stopped stroking as she said his name. He didn't answer her. He flinched and pulled away.

'Chris?' she pleaded hopefully.

'Sorry to disappoint you,' said Paul, his voice full of bitter sadness. 'It's me, making a fool of myself, again.'

'Oh. Hello, Paul,' she said quietly, wincing.

It was the weakest excuse for a smile she'd ever seen. But she couldn't blame him.

'Oh God. I'm sorry. I thought it was him.' She shook her head in disbelief.

He sighed. He looked like she felt: completely spent.

'You really like him, don't you? What is it about him? He's a total bastard, you know.'

'Paul, don't –'

His voice was calm but it was bordering on the edge of fury. 'Has he got more money than me? Is that it? Is it his flash car? Has he got a nice flat?'

'Give me a little credit. Do you think that's what I look for in a man? Do I seem that shallow to you?'

He sighed again. 'So what is it, then? Has he got a bigger cock? Does he do things I don't? The last two times I've fucked you, you thought it was him. So he can't be better than me in bed, can he?'

'Paul, please don't do this.'

His eyes drifted around, avoiding hers, and ended up looking down at his feet. 'I thought, after last night, maybe . . . It was so good.'

'Yes, I know.' She touched his arm. 'It was good.'

'It was amazing,' he corrected. 'I thought, maybe, we could start again.' Her silence made him look up. 'Seeing you like that, Natalie, all tied up and dressed in that outfit, and . . . You were so wild.' His eyes glazed at the memory. 'You were pulling on the cuffs and lifting your hips up, and you came so loudly, even with that gag in your mouth. It really turned me on, Natalie. I thought about it all night. I thought about you all night.'

'I'm sorry, Paul.' There was no way to do this other than honestly. 'It's over between us. It was fun while it lasted, and I do like you, very much. I hope we can –'

'Stay friends?' He nodded sadly. 'The two most dreaded words in the English language. He's done this to me once before, you know. He's like a jinx. Took away the last girlfriend I really cared about.'

'Oh, come on. You don't really care about me. We had fun last night, but you didn't even realise it was me. You've been sleeping with your pupils, that's how much you care.'

'OK,' he admitted. 'Fair enough. But does *he* care about you?'

'No. Obviously not, or he wouldn't have set us up like that last night.'

'Set us up? What are you talking about?'

'Oh come on, Paul. Haven't you worked it out by now? Chris set the whole thing up. It was all planned. He knew that the last person you'd expect was me, and that I'd be expecting him. He manipulated this whole thing the way he manipulates everything. He tried to drive a wedge between us and, let's face it, he has done.'

'Chris?' He snorted. 'He was nothing to do with it. I asked Margaret whether I could ... you know, and she gave me the key and took me upstairs. I had no idea you were expecting Chris. I was told anyone could ... you know – have you.'

She was confused. 'Chris didn't send you up to me?'

'Chris has been friendly lately, but not that friendly. We're sharing some of his clients now, but I can't see him sharing you, Natalie.'

She tried to clear the sleep out from her mind and take this in. 'So, let me get this straight. You didn't know it was me. I didn't know it was you. And Chris didn't know anything. It was a complete coincidence that you and me ended up together last night.'

'Complete and utter,' he said. 'Look, I hate the git, and the last thing I want to do is stick up for him, but he's not that sick and twisted. He didn't know I'd gone up to unlock your padlock.' Paul rubbed his chin thoughtfully. 'I actually got one up on him, didn't I? No wonder he left in such a temper.'

'He did?'

'Apparently. It was the talk of the party. Chris usually stays right to the bitter end, but he stormed

247

out early. Had to get some women from the club to give him a lift home – his car battery was flat, he'd left his headlights on.' He chuckled nastily. 'I heard this morning that he'd had to break his front door down. He'd left his keys at the vicarage. Wasn't his night, was it?'

She was more confused than ever now. Her blood ran hot, then cold. Had all her anger been misplaced? Had Chris meant to come for her, last night, and been thwarted by Paul? It was a bitter, bitter irony if that was the truth – if the man whose girlfriend Chris had poached was the man who'd beaten him to her fettered, willing body.

'Fancy a pizza?'

She smiled, shaking her head. 'Thanks. Some other time. I've an appointment to see a flat at eight.'

'You won't be moving back in with me, then.'

'No, Paul.'

His thin smile was grim but resigned. 'I'll see you tomorrow, then.'

'See you.'

'Natalie? Can I ask you a favour?'

'Anything.'

'Kiss me goodbye.'

Oh God. She could have cried at the sweetness in his voice. 'Come here,' she said, holding out her hand.

She rested her hand on his shoulder and kissed him. It wasn't a complicated kiss: no mind games, no ulterior motives, no shame or blame. Just a tender, longing kiss. No tongues. Just lips, gently pressing together in a last embrace.

They parted. She heard something, or rather felt it, and looked towards the door. Chris was standing there, surrounded in a dark gloom. He looked at Paul with hatred in his eyes, then looked at her. His eyes were empty.

'Chris?' she said, frightened by that look she hadn't

248

seen before. He stared at her for a moment longer before turning and disappearing down the stairs.

'Oh dear,' Paul said, with mock worry. 'I do hope he's going to be OK.'

'I'd better go and talk to him. Are you going to be OK?'

'I'll be fine.'

'You know, most women would kill to have you as their boyfriend,' she said.

'But not you.'

'You're great, Paul. You're funny and kind, and gorgeous.'

'Keep it coming,' he laughed. 'I'm enjoying this. Perhaps we should break up more often.'

'Oh, come off it. You don't need me to tell you that all the women fancy you. You can have your pick of this club, and you know it. You can have any woman you want.'

'But not you.'

'I'm sure you'll cope without me, Paul. You've got Mrs Spencer. And, from what my secretary tells me, you've had Mrs Regan, Mrs Formby-Lewes, Mrs Johnstone and a whole group of her pals for quite some time now. Don't be greedy. You don't need me as well.'

She went to find Chris. On her way to his office, she nipped into the ladies' changing room and checked her reflection, wanting him to want her as much as ever. Her pulse began to speed as she realised the woman looking back at her now was only a distant relation to the woman who used to look back from the mirror. She'd changed, and she liked the changes. Taking a slow, deep breath, she smiled at herself.

She knocked at his door and waited. Nothing. Knocked again. Waited, pulse racing. Perhaps he was wanking and hadn't heard. She pushed at the door. No one inside.

The tidiness shocked her. Chris's office was usually a mess of discarded tracksuits and trainers, with rosters and timesheets strewn all over the desk. Today there was nothing. No papers. No mess. Just an envelope in the middle of the desk.

Her breathing quickened as she picked it up. It was addressed to her. Inside it, written small on a big sheet of paper, were two words.

I resign.

He can't have left the building yet. She ran, clutching the piece of paper. She stumbled to a halt at reception. 'You seen Chris?' He's just gone. You might catch him, but you'll have to run. Ran down the path to the car park, heels sinking into the gravel. No car. No Chris. He's gone.

Jesus Christ Almighty. Fucking, shitting, wank. She ran back inside and up to her office. Panting, she dialled his number. Answerphone. She'd leave a message. He'd get it in a few minutes, when he got home. He'd come racing back for her.

'Chris,' she said after the beep. Then she realised she didn't know what to say. 'It's Natalie.' That was a start. 'I don't want you to resign. I . . .' Keep talking, or it'll cut you off. 'I'm not accepting your resignation. You can't leave. The club needs you.' She took a deep breath. 'Please, please don't leave now. Everyone at the club'll miss you. Oh bollocks, this isn't about the club, is it? *I* need you. I'll miss you desperately if you go. You can't go. I want you, Chris. I don't want Paul. Last night I thought he was you. I came to look for you, but you'd gone. It's over between me and Paul. He was kissing me goodbye when you saw us. It's you I want. You were right all along, Chris. I wanted you from the first minute we saw each other. You were right about lots of things. And I don't care if this sounds like a desperate, pathetic message. I am desperate. Last night, I realised –'

The machine ran out of tape and cut her off. 'Realised what?' she whispered to herself, not sure what she'd been about to say.

She put the phone down and waited. She'd wait until he called.

Something was wrong. He didn't call. She missed her eight o'clock appointment, although she didn't care. This was far more important. This was serious – he'd got home and got her message and ignored it. He really didn't want her. She picked up the phone and went to dial but put it down again, knowing she wasn't brave enough to hear his voice, cold and emotionless, telling her that he wasn't coming back.

What could be the reason? Her brain was too tired to think. She'd thought she knew what went on in Chris's mind, but she would never know. She sighed, the sigh of someone who'd just lost everything. Unaware that she was still clutching his note in her hand, she turned out the light in her office.

The club was emptying. In a daze, Natalie told the receptionist that she'd lock up, and she took the keys and wandered off with her thoughts. Customers passed her on their way out, but she didn't see them. She made her way to the far end of the club and on to court ten – Chris's court. The receptionist must have forgotten Natalie was still there, and turned the lights out from the control panel at her desk. But Natalie barely noticed. She didn't need light to see her memories.

Left alone in the suddenly silent building, she drifted to the net. When she touched it, she thought of him. When she looked up at the umpire's chair, where she'd sat and watched him and felt her knickers getting wet, she thought of him. When she breathed, she thought of him.

251

The silent darkness cleared her head. The words she hadn't said on his answerphone came to her, and she whispered them to him. 'Last night, I realised how much I wanted you. And how much I wanted you to have me. I was willing to give myself to you completely. The club can't survive for long without you, and neither can I.'

She closed her eyes. Her body swayed. She should have been pleased the tape had cut her off before she'd had a chance to make her admission – but she wasn't. After all, he'd already taken most of her. He might as well have had her mind as well.

Her eyelids jerked wide open. Her body tensed. A shot of adrenaline woke her. There was a noise, far away down the hall.

Oh Jesus. What a time for someone to break in. The front door open. The lights out. The alarm not set. The nearest phone a lifetime away from where she was standing. Oh God. Think.

They wouldn't come on to the court, surely. Nothing to steal here. She crept to the door, flinching at the deafening sound of her silent footsteps. She pressed herself into the wall by the door and strained her ears. Stay still, her mind told her body, which was desperate to run. Wait till they've gone. Don't move. Hold your breath.

But they were coming. Their footsteps were determined down the corridor – aiming for her. They knew she was there. How? What did they want from her? She'd give them the keys to her office; let them take the computer and the cash.

They were coming for her.

Her body won and she flung herself through the doorway, just as he arrived. He grabbed her arms and she flailed out blindly, fighting with him. 'Don't hurt me,' she begged.

'Why would I ever want to hurt you?'

She stopped fighting. She was out of breath. Her chest was heaving. 'Chris?'

He pulled her tight against his chest. His heartbeat was as fast as hers. His hands were in her hair, on her neck, down her back. He kissed her, telling her everything but saying nothing. Then, when the urgency of his lips and tongue finally slowed, he pulled away and looked at her through the darkness.

His fingers touched her cheek. He traced around her open lips and she reached for him, sucking his fingertips. His touch eased over her throat and to the button at her cleavage. Slowly, breathing hard, he undid her blouse and the cream silk fell to the floor. Feeling round her waist, he found the zip and her skirt was gone. He knelt and took off her shoes, one at a time, while she held on to his shoulder. Standing up again, he gently took off her bra and slid down her panties.

She moved to him. It was slow now. The panic and fear and desperation were gone. The only things left were the two of them, and their need. She pushed off his jacket and T-shirt. Knelt at his feet. Took off his shoes and trousers and his soft white shorts. He knelt down facing her. He eased her down to the floor.

Naked. Not just their clothes gone. Their souls had been stripped bare. They belonged to each other now.

He kissed her neck and her breasts, sucking the life out of her as he sucked on her soft nipples. He kissed her belly, kissed her mound, realised it was shaved and touched and licked it all over. 'Fuck,' he whispered, shocked by the nudity of her pussy. 'Oh *fuck*,' and his fingers and then his tongue were inside her. Her legs were over his shoulders, round his waist; and his cock was sliding into her pussy, her spine, her mind, and filling her soul.

Their lust took control and they were animals again – him pounding into her; her body and voice in spasms of surrender.

'Stay there,' he begged, leaving the warmth of his come on her inner thighs as he stood up.

'Where are you going?' He ran off into the blackness, towards their pile of clothes. 'Don't leave me again,' she said, as he returned.

'I had to get something out of my jacket,' he said. 'I took it with me last night. I was going to . . . I'd been thinking about it for such a long time, but . . .'

He rolled her over to face the floor. Sitting on his heels behind her, he pulled her up on to all fours, and did the thing he'd wanted to do last night.

It was cool and slimy on her arsehole. His fingers were quick and as they touched her secret hole she felt herself tensing. This would be torture. He was so big.

A finger first. Slowly, fighting it, her anus gave in to the pleasure and let him in. Another finger opened her further, then another, stretching her; readying her.

But she could never be ready. His cock was so thick. She heard him rubbing the grease on to himself and then he was prodding for entry. Patiently he pushed, an inch at a time, holding her still for him. Eventually her breath sucked in, her eyes closed tight, her mouth opened wide and he was inside her arse.

Inside her head. Oh, this was torture. Ecstasy so dark, so sharp and unbearable, it was pain. She could do nothing. He was merciful, sliding slowly in and out along the quivering, raw, nerve-lined passage that led through her guts to insanity.

It was too much. Too much. And then he began to fuck her. The darkness turned to light behind her eyelids. The insanity closed its fingers tight round her body and claimed her. She collapsed to the floor, her face pressed to the ground, her upper body bowed in surrender and only her arse left up in the air.

'You've got a fantastic arse,' he said, plunging between her cheeks. 'I've had dreams about your arse.'

She sobbed in reply. 'I can't take it. It's too much.'

But he carried on. 'You have to take it,' he murmured. 'I have to feel every part of you. I want to feel you surrender.' He got faster and deeper and his cock seemed to get bigger, until her brain was about to burst. She was already staggering blindly towards the edge when he took her hand and made her jump with him. He plunged in so deep, so hard, that the tangle of despair and pleasure unravelled itself and an incredible, impenetrable calm washed over her, like the silence on the way down. If an orgasm could flow from deep inside the arse then this one did, starting at the swollen tip of his penis and flooding her curled-up body.

He stayed there for ever, stroking her back, pulsing inside her. Neither one dared move, neither wanting to be the one to break the link between their bodies.

But eventually his penis slid out. Wetness spilt down her crack and mingled with the juice seeping from her pussy lips. She waited, twitching, as his fingers dipped into the overflow of their desire. 'I want to look at you,' he said, and then she was on her back again, looking up into his face as he lay at her side with his head propped up on his hand.

'You're so beautiful,' he said, soothing her with his voice but still torturing with his fingers. Reaching for her smooth pussy, he found her hard clit and flickered his thumb over it.

Her open knees tensed. 'I'm not beautiful,' she whispered. She knew she wasn't. 'You don't have to tell me that I am.'

'But you are,' he said, pressing with his thumb until her back rippled. 'You should see your face, when you come.'

His fingers flattened over her open cunt. He rubbed with his whole hand, pushing her tiny clit in rapid circles, massaging and pinching and flickering with his fingertips until her knees flopped down to the floor. Trapped by her own pleasure, she lay there, looking up at him, as she came.

He put a finger on to her tongue. She tasted herself, and him.

They lay together, naked and dripping with lust, until the moonlight shone through the gaps in the roof.

'I got your message,' he said.

'I got your note,' she said.

'Last night, when I found out Paul had gone upstairs, I couldn't cope. It was supposed to have been me. I was so jealous.'

'I came to look for you afterwards, but you'd gone.'

'I thought that was it for us. I thought you'd go home with Paul. I couldn't face seeing you with him again, so I left.'

'I didn't go home with him,' she said.

'Why didn't you come to my place?'

'I thought you'd set it all up. I thought it was some sort of sick plan you'd had. To make me give myself to you and then to give me back to Paul. It was so embarrassing.' She rolled on to her front and looked down at him. 'I thought it was you fucking me. And Paul had no idea it was me.'

'You thought I'd set that up?' He couldn't believe it. 'Did you hate me?'

She thought for a moment. 'I hated myself for wanting you. I thought you'd used me.'

'I thought you'd got back together with Paul. When I saw you kissing him, I had to resign. It would have driven me out of my mind, seeing him here every day, knowing you were his.'

'I'm yours now,' she said quietly. 'God, I never thought I'd say that to a man. Do you realise what you've done to me?'

He reached up and touched her hair. 'Do you know

what you've done to me? I can't look at another woman now without thinking about you. When I thought of Paul finding you tied to the bed, I felt physically sick.'

'I never thought I'd see you jealous.'

'I never thought I'd meet a woman who made me jealous of every man that looked at her.'

'And you are?'

He nodded.

'Oh God, that turns me on.'

He pulled her down and kissed her, rolling her over until he was on top of her. Natalie lay there and let him worship her, her body calm now after her orgasms; her mind easy in the knowledge that he wanted her so badly he was no longer in command of this.

Suddenly, he stopped. He scrambled to his feet and ran back to their clothes again.

He returned holding up a piece of paper. The piece of paper she'd been clutching when he'd found her. He tore it up into tiny pieces and they fell on her like summer rain.

'What's that?' she asked, knowing what it was.

'It's my resignation.' He dropped to the floor. His hand slid over her, into the warmth of her naked pussy. 'I'll stay. I'm yours, if you want me.'

'You can stay, on one condition.'

'What is it?'

'You take me to Wimbledon again.'

'To watch the tennis?'

'No.'

In the darkness, she felt him smile. 'You dirty girl,' he whispered.

BLACK LACE NEW BOOKS

Published in January

A FEAST FOR THE SENSES
Martine Marquand
£5.99

Clara Fairfax leaves life in Georgian England to embark on the Grand Tour of Europe. She travels through the decadent cities – from ice-bound Amsterdam to sultry Constantinople – undergoing lessons in pleasure from the mysterious and eccentric Count Anton di Maliban.

ISBN 0 352 33310 3

THE TRANSFORMATION
Natasha Rostova
£5.99

Three friends, one location – San Francisco. This book contains three interlinked and very modern stories which have their roots in fairy tales. There's nothing innocent about Lydia, Molly and Cassie, however, as one summer provides them with the cathartic sexual experiences which transform their lives.

ISBN 0 352 33311 1

Published in February

MIXED DOUBLES
Zoe le Verdier
£5.99

Natalie takes over the running of an exclusive tennis club in the wealthy suburbs of Surrey, England. When she poaches tennis coach Chris from a rival sports club, women come flocking to Natalie's new business. Chris is skilled in more than tennis, and the female clients are soon booking up for extra tuition.

ISBN 0 352 33312 X

SHADOWPLAY
Portia Da Costa
£5.99

Daniel Woodforde-Ranelagh lives a reclusive but privileged existence, obsessed with mysticism and the paranormal. When the wayward and sensual Christabel Sutherland walks into his life, they find they have a lot in common. Despite their numerous responsibilities, they immerse themselves in a fantasy world where sexual experimentation takes pride of place.

ISBN 0 352 33313 8

To be published in March

RAW SILK
Lisabet Sarai
£5.99

When software engineer Kate O'Neill leaves her lover David to take a job in Bangkok, she becomes sexually involved with two very different men: a handsome member of the Thai aristocracy, and the charismatic proprietor of a sex bar. When David arrives in Thailand, Kate realises she must choose between them. She invites all three to join her in a sexual adventure that finally makes clear to her what she really wants and needs.

ISBN 0 352 33336 7

THE TOP OF HER GAME
Emma Holly
£5.99

Successful businesswoman and dominatrix Julia Mueller has been searching all her life for a man who won't be mastered too easily. When she locks horns with a no-nonsense Montana rancher, will he be the man that's too tough to tame? Will she find the balance between domination and surrender, or will her dark side win out?

ISBN 0 352 33337 5

BLACK
lace

If you would like a complete list of plot summaries of Black Lace titles, or would like to receive information on other publications available, please send a stamped addressed envelope to:

Black Lace, Thames Wharf Studios,
Rainville Road, London W6 9HT

BLACK LACE BOOKLIST

All books are priced £4.99 unless another price is given.

Black Lace books with a contemporary setting

ODALISQUE	Fleur Reynolds ISBN 0 352 32887 8	☐
WICKED WORK	Pamela Kyle ISBN 0 352 32958 0	☐
UNFINISHED BUSINESS	Sarah Hope-Walker ISBN 0 352 32983 1	☐
HEALING PASSION	Sylvie Ouellette ISBN 0 352 32998 X	☐
PALAZZO	Jan Smith ISBN 0 352 33156 9	☐
THE GALLERY	Fredrica Alleyn ISBN 0 352 33148 8	☐
AVENGING ANGELS	Roxanne Carr ISBN 0 352 33147 X	☐
COUNTRY MATTERS	Tesni Morgan ISBN 0 352 33174 7	☐
GINGER ROOT	Robyn Russell ISBN 0 352 33152 6	☐
DANGEROUS CONSEQUENCES	Pamela Rochford ISBN 0 352 33185 2	☐
THE NAME OF AN ANGEL £6.99	Laura Thornton ISBN 0 352 33205 0	☐
SILENT SEDUCTION	Tanya Bishop ISBN 0 352 33193 3	☐
BONDED	Fleur Reynolds ISBN 0 352 33192 5	☐
THE STRANGER	Portia Da Costa ISBN 0 352 33211 5	☐
CONTEST OF WILLS £5.99	Louisa Francis ISBN 0 352 33223 9	☐
BY ANY MEANS £5.99	Cheryl Mildenhall ISBN 0 352 33221 2	☐
MÉNAGE £5.99	Emma Holly ISBN 0 352 33231 X	☐
THE SUCCUBUS £5.99	Zoe le Verdier ISBN 0 352 33230 1	☐

---------✂---------------------

Please send me the books I have ticked above.

Name ....

Address ....

....

....

.... Post Code ....

Send to: **Cash Sales, Black Lace Books, Thames Wharf Studios, Rainville Road, London W6 9HT.**

US customers: for prices and details of how to order books for delivery by mail, call 1-800-805-1083.

Please enclose a cheque or postal order, made payable to **Virgin Publishing Ltd**, to the value of the books you have ordered plus postage and packing costs as follows:

UK and BFPO – £1.00 for the first book, 50p for each subsequent book.

Overseas (including Republic of Ireland) – £2.00 for the first book, £1.00 each subsequent book.

If you would prefer to pay by VISA or ACCESS/MASTERCARD, please write your card number and expiry date here:

....

Please allow up to 28 days for delivery.

Signature ....

---------✂---------------------